Playing for Love

JEEVANI CHARIKA

ONE PLACE. MANY STORIES

HQ
An imprint of HarperCollins*Publishers* Ltd
1 London Bridge Street
London SE1 9GF

www.harpercollins.co.uk

HarperCollins*Publishers*
1st Floor, Watermarque Building, Ringsend Road
Dublin 4, Ireland

This paperback edition 2022

1

First published in Great Britain by
HQ, an imprint of HarperCollins*Publishers* Ltd 2022

Copyright © Jeevani Charika 2022

Jeevani Charika asserts the moral right to be
identified as the author of this work.
A catalogue record for this book is
available from the British Library.

ISBN: 9780008511555

To my family, always

Chapter 1

Samadhi Ranaweera sat with her portfolio bag clutched too tightly on her lap. She had finished her pitch to yet another niche handbag company and now they were deliberating. Even in her limited experience, she knew being asked to step outside while they discussed it was a bad sign. Mind you, she didn't know what a good sign might be.

This was the third company she'd pitched to this month. When she'd decided to start a small business, she'd had no idea how much work it would be. In her naivety, she'd thought between her years of experience as a project manager and the money from her generous redundancy package, getting the enterprise up and running would be an easy thing. But here she was, six months in and rapidly running out of time, money, and, to be entirely honest, enthusiasm.

Her fingers hurt from gripping the portfolio bag. She forced herself to unclench her fingers and shifted the position of the bag so that she could rest her arms on it. She was obviously doing something wrong. Her business plan had looked fine on paper, but she was losing something in translating it into action. Normally, when she needed advice on anything work related, she could ask her father or her big brothers. But they still thought she was working her regular day job. They would be horrified that she had chosen to launch her own start-up instead of getting straight back to hunting for a stable job. She'd have to sit through hours of lectures about being reckless with her future. 'Gambling', her father would have called it. Sam sighed. Perhaps he was right. She had gambled on this venture going well so that she could present him with her success. So much for that idea.

Around her, business carried on as usual. A woman pushed a trolley full of tote-style handbags that looked like they were from the latest season. Sam moved her feet out of the way and craned her neck to get a better view. It was her passion for handbags that had brought her down this path in the first place. After leaving her purse in the wrong handbag for the umpteenth time, she had started using a small inner bag that she could move from handbag to handbag. The inserts had made her life so much easier that she wanted to share them with the world. If only a bag company would partner with her so that her insert bags went into their designs, she'd be well on her way.

The offices she was sitting in were not huge – the company wasn't a big player in the market – but they were busy. Sam looked up at the big posters of their designs. They would work so well with her insert bags. She could make beautiful matching inserts to go with that season's colourways and women would be able to use more bags with less hassle. It was so obviously a good idea. Sometimes it felt like she was the only one who could see it.

She pulled herself together and sat up straighter. This negativity wasn't going to get her anywhere. She had to look alert and enthusiastic, just in case. All it took was one yes. Who knew, this might be the one company that said it.

When the man who had interviewed her came up, Sam stood and smiled at him. His expression was sympathetic. Her heart descended to her toes. Oh great. Another no.

'I'm very sorry,' the man said. 'It was an interesting pitch, but not something we can commit to right now, I'm afraid.'

She managed to keep her smile on her face. 'I understand. Thank you very much for your time.'

He nodded.

'You have my card, so if anything changes, do give me a call.'

'Of course.' He moved his arm, subtly directing her towards the door. 'Thank you for coming.'

Afterwards, as she sat on the Tube on the way back to her small office, with the portfolio bag leaning against her legs, Sam realised that they hadn't handed back her sample. She would have to sew another one. She leaned her head back against the window of the train and ran the whole interview through her head.

It always went wrong when they asked her about her manufacturing plans. None of the companies liked the fact that she didn't have a loan or an investor, but was trying to crowdfund the money she'd need. They all seemed to think that she was being wildly optimistic about how many random strangers would put money into her enterprise. To be perfectly honest, she was starting to wonder if they had a point. Raising money by crowdfunding had been a brilliant idea in theory – it would put her in touch with people who enjoyed fashion and were likely to shout about it on social media, and it would help her form her tribe as she went along. Except it wasn't working. She didn't know why.

Everything else in her business plan held up, but if this one step failed, it could scupper her business before it even started. At this rate, she was going to run out of the redundancy money that she was living on and would have to go and find a new job within a few months.

She sat up straight again and looked down at the bag resting against her leg. This was her dream. Shanthi Bags. If she made it work, she could make life easier for thousands of women. Millions, even. She wasn't sure when she'd started thinking about it, but it had been noodling away at the back of her mind for long enough that when she was offered redundancy, she had seen it as a chance to leave her soul-crushing day job and leapt at it.

3

Now Shanthi Bags was that much closer to being a reality, she wanted to succeed so badly that it was almost painful. Except no one believed she could do it. And sometimes she thought they might be right.

Luke Burneside changed into his cycling gear in the bathroom and went back to his office. It was late evening and the building was emptying out as people hurried off home, people from the many small businesses based here. His own assistant, Pete, had already left, so he had the office to himself. He checked the time. He could do a bit more work before he headed out.

Instead of putting his laptop in his backpack, he pulled up his chair and opened up the accounts for that quarter. Their takings were down. Again. He'd had the online event company for seven years now and it should have been making a good profit by now. But it looked like there wasn't going to be much to write home about this year. Again.

At least that meant he wasn't going to have to give any more money to his business partner either. He rubbed his face. At the moment, Bradley was rarely in the office, but he still owned part of the company. Luke worked all hours while Bradley did almost nothing. Luke needed to discuss this with him, but he kept putting it off. The very idea of confrontation made his heart pick up pace. He breathed in and out carefully, forcing his pulse to slow back down. Not today.

He made a few notes to remind himself of things he had to check, then shut the laptop down. Not being able to pay himself properly was a real pain. He grabbed his bag but in order to get his laptop in, he had to remove the envelope that he'd tucked inside that morning. It contained the details for his arrangement with the online gaming company Syren Corp. He mustn't forget to post that. He could have put it in the post tray at work, but he liked to keep his gaming life separate from his work. He didn't want anything to connect them. He slid the letter back into the bag once the laptop was in and put a reminder on his phone to post it.

It was nearly seven o'clock when he finally headed to the stairs to leave. Noticing the lights were on in the main meeting room, he peered in through the glass door. Kim, the receptionist, was in there, tidying up. She should have left ages ago.

He knocked and stepped in. 'What're you still doing here, Kim?'

She flipped back her corkscrew curls and gestured towards the cups and saucers she was gathering. 'Steering committee meeting overran.' She reached for a plate left in the middle of the table. 'Still, eh. Overtime.'

'Here, let me help.' Luke clipped his cycle helmet on to get it out of the way and began stacking the cups and coffee mugs on a tray. At the other end of the table Kim did the same.

He and Kim had started working at The Nest when the small-business incubator was still brand new. Luke and Bradley's fledgling company had been one of the earliest tenants and Kim had been the building's receptionist. They were part of the 'old guard' now.

They ended up with two trays stacked high with used cups.

'You go ahead to the kitchen,' Kim said. 'I'll lock up and follow.'

'Righto.' He picked up one of the trays and pushed his way through the door at the top of the stairs. As he descended, one of the towers of cups wobbled, but there was nowhere to rest the tray to steady it, so he carried on, praying nothing would fall over.

At the entrance to the next floor, he faced a door with a pull handle. He frowned and was considering putting the tray on the floor and sorting out the cup tower first, when someone pushed the door open. He looked up to see a woman holding it for him.

She was brown-skinned with black hair cut into a neat bob. Long eyelashes, plump lips, impressive eyes. Very impressive eyes.

5

Luke's mind went blank.

She moved into the stairwell and gave him a distracted smile. She gestured for him to go through.

He managed to say, 'Thanks.'

As he stepped forward, the cups wobbled.

The woman made a concerned face. 'Hang on.' She hitched her big handbag onto her shoulder and reached out to quickly rearrange the cup towers.

Luke stood there like a lemon, not sure what to say. She smiled at him and his world went sepia-toned for a second. He said, 'Thanks' once more, before hurrying through the door.

'You're welcome.' The glass door closed behind her as she kept walking.

Luke paused in the corridor with the kitchen at the end. The girl stopped at the reception desk, where she seemed to be signing out. She must work here then. He quickly carried on down the corridor before she noticed him staring at her.

In the office kitchen, which doubled as a staff room, he loaded the cups into the dishwasher, his mind not really on the task. Why was he so useless when it came to talking to people? He had just met the most beautiful woman in the world and he'd not said a word. And worse, he realised, he'd been in his cycling gear with his helmet clipped on and carrying a tray of dirty cups. That was a terrible first impression to make.

He pulled the bottom rack out and started putting the saucers in there. He would have to find out more about her. Maybe even work out a way to talk to her when he was wearing normal clothes. The easiest thing would be to ask Kim, who knew everyone. But that was out of the question.

He heard Kim coming into the kitchen and hastily straightened up before she made a comment about his arse.

'Don't change position on my account.' Kim grinned at him. 'How on earth are you still single?'

And that was why he couldn't ask Kim about the mystery

6

woman. He would never hear the end of it. He was used to her teasing by now, but there were limits. He made a face at her.

Kim ignored it. 'I can take over from here,' she said. 'And seriously, thanks for helping.'

'Not a problem. Do you want me to stay until you lock up?'

'Nah. I'll be fine. You go home. I'm sure you've got exciting evening plans.'

Luke laughed. 'Oh yeah,' he said. 'Wild, crazy plans. I'll see you tomorrow.'

He cycled home, microwaved himself some dinner, and rushed around getting chores done until it was time. Then he let himself into his spare room, which contained his gaming computer and microphone set-up. This was his favourite part of the day. It was when he could forget about everything else that was going on and become someone else entirely. He fired up the game he was currently playing, put on his headset, hit record, and became his alter ego. Blaze. Pro-gamer and YouTube star.

'All right there, folks,' he said, slipping easily into the strong Yorkshire accent of his childhood. 'How're we doing today?'

Sam removed her work from the sewing machine and broke off the thread. It was past midnight and her eyes felt gritty and sore. She grabbed the scissors and tidied up the long bits of thread before she turned her latest creation the right side out and examined it. It was a new demo bag insert. It gave her a tiny jolt of satisfaction every time she made one.

Until she could afford to hire someone to help cut and sew the handbag inserts, she had to make all the samples herself. At least it meant that she could make each bag unique. She smoothed the soft fabric down with her hands and smiled. This one was dove grey and orange. There wasn't another one like it. She liked a unique bag.

She stretched, feeling the tension in her shoulders. Enough for tonight. She would iron the bag into shape, sew on the 'Shanthi

Bags' label, and take photos for the website tomorrow. Running a small business involved a million tiny tasks, which always added up to more time than you'd think.

Once she'd finished tidying up, she was still too wired to go straight to sleep. So she made herself a hot chocolate and curled up on the sofa, ready to indulge in her one guilty pleasure.

Her cousin, Nirosha, had already gone to bed, so Sam plugged her earbuds into her phone and pulled up YouTube.

Her first memory of watching gameplays online was when she was 12 years old, sitting on the sofa next to her brothers as a walk-through of a game played in front of them. After their mother died, their father's grief had pervaded the house, making them tiptoe around it. Sam and her two brothers, left to themselves, stuck together. The boys played video games and Sam, not as keen a gamer as her brothers, tended to just observe. More and more, she watched one gamer's videos in particular – Blaze. She felt comforted by his friendly voice, his animated narrations.

Things were different now, of course. Thatha had remarried and the boys had gone off to their jobs. But Sam had carried on watching Blaze's videos whenever she felt down. As Blaze himself never featured on screen – the videos were of various games, with his voice narrating over the top – she could only imagine what he looked like. There were a few blurry photos of him, taken by people at conventions, which told her that he was tall-ish, slim. She had a lot of fun imagining what he might actually look like. It was silly, she knew, but you took comfort where you could find it.

She sat back and closed her eyes. The video game was less important than the sound of his voice. That voice had lulled her to sleep on many a night, especially in the weeks after her redundancy. She was half asleep by the time the gameplay ended. Then Blaze's voice came on, slightly louder than before and missing the raw edge it had when he was playing. 'And don't forget, if you want to be in with a chance to play alongside me in the never-seen-before game *SyrenQuest*, just hit the button below and enter the draw.'

Ha! For a second, she was tempted, but she wasn't really into playing and was pretty bad at most of the shooter games that her brothers had. She was more of a puzzle solver. She only watched Blaze's channel because she loved Blaze, not for the games. Her teens would have had a little less light in them without him.

Sam yawned and sat up. Now she was relaxed enough to go to bed. She looked at her phone, intending to close the YouTube page. The cash prize for the competition flashed up on the screen. She felt a pang of sadness. That amount of money would more than cover her first batch of bags and then some.

'I know you're thinking, "It'll never be me", but it might be,' Blaze said. 'Not only do you get to come and play with me or one of my pro-gamer friends, you get a ticket to the final, which has a convention attached to it, and … you get a Syren3 headset. And if you win, you get to take home all that lovely prize money. It won't cost you anything to join in. You've literally nothing to lose.'

She ended up watching the whole segment. She loved him. Imagine being able to meet him? To actually see him up close in real life. What would she even say? If by some miracle she ended up playing alongside him, there was no way she'd be able to concentrate with him within touching distance. There was no way she would be able to play well enough to win all that prize money.

'So go ahead and click the link,' he said. 'I'd love to meet you.'

A thrill ran through her. It was like he was talking directly to her. She couldn't help herself. She hit the link, typed in her email address, and agreed to whatever the T&Cs were. It was a futile thing to do. The chances of her being chosen in the lottery were miniscule. The chances of being paired with Blaze were even smaller. But it had been a shit day and just entering cheered her up. Now at least she could go to bed smiling.

Chapter 2

Three weeks later

Sam hurried through the rain-slicked street, her phone pressed to her ear. It was still a bit damp, but she was walking so fast that she was warm enough to open her coat. 'I'm nearly there. Has it started yet?'

In her ear, Niro said, 'They're just doing the intro about the new headset. State of the art. Lets you see the facial expressions of other players … blah, blah, blah.'

They were announcing the winners of the *SyrenQuest* competition today. Sam had intended to catch it at home with Niro, but she'd had to go and pick up her brochures from the printers, so she was heading to her office to watch it instead.

The façade of The Nest building was visible ahead. She tried to walk a little faster, which wasn't easy to do in heels. Sam ran up the steps, keeping her bag clutched to her chest. The atrium was a double-height space that contained a large cafeteria. It was light and airy and one of Sam's favourite places. The tables in the main atrium were full of people who had come in for a drink and a sit down. At the far end, where the floor above made a lower ceiling, was a more cosy seating area with a sofa and a TV screen.

The Nest had offices at a subsidised rate and Sam's was on the second floor, where the tiniest ones were. The smell of coffee wafted past. She hesitated. 'I'm in the building,' she said into the phone. 'I need caffeine. I didn't have time to grab any before I left.'

'Well, hurry up. They're explaining the game now and going through the professional gamers they've brought in.'

Sam smiled. She had introduced Niro to Blaze's channel. It was nice to have someone who understood her thirsting after him – something her brothers would never fathom. She and Niro made an odd pair. Sam was neat and looked very 'establishment', while Niro had a pierced eyebrow and purple streaks in her black hair. But they'd always got along well. A few weeks ago, when she'd got the email telling her that her name had been drawn to be one of the rookie players in the *SyrenQuest* competition, it was Niro who'd celebrated with her. Over the last few weeks, with all the paperwork that she'd had to sign, she would have dropped out if it weren't for Niro. And now she was a whisper away from her dream of meeting Blaze in real life.

She still couldn't believe she'd won a place. There was no way on earth she'd win the prize money, but it would be fun to go to the convention and meet Blaze. For Blaze to be her actual game partner was too much to hope for. She would find out who she would be paired with today – any minute now. Part of her was desperate to know, but another part just wanted to hang on to the futile dream of playing alongside Blaze for a little longer.

'They're starting. I think they're going to announce the pairings at the same time as they announce who's on the newbie shortlist,' said Niro.

Well, that made sense. She had known that she was one of the contestants for a week now, but she had been sworn to secrecy until the formal announcement (Niro didn't count, as far as she was concerned). 'Okay, well, I'm nearly at the head of the queue for coffee now,' Sam said.

She glanced across the room at the big screen on the wall.

A group of guys whose companies had offices in the building had taken over the sofa. One of them flicked through the channels. 'Here we go,' he said. The all-too-familiar advert for the *SyrenQuest* competition came on-screen. There was no audio, but Sam had seen the ad often enough to know the theme song by heart.

'Someone's just put it on the screen in the cafeteria,' Sam said to Niro. 'I'll try and watch it here rather than upstairs.'

'Are you excited?' asked Niro. 'After today, you finally get to tell people about it.'

Sam laughed. 'Who would I tell, Niro? You're literally the only person I can talk to about it. And you promised you wouldn't tell anyone.' She reached the front of the queue and ordered. A quick glance. One of the guys was poking around behind the screen, probably trying to turn on the sound. 'Okay. I've got to go now, Niro.'

'Good luck, good luck, good luck.'

The sound on the telly came with a blast of noise that made the barista jump and nearly spill Sam's coffee. The guys on the sofa turned and shouted 'sorry' to the room in general. No one responded.

Sam added a dash of cold milk to her coffee and sauntered up to where the guys were sitting. On the screen, the head of Syren Corp was talking about the list of professional players who were going to be 'ushering' the newbies through the game. Sam bristled a little at that. She wasn't a complete novice at video games, nor were any of the other amateurs, probably. And in fact, no one had actually seen *SyrenQuest* yet, not even the pro-gamers. So they were all new to it anyway. It was a ridiculous distinction. She blew on her coffee and watched the first couple of pro-gamers being introduced.

'Next up … this YouTuber is a fan favourite,' the man on TV said. 'He's been streaming his gameplay since he was a teenager. He's known as the gaming world's Mr Nice Guy. It's … Blaze!'

12

Blaze's avatar came up on-screen. As always, he'd chosen a character who was tall, slim, and had something of the pirate about him. This avatar had a neat beard, long blond hair tied back in a ponytail, and a Zorro-style mask. It was similar to avatars he'd chosen before, in other games, but this time it looked almost real. It had tattoos on the arms, too. Syren Corp must have designed it especially for him.

From now on, her imagination would always think of him like that. Sam smiled. That was no hardship.

She herself had been allowed to customise her avatar using some limited options available in the game. She'd chosen to be a blue pixie, with pointed ears and a long blue plait. She had tried to choose some sensible armour. Not easy, because female combatant armour was never practical. Seeing as she would have to dress up as her own avatar in the unlikely event that she made it to the final and went to the convention, she felt she should wear something that she would actually be able to carry off in real life, even if she was painted blue.

On screen, the man asked the computer to randomly select one of the pro-gamers and one of the newbies to play with. The idea was that the pro-gamer and the newbie would work together. There were sixteen pairs, and four rounds. The final would take place at *SyrenQuest* Live, which was going to happen in two weeks' time.

Sam leaned forward and noticed that one of the guys – she thought his name might be Pete – was writing down the names of the people selected, and who they'd been paired with. 'What are you doing?' she asked.

He looked up. Remembering that she was at work, she added, 'What's all that?' She raised her coffee cup towards the screen. She had decided long ago to keep the gaming as her secret hobby. If people didn't know about it, they couldn't make fun of her for it.

'Oh, it's the latest thing in the games world,' said Pete. 'It's a new headset that Syren is bringing out. Quite interesting tech actually. They're doing a soft launch through a video game competition a few months before the big conventions start. It's very cool. Everybody's watching it.' He tapped the notebook and looked sheepish for a second. 'We're running a book on it.'

Of course they were. Out loud, she said, 'Wow. That sounds interesting.'

'You're Sam, right? With the handbag business?' asked one of the others. 'Do you … play?' He said it in a dubious tone, as though someone couldn't possibly be interested in handbags and computer games at the same time.

'Oh. No.' She shook her head. She stopped talking and stared at Blaze's avatar rotating on the screen. They were choosing who would be playing alongside him. Names scrolled past too fast to read. The computer would stop any second now. She wondered what it would be like to meet him in real life. She had spent so long with his voice in her ear that she felt like she knew him. But to him, she would be a nobody. Meeting him could potentially be cripplingly awkward. On screen the avatar smiled, the eyes behind the mask sparkling green. Oh, but meeting him would be so much fun.

'That's Blaze,' the guy on the sofa said helpfully. 'He's awesome. I used to watch him when I was a kid. I almost grew up with him.'

'You make him sound like he's really old,' said another. 'He's only in his late twenties, you know. He's just been going a long time.'

The computer rapidly cycled through the remaining amateur gamers, and stopped on a name. Bravura9.

'Bravura9 will be paired with Blaze.'

Sam stifled a little squeak. Bravura9 … was her.

Luke spotted the *SyrenQuest* logo on the TV at the far end of the cafeteria. He had started streaming the big reveal on his phone, but when Pete had texted to say he and the guys from the office opposite had put it up on the big screen, it seemed only right to come downstairs and watch it in company. Of course, Pete had no idea that Luke was actually taking part in *SyrenQuest*. No one here knew that he was Blaze, but the guys on the sofa knew he was interested in video games. As far as they were concerned he was just the quiet chap who ran an online events service company. He liked to keep it that way. YouTube fame was great, but he didn't want it leaking into his real life. His channel was his escape from the real world.

When he came out of the lift and turned the corner, his step faltered. *She* was standing there watching it too. She seemed to be asking the guys what was going on. For a second he didn't know what to focus on. The game announcement, or Sam, the girl he'd been trying to pluck up the courage to talk to for the past three weeks. Now would be a good time. He should just go up to her and say hello. It's not like it was a big deal or anything. It was a normal, everyday thing to do. He took a deep breath and went across to join them. He walked in what he hoped was an easy, laid-back stride. Nonchalant was what he was going for. She didn't even look at him – she seemed to be fixated on the screen.

On the TV, a voice said, 'Blaze.' His body automatically responded to hearing his other name. He turned too fast and his arm jostled Sam's elbow. She gave a yelp as hot coffee slopped over her hand.

'Oh my god, I'm so sorry,' Luke said. 'Are you okay? Did you get burned?'

She gave him a brief glare and shifted the coffee to her other hand. She shook the liquid off and flexed her hand. 'Ow.'

'I'm so sorry,' Luke said again. Well, he'd got her attention all right. Way to go, Luke. On the other side of the sofa, the guys were giving him pitying looks. Pete passed him a napkin, which he offered to Sam. 'Here. Can I get you a fresh coffee or something?'

'No. It's fine. Don't worry about it.'

'I'm Luke, by the way.'

'I know.'

'You do?' How did she know who he was? Was this a good thing? His imagination raced. Did she remember him as that idiot in the cycle helmet? Heat rose in his face.

'You gave a talk about online event strategies last month.'

Oh. Right. 'You went to that?' Of course she went to that. She'd practically just said so. Luke opened his mouth to say something less stupid, but she cut him off.

'Look. I'd better get going.' She nodded to the other guys. 'Thanks for explaining the … er … thing. I'll see you guys around.'

She hurried away, still flicking her hand as though to cool it down. If she walked any faster, she'd be jogging.

Luke turned round to the guys. 'Ugh. That's not how I wanted to introduce myself.'

Pete shook his head. 'I think you blew it there, boss.'

Luke sighed. 'So, what's happened with this tournament then?' With all the excitement, he'd missed finding out who they'd paired him with. He would have to look it up online when he got back upstairs. What a mess. He should have just watched the reveal on his phone like he'd intended. He walked round the sofa and dropped down next to Pete.

On the screen, the next pairing was announced. Pete wrote it down in his notebook. 'We're doing a sweepstake,' he said, distractedly. 'You in?'

'Sure. Why not? Let me know when you've got the full list.' He looked towards the lift. Sam had disappeared from view. 'I don't suppose any of you know what that girl's company is called, do you? I feel I should go and apologise properly.'

Pete gave him a pitying look. 'Seriously?'

'What have I got to lose?'

Pete shook his head. 'Her name's Sam. Her company is called Shanthi Bags and she has one of the offices on floor two.'

'Shanthi Bags,' Luke repeated. 'I'll go find her office and apologise.'

Pete sighed. 'Just don't come off all stalkery, okay?'

'Of course not. I will be the epitome of a polite, normal person.'

Pete patted him on the shoulder. 'Good luck with that.'

Chapter 3

Sam went upstairs to where the public area of The Nest ended and the business-specific section of the building began. Kim looked up from behind the reception desk. 'Morning, Sam, what have you got today?'

Kim always asked that question. In response, Sam put her handbag on the counter. 'You've seen this one before. It's the cream-and-orange bucket bag. Like the Juicy Couture one, but older.'

Normally, she would have stopped to chat. Kim was a handbag enthusiast and had even pledged to Sam's crowdfunding campaign to finance the first batch of Shanthi Bags. 'Sorry, I can't stop today, Kim. I have a ton of stuff to do and I'm late already.'

Kim waved her in the direction of the main door, as though giving her permission to move on.

'I'll see you later.' Sam buzzed herself into the office floor and practically ran to her little room.

Once inside, she shut the door, put what was left of her coffee on the table, and let out a long, shaky breath. The excitement that she'd been carefully tamping down for the last fifteen minutes bubbled up and popped into a huge grin. She was going to play with Blaze. 'Yes!' She punched the air. 'Yes, yes!'

Her phone rang. It was Niro, who shrieked, 'Oh my god!'

Sam gave a little squeal and danced on the spot. 'I can't believe it.'

'Did you get to see it happen?'

Sam stopped dancing. 'Sort of. I saw the announcement, but I was with people, so I had to pretend that I didn't know anything about it. And then this guy hit my elbow and I spilled my coffee on my hand.'

'Is it okay? You can't play with a burned hand.'

Sam prodded the back of her hand. It was a little sore, but didn't hurt as much as she'd expect a burn to. 'I think I'll be okay.'

'What a git, spilling your coffee!'

Sam thought of Luke. 'Not really,' she said. 'I think he's a bit clumsy. I saw him give a talk a while ago, and he was so nervous. Someone had to ask him to speak up a couple of times. Once he got going, he was good though. I think he's just shy.'

'Oh, I remember you talking about that. You thought he was interesting …'

Sam laughed. 'His talk was interesting. Not him.'

'Pity. Otherwise you totally should have got him to buy you another coffee … and one thing could have led to another.'

'Nope.' Sam shrugged off her coat and plugged in her laptop. She really had to stop watching romcoms with Niro. 'I have stuff to do.'

'Me too,' said Niro. 'But I'm taking this as an early lunch break. How's your crowdfunding going?'

'Not great, the last time I looked.' She pulled out a packet of papers from her bag. 'I've picked up my brochures.' It was collecting these that had made her late coming in. She pulled one out and opened it. Niro, a freelance photographer, had helped her design it. Sam used the virtual brochure in her email pitches, but she needed something to take with her if she actually got someone to agree to meet with her.

'These photos are amazing, Niro. They look so professional.'

'I *am* a professional,' Niro pointed out.

'I didn't mean—'

'It's fine. I know what you meant.' Something pinged in the background. 'My lunch is ready. I'd best go. You have a lovely afternoon. What are you doing today?'

Sam tried to gather her scattered thoughts. 'I … am going to pitch some more blogs and podcasts and see if I can get any more pledges for the crowdfunding campaign.'

'You know, if you just come clean and tell your dad and stepmum, I bet they could help you get it funded in no time.'

The mention of her parents burst Sam's happy bubble. 'No, they won't. They'll just come round and berate me about wasting my life. You know they will.'

Niro sighed. 'Okay. Well, I'd better go eat this. You have a productive day and come back all psyched up to try out this funky headset they sent you.'

Sam smiled. 'Yeah. See you later.'

'Laters.'

After Niro hung up, Sam stared at the home screen on her computer for a few seconds, unable to focus. Every thought seemed to circle back to how she was going to be playing alongside Blaze.

'Focus, Sam. Focus.'

There were several new emails in her inbox, most of them from people she'd sent pitches to. She was working her way through her 'most wanted' list alongside her more pragmatic, small-designer list. Most of the bigger places didn't even bother with meeting her and rejected her by email. Polite rejection. Polite rejection. What a surprise, another rejection. Oh dear. Impolite rejection. Rej— wait. She went back a couple of emails. This one wasn't a rejection.

We would like to offer you a chance to demonstrate your product and how it would fit with our brand.

Raven Millehouse
Head buyer, Boutique Belvoir Ltd

She checked the name. Sam's hand flew to her mouth. 'No way.' This was a department store that had its own brand of luxury handbags. They were willing to meet her to talk about using her bag inserts with their handbags. This was turning out to be the best day!

Hot on the heels of triumph came the fear. She pulled up her crowdfunding page. She wanted at least a third of the funding to be in the form of small pledges from people who wanted one of the earliest batches, so she could show that there was a demand for her product. Her forecast meant she should have hit that by now. She was nowhere near her target. The crowdfunding site had a time limit and it ran out in just over a month. When she set it up, she had been sure that would be plenty of time, but now she had doubts.

She needed to approach more magazines and fashion podcasts to get her message out there. She had a list from her market research, and she was carefully tailoring her pitch to each one. She would have to work through them faster.

Except she had committed to playing video games in the evening – not for fun, but for the competition. Her chest clenched. She forced herself to breathe slowly.

She could throw the competition and get out after the first round. But that would mean making an idiot of herself in front of Blaze. She wanted to impress him – which meant practising her moves and taking the gaming seriously. Besides, if they won … she could use the money to get her first batch made, even without the crowdfunding. For a second, she let herself imagine it. But no. There was no chance she could win, even with Blaze there to 'usher' her. Everyone else was brilliant too.

She was just going to have to work as many hours in the day as possible to make up for losing her evenings. 'Aargh.' She leaned back in her chair and pressed her hands to her face.

At that moment, someone knocked on the door. She turned to see Luke standing there, looking hesitant.

'Bad time?' he asked.

She drew a deep breath. It *was* a bad time, but perhaps a few seconds of talking to someone would get her out of the tailspin she'd got into. 'Erm … no. No. How can I help?'

He stepped inside, leaving the door ajar. 'I came partly to ask how your hand was.'

Her hand? Oh. The spilled coffee. She had completely forgotten about that. 'It's okay, I think. Thanks for asking.'

He shifted his weight. 'Can I … buy you another coffee sometime?'

She looked at him. He was tall, with unruly dark hair, pale brown eyes, and glasses. Whenever she saw him, he had a slightly harassed air about him, as though he was worrying about something. When he'd given his talk, he had been a soft-voiced mess for the first ten minutes, but once he warmed up, his whole demeanour had changed. This was a guy who was confident in his work, but not in much else. Which was really not her type.

'Sure. Not now, obviously.' She gestured towards her computer.

He took a step further into the office and put his hands in the back pockets of his jeans. 'Of course. But maybe tomorrow?'

Sam glanced at her computer again. He seemed nice, but she didn't have time for awkward flirting right now.

He seemed to pick up on her hesitation. 'You're busy. Fair enough.' He leaned forward and looked at her screen. 'You're crowdfunding?'

'Yes. Not very successfully, it seems.'

'Can I?' He gestured towards the screen. 'I've helped a few clients with theirs.'

'Be my guest.'

He crouched in front of the screen and scrolled through her site.

'I was hoping to have reached at least a third of the target by now, but …' she said.

'You make handbag liners?' he said, a little distantly. He was reading as he was talking.

'No. Bags to go within bags. So you can change handbags without losing the vital stuff.' She moved her chair so that she was next to him. 'You know. When you want to change bags, you swap the inner bag into the new handbag and off you go. Much less faffing.'

He glanced at her and smiled. 'I'll take your word for it.' He looked back at the screen. 'But why?'

'What do you mean, why? I've just told you. Lot less faff.'

'No, I mean, why *you*? Why this way? Why set it up as a business?' He stood up again. Now he was towering above her.

Sam looked up. 'I want other people to be able to swap handbags quickly and easily …' Wasn't it obvious?

He turned a chair round and sat down so that he was facing her. 'You need a story,' he said, pointing towards the crowdfunding site. 'Something about why you came up with this business. Why it's important to you. I'm guessing you've gone through your friends and family for donations. They're investing in you, rather than the thing. When it comes to strangers, they'll be investing in both the thing and in you. So if you can tell them a personal story about why this is important to you, it'll make them more inclined to give. Does that make sense?'

'I think so.' She considered the site that she'd spent so long putting up. She'd learned how to do it all by reading blogs and other guidance. It was entirely possible that it needed work.

'Your product photos are perfect, by the way. Really nice.'

'Oh, my cousin did those.'

'They're great.'

The conversation faltered for a moment, before Luke said, 'I'd … better let you get back to it. There are a few things you could do with the layout to improve flow. I'll mock something up for you, if you like.'

She didn't know what to say.

'I'll bring it round tomorrow. Nine-ish?'

'That would be amazing. Thank you. But … why are you doing this?' If it was just an elaborate way to ask her out, then it seemed weird for her to take advantage like that. Besides, she didn't have time for dating right now.

He considered for a second, then said, 'Partly, it's a community thing that we do here. You know, helping each other to "fly the Nest". I started out in a tiny office like this one – just me and my business partner.' A fleeting sadness passed over his face. 'People here who were more established helped us with advice back then. I try to pay it forward.'

'That's very kind.'

'Partly, I feel bad that I spilled your coffee.'

At this, Sam laughed. 'If you can help me get the crowdfund going, you will have more than paid back for the coffee.'

He grinned. 'I'll see what I can do. I'll see you tomorrow, a bit after nine.' When he smiled, his face lost that slightly wary look, making him quite handsome.

'See you tomorrow.' She watched him close the door and turned back to her crowdfunding page. Now that he'd pointed it out, she could see that he was right. She'd been so busy making sure she told people all about the product and how useful it was, she'd forgotten to tell them anything about herself.

The next problem was whether she wanted to tell people about her reasons for starting this business. It was far too personal.

Luke returned to his office feeling optimistic. She hadn't said yes to coffee, but she had been happy to meet him tomorrow. For him, that was progress.

In the office, Pete was on the phone. Luke quietly sat down at his desk and pulled up his project list. He had deliberately blocked his schedule to watch the *SyrenQuest* announcement. Now he needed to get back to work.

Behind him, Pete laughed. Luke glanced over his shoulder and shook his head. Pete was so natural in his interactions with people, even on the phone. Luke himself hated the phone. Give him a computer and he was happy, but speaking to real people, or worse, trying to sell to real people. No, thank you. When he and Bradley had started this business, they'd split the tasks so that Luke did the coding and design work, and his partner did the selling and schmoozing. It had worked well until Bradley gradually stopped coming into the office. These days, Luke rarely saw him. There wasn't any evidence that he was doing any work at all. The only reason the company had stayed afloat was because a lot of their existing customers came back every time they needed someone to run an event.

'Fantastic,' Pete said. 'I'll just drop you an invoice for the deposit and we'll get cracking on this right away.'

Luke's shoulders dropped a fraction. Good. They got the job. Pete had been working for him for six months. He had originally been hired as part of an apprenticeship scheme run by The Nest, where The Nest paid part of the salary for a junior employee for a year. The company got a helping hand, the fresh graduates got work experience – everyone won. The plan was that Pete would take over the design work while Luke handled all the tech stuff, but it had quickly become apparent that Pete was a people person. So now he did all the customer care, which Bradley should have been doing, while Luke's workload stayed the same. Luke had no idea what was going to happen when the year was up. He couldn't manage by himself. Besides, he liked having Pete around to share the office.

'That's brilliant,' Luke said to Pete. 'You're really good at this.'

Pete grinned. 'Not really. I'm average at it. You are just very bad at it and it makes me look good by comparison.'

He couldn't disagree with that.

Pete grabbed a pen and wrote the client's name on the white-board and started to block out time for the project. Luke watched him. Bradley should have been doing that too.

'How'd it go with Sam?' asked Pete. 'Do you have a date?'

'Sort of,' said Luke.

Pete turned around. 'What do you mean "sort of"? Did you ask her to meet you for coffee or not?'

'I did. But then I offered to help her with her crowdfunding campaign. So I'm meeting her tomorrow to give her notes on how she can improve the page.'

'Unbelievable. All you had to do was say, "Do you want to have coffee?"'

Luke shrugged. 'But this way, I get to see her more than once. The best way to get to know someone is to work with them, right?'

'I suppose.' Pete laughed. 'When I first met you, I thought you were a bit nerdy, but cool in your own way. Now that I've worked for you for a few months, I know that you're very nerdy and … really not that cool.'

Luke laughed too. 'See. It works. You know me better now.'

They both returned to their work. Yes, he definitely needed to talk to Bradley. He couldn't afford to pay the full amount of Pete's salary when the apprenticeship ended, unless his partner reduced his take. Damn. There was no one else who could talk to Bradley for him. He had to do it. The very thought of it made him feel sick.

He opened up a new email. May as well get it over with. Like pulling off a plaster. Should he call? The idea made him go cold. No. Email was better.

He typed in Bradley's email address then wrote:

We need to talk. Meeting at the company office at 9.30 on Wednesday?

To his amazement the reply came back within a few minutes.

Hello stranger. Yes. A chat is long overdue. Wednesday is good. Can't do 9.30, I have a previous commitment. I'll come round at 11.

26

Luke stared at it. The assumption that he was free at eleven rankled. But there was no point prolonging the discussion. So he wrote back and confirmed that Wednesday at eleven was fine with him.

It took a whole minute of mindful breathing to calm his heart rate back down again.

Chapter 4

The first time the contestants were allowed to try out the game was that evening. There was an 8 p.m. start. At 7.30, Sam opened the box and lifted out the Syren3 headset. This special edition set was white with the year written on a teal flash along the side.

Niro plugged the player into the TV. 'You know, if you ever decide to sell that, it'll probably be worth a fortune. There are only thirty-two of those in the UK. If the headset takes off, it'll be a collector's item in no time.'

'Why would I want to sell it?' Sam turned the headset on and brought up the settings on the screen.

Niro shrugged. 'Dunno. If you get trashed in the first round, you might be so scarred that you don't ever want to look at it again.'

Sam paused in the middle of raising the headset to put it on. 'What sort of pep talk is that?'

Niro sat down, cross-legged, on the sofa and pulled a bowl of popcorn onto her lap. 'I'm not saying it'll happen. Just giving you a scenario where you might want to get rid of it.'

'Nope. Even if I humiliate myself in front of Blaze, I'm not getting rid of this. It'll remind me of the only time I got to meet him in person.' Sam gave the headset a gentle pat.

'I don't get why you love him so much. You don't even know what he looks like.'

Sam inclined her head to acknowledge that. 'I'm hoping he looks at least a bit like his avatar,' she said. 'But I know his voice. I know his sense of humour. I know his competence … so, weird as it sounds, I do know him.' It was hard to explain. Blaze was extremely good at what he did and that was very sexy.

His voice was tied up with fond memories of her middle brother, Gihan, teaching her how to play different games. They had played *Tomb Raider* together, with Sam doing the puzzles and Gihan killing things. Watching Blaze, to her, was like hanging out with her brother's best mate. A place to pretend she was playing. He was virtually family to her, but to him, she meant nothing. Now she was going to play alongside him. He would realise she existed. It was like meeting a movie star.

'So, how does this work, then?' Niro asked.

Niro picked up a pair of 3-D glasses that Sam had kept from the last time she went to the cinema. She would be watching along on the TV screen.

Sam settled the Syren3 onto her head and adjusted it so that it didn't wobble. 'So … I turn this on.' She sat down and worked through the menus on-screen to get to the demo. 'Okay. Let's see what this looks like.' She pressed the button on the side of the visor and entered the demo.

The graphics were 3-D and very detailed. It took a few seconds for her brain to get past the uncanny valley feeling. The demo was set in the grounds of a manor house. She practised moving around and found the commands that appeared in front of her easy enough to follow. She spent a few minutes doing the standard moves. Niro said something.

'Hang on.' Sam adjusted the sound balance, so that she could still hear her cousin. 'What did you say?'

'I said, it looks pretty good. It took my eyes a few minutes to adjust to the 3-D thing, but it's really good. You're doing well with all the running and jumping and … stuff.'

'I need to practise,' said Sam. 'I'm quite slow.'

'I'm impressed though,' said Niro. Her voice was muffled and disembodied compared to the sounds coming through the headset. 'I wouldn't be able to do that.'

'Yes, but I'll be playing with Blaze and he's a pro. I don't want to slow him down too much.' She tried punching something. 'This character seems to be good at running and climbing, but rubbish at fighting.' She tried another combo. Instead of the flying kick she was expecting, she managed only a small jump. 'Okay. I really need to work on my fighting skills.'

'That's not so bad,' said Niro. 'At least you're nimble.'

After a few more minutes of intense practice, a banner flashed up to say there was a live event in five minutes. 'Oh shit.' Sam hit the button to flip up her visor.

'What?' said Niro, who had just picked up a handful of popcorn. 'It's only the kick-off. You've been waiting for this for days.'

Sam's breath was short. 'I'm going to meet Blaze.' She felt hot and breathless. She flexed her fingers. 'I'm finally going to meet Blaze. Oh my god.'

Niro stared at her. 'It'll be fine. He's just a guy. To him, this is just a job. Be cool.'

'But what if I screw up and play really, really badly?' Sam swallowed. Her throat was like the Sahara.

'Then you screw up. It's fine. It makes no difference to your real life. You still get to play and be part of it. Half of the other people in this game will be in exactly the same position, okay? No big deal. Besides, all you're doing today is meeting up, right?'

'But—'

'Just get on with it.' Niro waved her handful of popcorn at the screen. 'Go on. I want to watch.'

Heart pounding, Sam lowered the visor and clicked back into the alternate world.

Luke entered the game. He would be meeting his game partner for the first time. He had done a search on Bravura9, but hadn't found much, other than that they always seemed to choose a female avatar – so he was assuming she was a woman. She barely had a presence on social media or in the gaming community. A quick search on his own feeds had shown a few comments from a Bravura9, but that was it. So, a relative newbie then. She probably wouldn't be much help in the game, but that was okay. As a pro-gamer, he was being paid regardless. He wasn't the most accomplished player among the pros anyway. Two of the guys were proper e-athletics champions. Luke knew that he was only there because of his YouTube following.

Sensing something move on the periphery of his vision, he turned. Bravura had entered the game. She was an elf, with pointy ears and blue skin. He raised a hand and said, 'Hi.'

The avatars were animated and had ultra-smooth skin and oddly textured clothing, but the expressions were unusually nuanced. Bravura stared at him, her eyes wide and her mouth a small 'o'. The facial rendering on these headsets was excellent. The poor kid looked terrified.

'It's nice to meet you,' he volunteered.

She winced, as though someone had kicked her. 'I …' She cleared her throat. 'Hi. I'm Bravura. Which you know, obviously, because we were paired up for the game. It's an honour. A complete honour to meet you. I've watched all your videos. I'm a big fan. Huge.' She was talking very fast and sounded breathless.

Blaze smiled. He had come across this reaction before, but it was usually from 10-year-olds. 'That's great to hear,' he said smoothly.

'Wait, are you broadcasting this? You are, aren't you? Of course you are. It's part of *SyrenQuest*.' A blue hand flew to her mouth. 'I'm on YouTube. Oh my god, I need to stop talking.'

Oh dear. He felt sorry for her. To him, being on YouTube was fun. A chance to leave Luke behind and become Blaze, but it must be scary to put yourself out there if you weren't used to it. 'How about we run through one of the training exercises, just to see where our relative strengths and weaknesses are?'

'Oh, yes. Good idea.'

They ran through a few challenges together, Blaze narrating everything as they went. Talking to himself on the channel came naturally to him, but not to his co-player, it seemed. As far as he could tell, Bravura was concentrating fiercely, which didn't lend itself to chatting much.

He observed her play. The character was pretty nimble, but her reflexes weren't great. The fighting moves were … bad. Terrible, in fact. His heart sank. He would have to work hard to make sure she survived any combat, or they wouldn't make it past round one.

Oh well, he'd known this was a possibility when he'd signed up. He would get paid regardless of the outcome, so there was no need to stress. Right?

The introductory session ended and Sam flipped her visor up. She slowly leaned back against the sofa.

'So … how do you feel that went?' asked Niro, her tone cautious, like someone approaching a skittish cat.

'Oh my god, I was awful. And I was such a gibbering mess.' When she closed her eyes, all she could see was Blaze's expression while he was watching her. He hadn't looked angry, just resigned. Like he knew they were going to tank and he was making his peace with it. How humiliating.

'It wasn't so bad …' Niro began.

Something flashed on the screen. Her phone buzzed at the same time.

'What's that?'

'The game chat, I think.' Sam flipped her visor down and opened the chat. There was a message from Blaze.

Hi. It's pretty overwhelming being filmed, huh? Don't worry. You'll be a natural in no time. Just pretend that the only people around are your friends. Chat a bit. Keep it light. Maybe practise the fight moves before round one. Looking forward to working with you. B

She knew that the same message would be on the chat app on her phone.

'What does it say?' Niro nudged her.

Sam realised that the chat messages weren't displayed on the TV screen. She read it out loud.

'That's nice of him, trying to put you at ease,' Niro said.

'Especially after I was so bad.'

Niro gave her a hard look. 'You have to stop beating yourself up about not being instantly good at things.'

Sam shook her head. 'I need to practise quite a lot so that I don't let him down.' Carefully, she switched the headset off and removed it. 'I was hoping to spend the evenings doing more research for my Shanthi Bags pitches. Maybe I should start going in to work early, so that I can have the evening as game time—'

'Uh-huh. So, are you going to reply to him?'

She should message him back. He had been so kind. It would be churlish to stay quiet just because she was embarrassed at making an idiot of herself. When Sam didn't respond, Niro said, 'You have to reply to him. Come on! This is your chance to chat one to one.'

'What do I say?'

'I don't know. "I'm looking forward to working with you too" maybe?'

Sam opened the chat app on her phone and typed that out. She added, *I'm sorry I was so clumsy. I'll do better next time.* 'Should I say anything else?'

Niro shrugged. 'Such as?'

'I … don't know.' She stared at the lines that she'd typed. It would have to do. 'I'm going to send this before I chicken out.' She hit send and closed her eyes.

There was no reply from Blaze. Of course not. There wasn't anything else to say. 'I should have asked him a question,' she said.

'Don't worry, that might have looked a little weird anyway.' Niro tilted her chin towards the game console. 'Are you going to practise tonight?'

Sam looked at the headset and sighed. 'I should, but I told Luke I'd think about how to make the crowdfunding site more personal.' She collected the headset and wrapped it up in its original bubble wrap. 'I really need to do that.'

Luke opened his chat app to catch up on his messages.

There were a few from his friend Flick, who was another pro-gamer on *SyrenQuest*. He had known Flick through game chats for a while. About two years ago, he had met her at a convention and they'd got on well in real life.

Flick: *So, how's your newbie? Any good?*

Blaze: *No. Bloody awful. Yours?*

Flick: *Not bad TBH. Fast. Decent reflexes.*

Blaze: *Yeah, I'm going to be out of this in round one.*

Flick: *Haha. You'll just have to be good enough for both of you.*

Blaze: *Like I said. Round one max. She's awful.*

Flick: *I hope you didn't tell her that! This is just a paid gig for you, but to a newbie this must be terrifying.*

Blaze: *Of COURSE I didn't tell her that! What do you take me for?!*

Flick: *You're being uncharacteristically grumpy, that's all.*

Blaze: *Sorry. Real life stress.*

Flick: *I'd offer a listening ear, but I know you value your privacy, so accept a virtual hug instead.*

Blaze: *Gratefully accepted. Listen, it looks like she's replied. I'd best go respond.*

Flick: *Be nice to the girl.*

Blaze: *She's a fan, by the looks of it. I'm always nice to my fans.*

He saw that Bravura had replied to him apologising for being crap. Now he felt bad for being rude about her, even though he'd only said it to Flick, whom he could trust to be discreet.

It sounded like Bravura could do with encouragement. As Flick said, he was getting paid anyway. While winning the prize would have been brilliant, it was unlikely that he would. So why ruin someone's fortnight over it?

Blaze: *Don't worry too much. It's just a game. Have fun. I'll speak to you tomorrow before the start.*

There. Hopefully, that would help. With any luck she would be less nervous the next time they met in the game.

A few minutes later, Sam had tidied the hardware away and the living room was back to normal. Niro had swapped her popcorn for a blanket and was settling down to watch something on Netflix. Sam stood in the kitchenette and stared at the message from Blaze on her phone.

Don't worry too much. It's just a game. Have fun. I'll speak to you tomorrow before the start.

Sam couldn't help smiling at that reply. It was just a game to him. It was the experience of a lifetime for her. 'Niro.'

'Shh.' Niro flapped her hand, not taking her eyes off the screen.

'Sorry.' Sam took her little secret and went up to her room. The idea that Blaze even knew she existed seemed like a miracle. The fact that he was messaging her directly was almost too huge to comprehend. She wanted to tell someone about it, but there wasn't anyone. Well, apart from Niro, who had indulged her a lot over the past few weeks, but clearly needed a break right now.

Inside her bedroom, she leaned against her door and read the messages from Blaze again. *Maybe practise the fight moves.* No kidding. She had been unbelievably slow and clumsy with her playing. *It's just a game.* Hah. No it wasn't. There was quite a big prize at stake. Besides, she didn't want to be the one responsible for dragging him down in front of his peers. She would have to spend her evenings practising. She could improve, she was sure. Maybe it was a good thing she'd been so terrible today. It meant that when she saw him again, he could be impressed with her progress.

She lifted her gaze to the rest of the room and her dream popped. Who was she trying to kid? She had a business to run. With only five weeks left on her crowdfunding campaign, she needed to keep her head down, and find more supporters and, ideally, a handbag company to partner with. She didn't have time to spend on video games. She pushed herself from the door towards her mother's wardrobe.

Since she paid slightly more rent, Sam got to have the bigger room in the flat. It was a Georgian house, one that had been split up to make the apartments, so the rooms were larger than in newer houses. It meant that Sam could have two wardrobes. One from Ikea and one that had belonged to her mother. If she'd had space for only one, she would have kept her clothes in a pile on her desk, just so her mother's cheap and flimsy old wardrobe could live with her.

When she opened the wardrobe's doors, she took a deep breath as she always did. That first movement of air always brought with it a smell – a hint of perfume or of leather that reminded her of Amma. The inside had been modified so that it held rows of shallow shelves and hooks. They were all full of handbags. Sixty of them. Amma's collection only had fifty-six, but Sam had added four of her own. There were bucket bags, shoulder totes, clutches, tiny Nineties-style baguette purses, even a silver backpack. Nearly all were from the high street, although there were a few factory rejects from designer brands bought on trips to Sri Lanka. The value in the collection lay in what the bags meant to Sam.

She had been barely 12 when her mother died. Her brothers had been 14 and 16. Their father had withdrawn with grief. He was there, making sure they had food and whatever else they needed, but he never wanted to talk to them, and certainly not about their mother. So they talked to each other. Sam had spent many an evening curled up with a book while her brothers shot at things on a computer. After a year or so, their father met their stepmother, a nice woman who took one look at the children who were glaring suspiciously at her and made it her business to make sure they got their father back. She hadn't fully succeeded in that, but Sam and her brothers loved her nevertheless. She had been a kind and steady presence when they needed her the most.

Sam pulled the bag she'd taken to work off the bed and removed her Shanthi bag from inside it. She did a quick check to see if she'd left anything in the larger bag before she wiped it down and put it back in the cupboard. Hmm ... which bag to take tomorrow?

She chose one, popped in the Shanthi bag, and put it back on the bed. Instead of closing the wardrobe, she sat on the floor and looked at it.

Sometime in her late teens, she and her stepmother had got the boxes of handbags down from the attic and sorted them so that Sam could use them. Sam's memories of her mother were hazy now, but sometimes, a particular light on a particular bag would trigger a memory so strong, she knew she hadn't really forgotten. The best way to feel a connection to Amma was to carry one of her bags with her, every single day.

Her idea for Shanthi Bags came from the many times she'd switched bags and found that she'd left her purse or her keys in the old bag. She had made herself a small pouch, to begin with. Over time, it had evolved into the current design of a soft bag with an elasticated pocket for a mobile phone, another for lipstick and a packet of tissues, and enough space in the middle to take a decent-sized wallet and other odds and ends. For the prototype bags, she'd chosen brightly coloured fabrics, so that the inserts themselves were desirable objects, rather than something plain and functional. She'd called them Shanthi, after her mother.

Luke had asked why she had started her business. This was her why.

She chewed her lip. Did she want to share that? It was such a precious connection that it seemed wrong to use it for something as tawdry as advertising.

Chapter 5

Luke tried to stifle a huge yawn and failed. He'd been up late last night, messing around on the *SyrenQuest* training site. He had hoped to be a bit more alert for his meeting with Sam. He slumped at a table in the cafeteria, with his coffee by his elbow, and pulled up the *SyrenQuest* chat app on his phone. There were a few more messages in the pro-gamer group, but nothing interesting.

He put his phone away and looked up to see Sam getting her coffee. She smiled at him and his pulse suddenly got louder. From past experience, he knew that 'be casual' was a recipe for disaster, so he decided he'd just be his normal intense self. He pulled out the notebook where he'd sketched a few layouts and suggestions on how to redo her crowdfunding site.

'Good morning.' Sam pulled up a chair to sit at the opposite side of the table.

He noticed that she was using a reusable cup with a lid. He pointed to it. 'In case of spillages?'

She grinned. 'I learn from my mistakes.'

He nodded and smiled. She was very pretty. That smile was incredible. The smile faded and was replaced by a look of puzzlement. Oh dear. He was staring, wasn't he?

He looked down. 'I ... er ... made some notes. Here.' He

turned it around, so that it was the right way up for her and started explaining what it all meant. As he spoke, he could see the expressions that flitted across her face – some of what he was saying clearly meant something to her, but some of it was way off the mark. That was okay. No client ever liked a hundred per cent of the suggestions. He never normally cared, but it was important to him that she liked what he'd produced.

'What do you think?' he asked.

She nodded, slowly. 'A lot of it makes sense.'

'You could use the images that you already have. You might need some more, though, including some of you perhaps. There are plenty of examples of the bags.'

Her lips pressed together.

He could sense the hesitation. 'You don't agree?' he prompted.

'I sell bag inserts. I think the website should focus on the product. Not me.'

Ah. That old chestnut. He had seen this before when he'd helped people. They were all about the product or service. It was nearly always easier to convince men to feature themselves on their websites than women. 'Remember I said that people buy from people they like and trust? How can they get to like and trust you if you're not visible? Your current site doesn't even have much of an "about us" page.'

She inclined her head. 'I suppose I could expand that a bit.'

He took that as a win. 'You could. In fact, you should.'

She looked down and rotated her coffee one way and then back again. Oh dear. She was avoiding eye contact. He should probably shut up now. Except, he was right. Her project had so much potential, it would be a shame to see it fail for want of something so easily fixed. All she needed was a personality and a story to get people talking about the product.

'You're intelligent, articulate, and attractive. You'd be the perfect figurehead to give to this project.' He said it quickly, so that it sounded like a fact and not like he was hitting on her.

She made a face. 'I'm not really comfortable with that,' she said.

Luke leaned back. 'Okay. How about, you do some research on crowdfunding projects that have been successful? See how much of it is about personality and see if they give you any ideas on how you can build more of a personality-led brand without giving up too much of yourself.'

She didn't reply.

Around them, the cafeteria filled up. The buzz of conversation and the clink of crockery rose around them. Should he say something? Was this silence a bad sign?

'Sam?'

She raised her eyes, her expression guarded. 'Okay,' she said. 'I'll think about it.'

'Great. Just tell me when you're ready and I'll update the site for you.' It wouldn't take him long to make the changes, because he was used to doing it. To someone new, it would be overwhelming. 'For now, I can just tweak it a little so that it flows better. If you like.'

She shifted in her chair. 'That's very kind, but I can't afford it. I have no budget left to pay for website stuff.'

'Oh, it's on me,' he said. 'I told you. Paying it forward. You do someone else a favour when you're established.'

'Oh, in that case … Thank you. You're a star.'

He shrugged, modestly. She glanced at her watch. Luke's mood deflated. Was she in a hurry to get away?

'Do you need to run?' he asked, trying to keep the disappointment out of his voice.

Sam looked up at him and seemed to come to a decision. 'Yes, but I think I should drink my coffee before I go up, otherwise it'll just go cold.'

'What are you up to today?'

'Same as every day. Writing pitches, ticking off the rejections.'

'Keep at it,' he said. 'It only takes one person to say yes and things will change.'

'Fair point.' She took a sip of coffee. 'So what about you? Exciting plans for the day?'

He grimaced. 'I have a meeting with my business partner.'

She raised a quizzical eyebrow at him as she slipped off her seat and started gathering her things.

'I haven't had any emails from him or any input into a project for six months now. I keep cutting him slack, but I think I really need to do something about it now.'

The look she gave him was sympathetic. 'That does sound like an untenable situation – and unfair on you.'

Luke blew out his cheeks. 'Yeah. But I hate confrontation. Plus, Bradley is so … charming. Whenever we argue, I end up being the bad guy.'

'That's tough. Could you frame it as a business thing only and not bring up your friendship and how it's affected by this?'

'That's what I intend to do. I just hope I can hold my nerve.'

'I'm sure you can,' she said. 'I have to go. Thank you for your suggestions.' She picked up her cup. 'Good luck with your meeting.'

'Thanks. Let me know when you have pictures and the copy for the site and I'll slot them in.' He picked up his own cup and drained it. Sam had left and was standing waiting for the lift. Luke thoughtfully put his cup back down. That went well. He hadn't said anything weird. All good.

Sam glared at her crowdfunding page. No pledges since yesterday. This was a new low. Luke had some good suggestions, but she didn't agree with all of them. Especially his insistence on making the crowdfunding site all about her. Why? It made sense that it should be about her product.

She closed the page and laid her forehead on the desk. This was not how this was supposed to go. She was supposed to create a vibrant and fun community of people who loved handbags, not feel like she was scrabbling around begging for support.

Maybe her father was right. Maybe the best thing was to stick to a regular job where you put in the hours and got paid – regardless of how you felt about your work. There was no creativity, no buzz. But you got a reassuringly regular paycheque at the end of each month.

Sam stood up and walked over to her cork noticeboard. It was covered in various notes she'd left for herself, but also, in the bottom right corner, a photo of her mother. It had been taken when Sam was about 6. She was in the photo only as an arm and a blur as she ran out of shot. Amma was laughing. Her face wasn't even very clear in this photo, her hair was spilling onto her face and her hand was raised to push it back, obscuring her mouth. But the way her head was thrown slightly back, the way her eyes were creased at the edges … Sam could almost hear her laugh.

Amma had taught her about hopes and dreams and being creative. Thatha, on the other hand, always advised caution and common sense. With Amma gone, Sam's adult life only had caution left. Taking a risk like she had done with Shanthi Bags was a tribute to her mother, but at the same time, it felt like a betrayal of her father.

Unless she made a success of it.

Which brought her right back to her struggling crowdfunding campaign and her lack of a retailer to partner with. Not to mention letting herself get distracted by this gaming competition. It was as though fate had conspired to give her a pathway to two things she really wanted – to run her own creative business and to meet Blaze – but it was forcing her to choose one.

Well, stuff that. She would do both. Neither of her parents had taught her to fold at the first hurdle. She was going to run at both those goals full tilt and see what happened.

She went back to her desk and looked again at the notes from her meeting with Luke. She was convinced that Luke was wrong about people needing to see her on her crowdfunding page, but his was the first bit of professional feedback she'd had on her campaign. It would be stupid to dismiss his advice without even checking. She searched for some successful crowdfunding campaigns and scrolled through them. They all had a lot about what they were selling, but … the creators were there posing with their products, beaming with drinks in their hands, making cutesy faces at their pets. Frowning, she read a few 'about' sections. Personal stories. Some were heartwarming, some were inspiring, but all of them were very personal. They all fleshed out the people behind the business. Dammit, Luke was right. They did all have that in common. It was almost as though the personality came first, and the product second.

But she didn't want that. So, what could she do?

Sam put her head back on the desk.

Luke half expected Bradley to not show up for their meeting. He popped to the front desk and told Kim to give him a call if Bradley came in. 'He has an access card, but I guess he'll have to sign in.'

'I haven't seen Bradley in ages,' said Kim. 'It'll be nice to see him. What's he doing now?'

That's what he wanted to know too. Luke bit back his bitter reply and instead said, 'I'm not sure. Partly why we're meeting.'

Kim flicked a curl out of her eye. 'Did you catch up with our Sam yesterday?'

He didn't ask how she knew. She always knew everything that happened in the building. It was like a superpower. 'I did, actually. Thanks.'

'And?' Kim waggled her eyebrows at him. 'Do I sense some gossip in the making?'

'No!' It came out too emphatic. 'No,' he said again, more calmly. 'I had to apologise for spilling her coffee. And I said I'd help her with the crowdfunding project. No gossip.'

Kim leaned forward on her elbow, chin resting on her hand. 'But would you like there to be? Do I sense love in the air?'

Luke shook his head. Kim was always doing this. She liked to tease people, but she seemed to particularly enjoy teasing him. 'You're obsessed with matchmaking, you are.'

Kim shrugged. 'Keeps me entertained. It's not like I can shop around anymore, is it? Tell you what,' she said. 'I'll put in a good word for you when I next see her.'

'Please don't—'

The switchboard phone rang and Kim had to answer it. Luke took the opportunity to go back to his office.

L&B Online Event Services had an office on the third floor. Unlike the tiny offices downstairs, these were intended for companies with three or more employees. In theory, this meant having space for three desks and a small meeting space. But Luke used the meeting room to store the equipment, and Bradley's desk was mostly used as a dumping ground for stuff that needed to be sorted out later.

Luke sat down at his desk and tried to concentrate, but his thoughts kept circling back to his upcoming meeting with Bradley. It sucked all his energy, distorting his brain like a black hole. When Bradley walked in the door, it was almost a relief.

'Hello, hello.' Bradley surveyed the place as though he owned it. He already had a hot drink in one hand and a couple of biscuits in the other. He must have charmed those out of Kim. 'Luke. It's been too long.' He stopped beside Pete. 'You must be Pete,' he said. 'I'm Bradley. It's nice to meet you.' He transferred his biscuits to the same hand as his mug and shook Pete's hand. 'How're you finding working with this guy?'

Pete's gaze darted sideways to Luke. 'Er … fine.'

Luke stood up. Bradley had been back less than a minute and already Luke wanted to punch him. Where was the easy-going guy that he'd gone into business with? 'I've booked us a meeting room, Brad. Shall we?'

Bradley made a face at Pete. Luke ignored it. To his quiet delight, Pete did too.

When they got into the meeting room, Bradley sat down and dipped his biscuit in his tea. 'What's all this about, Luke?'

Luke started to sit down, then changed his mind, leaving him for a second in an awkward crouch. He stood up properly. 'I'll get straight to the point,' he said, exactly like he'd practised. 'You haven't come in to work for ages and things have to change.'

'I'm here now,' said Bradley, smiling.

'Only because I asked you to be. And in all honesty, I'm surprised. I half expected you to ignore me like you normally do. I've even drafted a formal letter.'

'Really?' He shook his head. 'There's no need for that. You could have just called me.' He dipped the second biscuit. 'What does your letter say?'

'It reminds you that the agreement we both signed includes a clause that says you will work for the company an average of three days a week. You haven't done anything for over a year.'

'Ah, but you don't know that,' Bradley said, with infuriating cheeriness. 'I could have been pitching to loads of clients, for all you know. I don't have to tell you exactly what I'm doing. You're not my boss.'

Luke felt the heat rising in his face. His heart raced. 'I'm not your boss. But I am your business partner. And right now, I'm the only one doing any work here. Do you know how many balls I've had to pick up because you'd dropped them? How many suppliers I've had to smooth over because you didn't process the invoices like you were supposed to?'

Bradley shrugged. He didn't seem to be listening. 'So, I slipped up a couple of times. Nobody's perfect, Luke. Not even you.'

'I'm not …' No. This was a distraction. Luke sighed and sank into his seat. A change of tactic was required. 'Look, Brad. I don't want to have to come after you for breach of contract. This isn't like you. Is everything okay?'

Something changed in his former friend's posture. Oh. It

sounded like a little sympathy was having an effect. 'Brad? Are you in trouble?'

Finally, Bradley made eye contact. 'In a manner of speaking, maybe,' he said. 'I … got into some debt. I couldn't pay it off, so I picked up more freelancing work, which is going well, by the way. I get dividends from here anyway, so I focused on that for a bit.'

'But that's hardly fair,' said Luke. 'And it's also not what we agreed.'

'It's a tough world out there, Luke. It's not all fun times and video games.'

Ouch. Low blow. During his university years, his YouTube channel had become profitable enough for him to seriously think about making a living off it. As a result he had taken his eye off his degree and only scraped through the course that he should have aced easily.

Bradley spotted his discomfort. 'I don't think you're in any position to lecture me about getting distracted from the important things, are you?'

Luke struggled to recover his composure. 'That was a long time ago. Since we started this company, I have given it my all and you know it.'

Bradley didn't disagree with him. He couldn't because it was true. Luke could hear his pulse roaring around his head. Bradley, as usual, was calm and so bloody charming.

'Tell you what,' said Bradley. 'I agree with you on one thing. This arrangement isn't working. I don't like doing this work and you don't want me here, so why don't we come to a compromise. Why don't you buy me out?'

Luke blinked. He hadn't expected things to get to that quite so soon. It was a good suggestion. Although, it depended on how much Bradley was asking for. 'It's a bit sudden, but okay,' he said. 'Let me ask the accountant to run the numbers and we'll come up with a figure.'

Bradley smiled and nodded. 'It'll have to be soon, though.

So how about three weeks from now? If you can't buy me out by then, I have another buyer interested.' He stood up. 'I think we're done here.'

'Hang on—' Three weeks wasn't much time. Especially if he had to find extra money.

'It was good seeing you again, Luke. I'll be in touch.' He grinned and left.

Luke stared at the door. Bradley had just walked out on him. His first thought was how rude that was. His next thought was that Bradley had tricked him. He had clearly come in planning to tell Luke he was selling up. The three weeks was a sop; a way to make Bradley look like less of a bastard. He was banking on Luke failing to raise the money in that time. Luke fumed quietly. He wasn't going to chase his former friend down the corridor. He wouldn't give him the satisfaction.

Whatever Bradley's reasons for giving him three weeks, the opportunity to own the whole of the business was too good for Luke to pass it up. Besides, if Bradley sold up to someone else, Luke would have to share ownership with a stranger. That would be awful. Right now, he got to run the company – which was essentially just him and Pete – how he liked. If someone else got involved, things would change. He definitely did not want that.

Three weeks was hardly enough time for him to raise the funds he'd need to buy Bradley out. He had some idea what Bradley's share was worth, and he didn't have that kind of money.

Unless … Luke slowly let out his breath. Unless he won *SyrenQuest*.

He sat with that thought for a few minutes. He was normally careful to keep his Blaze-related money away from the company. The YouTube money paid his mortgage and allowed him to live a decent life despite his company earning minimal profit. He didn't have any slack there. He had savings, though it would take some time to release them. But *SyrenQuest* wasn't factored into his budget. If he won that, he would have enough money to invest in his company.

Winning *SyrenQuest* would be a long shot. His partner in the competition wasn't the greatest of players, but *he* was pretty good. From what he could tell after that single practice session, this game was more like an adventure quest than a shoot-'em-up. So the fact that Bravura wasn't a good fighter might be less relevant. They hadn't played together before, which made life difficult. Then again, none of the other teams were used to playing together either, so maybe his chances weren't as bad as all that.

He drummed his fingers against the desk. The first round was that night. The competition was run so that they all played the same scenario in parallel. The eight teams who finished in the shortest time would go into the next round. So … he just had to remember to keep good time. Bravura's character was a small elfin thing. He could carry her and run if he needed to.

It wasn't the soundest of financial plans. But he only had a few weeks, so this was the best he had.

Sam worked steadily into the evening, writing more pitches for Shanthi Bags. Sitting at her computer for so long was making her shoulders stiff, so she stood up, flexed her neck, and swung her arms around to loosen up. It was probably time to call it a day. She wanted to get home in good time so that she could eat and have another quick practice on the *SyrenQuest* training scenarios before the competition started that evening.

A few minutes later, she was ready to go. On her way out, she met Luke coming down the stairs, also leaving. He was dressed in cycling gear, for his commute home probably. She couldn't avoid him without being obvious, so she nodded to him in greeting. They fell into step as they walked up to the front desk to sign out.

'How are you getting on?' he asked.

'Not bad,' she said. The silence that followed was awkward.

There was someone else ahead of them, signing out, so they had to stand together, waiting.

'Thanks for your notes,' she said to him. 'They've been really useful.'

'That's great.' He smiled. 'I'm glad it was helpful.'

'It was. I'm glad you spilled my coffee now. You've definitely more than repaid me. In fact, I probably owe you coffee for your help.'

Whatever Luke was about to say next was interrupted by Kim. 'Hello, you two. Calling it a day, are you?'

It was their turn to sign out. Luke pulled the entry book and pen towards him. 'Uh-huh.' He bent his head over the book.

'Are you coming to George's birthday drinks later?' asked Kim.

'No,' said Luke.

Kim looked at Sam.

'I … don't know who George is,' she said.

'Doesn't matter,' said Kim. 'I'll introduce you. You should come. It'll be a good way for you to meet the rest of the people in The Nest.'

'The socials are pretty fun,' said Luke. He pushed the book towards Sam.

'So, does that mean you're coming, Luke?' asked Kim.

'Oh. No. I can't. I have a thing.' He pulled his cycle helmet on and clipped it under his chin.

'I can't either.' Sam signed out. 'I've got plans, too.'

Kim looked from one to the other. 'Wait a minute. Have you both got plans … together?'

Luke's eyes went huge. 'No, of course not,' he said, colouring slightly.

Kim's sceptical expression didn't do anything to help. She was so obviously teasing and Luke seemed to be walking straight into it.

Sam felt sorry for him. 'I don't know what Luke's doing,' she said. 'But I will be at home, in front of the telly. I promised my cousin I would hang out with her tonight.'

'I'd best be off. I'll see you guys tomorrow.' Luke practically fled.

Sam and Kim watched him go.

'It's almost too easy.' Kim chuckled as she sat down. 'He gets so embarrassed, bless him.'

'Poor guy,' Sam said.

'Seriously, though, is there anything going on? He was looking for you the other day. You guys seem to be quite chummy just now …'

'He's giving me some help with my crowdfunding campaign.' Sam hitched her bag onto her shoulder.

'Oh, well, that's dull.'

It was? 'I thought it was kind of him, actually.'

'I'm sure it was. Luke's always doing stuff like that. I doubt there's any new business here that he hasn't helped out in some way. He's a good guy. Not bad-looking too, once you get past the shyness. And, you've seen him in cycling shorts. Phew.' She pretended to fan herself.

Sam laughed. 'Sounds like you have a thing for him, Kim.'

'Too late for me,' Kim said, pointing to her wedding ring. 'But you …'

'Goodbye, Kim.'

'Think about it,' Kim shouted after her.

By the time Sam got outside, Luke was nowhere to be seen. She couldn't help feeling that it was mean of Kim to tease him. Also, why on earth did Kim think that she liked sweet guys? An image of Blaze's rakish grin on his avatar flashed across her mind. Her perfect man was handsome, super competent, and nice. If she was going to play alongside him, she was going to have to get herself home.

Chapter 6

Round One: You must obtain the first key. It is expected that you will complete the quest in under three hours. All players will start at the same time. The eight teams with the shortest game times will progress to Round Two.

Luke stared at the instructions. Was that it? No other clues? Just a picture of the key. He frowned at the object on the screen. From the side, it looked like a slice of it was missing. When he rotated it, he could see a small hole at one end and a peg on the other. This was a component of something else. They probably had to collect the pieces and make the final key.

He knew how the characters moved and how realistic the graphics were, but apart from that, he had no idea what he was getting into.

He messaged Bravura.

Blaze: *What do you think? Not much of a clue.*
Bravura: *It looks like the key is a part of something bigger. I'm guessing we're collecting the bits and making a key at the final stage.*

Good. She thought the same as he had. Useful to know.

Bravura: *There're some markings on it. They look like hooks. Or sickles of some sort.*

Were there? He rotated the key again and zoomed in. Oh yes. What he had taken for texture markings resolved themselves into a stylised drawing of curved hooks. How had he missed that?

Blaze: *Good spot!*
Blaze: *Looks like speed is the thing we need for this.*
Bravura: *I may not be much in a fight, but one thing this character can do is run fast. :-)*

In their initial meeting, Luke had assumed that Bravura was going to be someone who he needed to carry along with him. Getting a teammate through a public lottery was always dangerous. Most people who entered would be good players, but there was always the risk of opportunists entering, just so that they could get hold of a limited edition headset. At least Bravura was keen to play and her observation skills were apparently better than his. Perhaps this wasn't going to be such a disaster after all. He had come into this expecting it to be nothing more than a bit of fun, but now that he actually needed to win, things had changed.

Sam rubbed her hands on the side of her legs. Nearly time. She hadn't had time to practise, so she was just going to have to do what she could. She bounced lightly on her feet and stretched her neck from side to side.

'Good luck,' said Niro, who was sitting on the sofa again.

'Thanks.' Sam puffed out a breath, put on her headset, and became Bravura. At first she was standing in a field at sunrise. The theme song played and the lyrics scrolled overhead. She read them, even though she already knew them by heart.

Welcome to the Quest, my friend
Be the fastest to the end
The paths depend on which you choose
When one dies, you both lose

Choose the right, not the wrong
Spare the young, heed the song
One last thing you have to know
Where one goes, you both go
Where one goes, you both go

When she lowered her gaze again, Blaze was standing several metres away. He looked at her. 'Ready?'

His voice was clear in her headset. It was like he was standing right next to her, instead of metres away.

'Ready as I'll ever be,' she said.

The words 'Quest One' appeared in the sky and the scene changed.

She was standing in what looked like an old stone dining hall. It was a single, large room, with well-spaced sconces dividing the room into light and trembling shadows.

She turned. Blaze was standing next to her, frowning. This was the first time she'd seen the avatar actually playing, rather than messing about practising. There was a whole new intensity to him. If he'd looked attractive before, having an actual expression on his face only made him sexier. Even if that expression was a frown.

He took a few steps into the room. Oh yeah. Game. She wasn't there to gawp at Blaze. If she was going to get to know him, she'd have to play. She turned and took in the smashed crockery and the overturned benches. 'Looks like it's been ransacked.'

Blaze peered around, still frowning. 'Everything of value must have been taken.'

'But they must have made us start here for a reason,' she said. 'There must be something in here we're meant to find.'

His frown gave way to a raised eyebrow. 'That's a good point. You take that side, I'll take this one.' Without waiting to check, he strode over to his side.

Sam shrugged and started to methodically straighten things up and search for anything that looked like it might be useful.

After a few minutes, Blaze said, 'This is useless. There's nothing here. We should try outside.'

'Why would they start us off here, if there wasn't anything we were meant to find?'

He shrugged. 'I don't know. I only have the same information you have.' He headed towards the door.

Sam stared at the table. The tablecloth was still on it. 'Everything is smashed up, but the tablecloth is intact. This might be useful. I don't know what for, but—'

'Grab it then,' said Blaze. 'Come on. We're against the clock. We can't waste time dawdling.'

He drew his sword, threw open the wooden door, and crouched, ready to fight.

Behind him, Sam did the same. Nothing happened. They both straightened up.

'Okay,' said Blaze. 'Let's go.'

Outside, it was daylight. They were in a clearing, and a path led away from it. Above them a glowing wayfinder diamond in the sky showed them which way they had to go.

'Path?' said Sam.

'Path,' Blaze agreed. He set off, not waiting for her. He was narrating what he was doing, for the benefit of his channel. She knew this was how he always played – rush in first, think later – but they were supposed to be a team here. She felt like she was being babysat.

The path ahead forked, but the wayfinder was in the middle. They had no way of knowing whether left or right was the correct path. He stopped and glanced one way, then the other, one hand always on the hilt of his sword. 'Which way?'

'I don't know,' she snapped. 'I only have the same information you have.'

He turned to look at her. Was that a hint of a smile? 'Touché,' he said.

Both paths led into deep woods.

'In that case, let's go … left.' He strode down the path into the trees.

Sam bit her lip and followed him. What other choice was there? She had almost caught up with him when something landed on her. She hit the ground with a crunch. Turning her head, she saw a confusion of legs and claws. These things looked like sloths, with long arms and cruel claws, but unlike the real thing, they moved fast.

A movement at the corner of her vision. She rolled. A claw raked the ground where her face had just been. She scrambled to her feet and pulled out her weapon. The creature attacked. She was nowhere near fast enough. It caught her shoulder. Her health bar flashed up in front of her at less than half and dropping. The creature turned to charge again. She looked around for something to climb or run to.

A few metres away, Blaze was fighting three of them at once. As she watched, one of the creatures fell. She ran for the cover of the trees, but something caught her from behind. She turned her blade around and plunged it backwards under her arm. The grip loosened. She did it again. It must have made contact because the creature dropped and stopped moving. But it had already hurt her – her life bar flashed red. She stared, aghast. Was that it? Her one chance to play alongside Blaze and she was going to die in round one?

'For heaven's sake,' Blaze said.

She looked up and saw the disgust on his face as he whirled past. That guy was fast. No time to feel sorry for herself. There was a small health potion in her inventory. She grabbed it just before her health bar reached zero and recharged it halfway. Back on her feet, she turned to help Blaze, but there was nothing left to fight. The creatures were on the ground, already fading away.

'What was that?' Blaze shoved his blade back into its sheath. 'Did you practise at *all*?'

Bravura said nothing. No. This was harder than she was expecting. She hadn't practised. She didn't deserve this chance she'd been given.

'I—'

'Never mind,' he said, wearily. 'If they don't want us going that way, then it must be the right path. Come on.' He set off.

She wanted to cry, but she was here in the game. Where one goes, you both go. She followed him, trying to keep focused.

She turned to look at the ground where the murder sloths had been. All that was left of them was a few black claws, big, curved things that could tear through anything. She picked a couple up. You never knew.

'We are judged on how long we take to complete this task,' Blaze said, his voice tight.

He wasn't telling her off exactly, but he sounded like he was keeping a rein on his anger. Sam caught up with him. He was narrating as he went again, so at least she didn't have to compound her humiliation by making conversation. She walked along in silence.

This was a disaster.

Sam took off her headset. They'd paused the game so that they could take a ten-minute toilet break. Once the headset was off, Sam realised just how tense she was. Plus, she really needed a wee. When she got back, she asked Niro how she thought things were going.

Niro made a face. 'You're still alive …'

Sam rolled her shoulders, trying to loosen them. 'That bad?'

'I get that meeting this guy is your dream, but you're not really putting your back into it, are you?' said Niro. 'I've seen you play video games before. You're not normally this bad.'

'The game's new to me. And he makes me nervous.'

'I can see that,' said Niro. 'Plus, he's talking all the time and you're not saying anything. Perhaps you should try some banter.'

'Banter?'

'Just talk to him. Chat. It might make you less stiff and awkward. It would make watching it a bit more entertaining for the rest of us.'

'That's the thing. Whenever I say something, I'm horribly aware that millions of people will see it.'

'So what?' said Niro. 'No one knows it's you. It's just some blue chick with pointy ears. She could be nothing at all like you. Get in there. Live a little.'

Sam picked up the headset, which was one of only thirty-two like it. Niro had a point. She should live a little.

'Look!'

They were back inside the game. There was a monolith visible through the trees. The wayfinder hovered directly above it. Clouds moved across the sky, making the light shift. Something gleamed at the top of the monolith.

They ran through the forest until they were standing at the foot of it.

'I guess we have to figure out how to get up there now.' Sam approached it. 'It's not going straight up. There's a slight incline.' She reached out to touch the surface, which gave her no information whatsoever.

They walked around it. There was a furrow, a bit wider than the width of a person, running all the way up. 'I wonder if you could use that to brace yourself,' said Blaze.

'Like climbing up a door frame?'

'Exactly.' He tried it. He made it up only a few feet before he slid back down again. 'Nope.'

'It's too high to jump,' said Sam. 'But what if you threw me? This character is light and agile, right?'

'Let's give it a try.' Now that things were happening again, Blaze seemed to have cheered up. He cupped his hands and crouched. She took a short run and vaulted upwards from his cupped hands. She got higher than she expected, but she was still a long way off. She twisted and landed on her feet.

'Perhaps we could rig something to catapult one of us up,' she said. She opened up her inventory and scrolled through. The claws. Hmm. She took one out.

'Where did you get that?' he asked.

'Picked it up while I was dawdling.'

He winced. 'Good call. So you think we could use it to climb?' He looked dubiously at the monolith. 'We don't know what it's made of …' He pulled out his sword and stabbed the monolith. His blade sank into the surface. 'Oh. Cool.' He tugged it out again.

The moment the sword came out, something screeched. Sloths poured out from the trees.

'Go, go, go!' Blaze shouted. 'I'll hold them off. You climb.'

She grabbed two of the claws and tossed him the third. Then, without waiting to see what was happening, she launched herself at the monolith and started to pull herself up. It wasn't exactly a quick way to get up. She had to use one claw to brace herself and then extract the other and stab it in further up.

At the base of the monolith, Blaze was a dervish, fighting the creatures as they came at him. Sam glanced down. There were too many of them, surely. But now she could see that they had spotted her too. They started climbing up behind her.

'They're coming after me,' she said. To her surprise, her voice was calm. She stuck both claws in to give her a decent foothold and pulled out her own sword. Unlike Blaze's wide, cutlass-type thing, her sword was made for stabbing. So she stabbed, aiming for the eyes. The first sloth fell and took a couple of others down with it.

'Nice one,' Blaze grunted.

She looked down. 'There are more coming,' she said. 'Climb. Where one goes, we both go, remember?'

He backed up to the wall. She stabbed another sloth. It fell just short of where Blaze was. He somehow managed to fight off the others and simultaneously grab the claws from the fading dead one and ram them into the monolith. This gave him footholds to get a bit of height. Okay. So he had a strategy.

Sam turned back to her task. It seemed to take forever to get to the top, but she eventually reached it. On the plateau at the top was the key, rotating on a blue glow. She grabbed it. 'I've got it.'

'Aargh.'

She dropped on her belly and looked over the side. Blaze was not far behind her, but there were too many sloths in the way. She wrenched one of the claws she'd been using out of the surface and threw it at the creature nearest him. She had aimed for its face, but hit it in the arm instead. The creature lost its grip in that arm and flailed around, hanging from one set of claws. At least the thing was distracted for a second. Blaze grinned and threw himself sideways. He used the claws the distracted creature was hanging from as a stepping stone to get himself higher. A few seconds later, she was hauling him up onto the flat top.

The minute he stood up, the clouds gathered into a swirl overhead, turning the world dark. Light flashed in the core of it. The wind whipped around them, so strong that she grabbed hold of Blaze before she lost her balance.

'What now?' Sam said.

'I don't know. I only have the same information as you do.'

She rolled her eyes. 'We have to get off.' Cautiously, she leaned forward to look over the side. The sloths were all dashing for cover. 'Somehow, I think staying up here isn't an option.'

Blaze turned. He grabbed her arm, fingers around her elbow. She changed her grip to match. So now they were keeping each other steady. 'We can't jump. It's too far down. It's very windy, but I don't think it's strong enough to carry us along.'

'What's in your inventory?'

They both checked what they had. One key, medical packs, swords, rope, food packs … and one tablecloth. 'Wait,' Sam said, extracting it. 'Do you think that we could use this as a parachute?'

There was a crash and a bolt of lightning struck a few feet away from them.

'I guess this is where we find out. You take those two corners. I'll take these two. Hold on tight.'

She grabbed the corners. They stood together at the top of the edifice.

Blaze said, 'Face away from the wind.'

She did. The wind was strong enough that her plait was blowing in front of her. 'Ready.'

'Three. Two. One. Jump.'

Sam squeezed her eyes shut and leapt. They plunged downwards and then, astoundingly, slowed down. The cloth billowed out at an angle above them, pulling them along. The wind blew them over the treetops, past clearings and rivers, and then suddenly dropped. They drifted down to the ground in the middle of a meadow.

The minute her feet touched the ground, the scenario ended and they were back in the training area. Their time – '2 hrs 46 mins' – hovered in the air above them.

She started up at it, mesmerised. 'That's pretty good, right?'

Blaze shrugged. 'We won't know until everyone's finished.' He sighed. 'Well, I guess that's us done for a bit.' He turned to face her and held out his hand. 'It was nice playing with you.'

Sam blinked. So polite, yet so cold. She had listened to him for years so she knew what he was normally like. This was not the usual exuberant Blaze. He was pissed off and trying not to show it.

'I'm so sorry. I was useless in the fighting.'

'Well, now we know our strengths and weaknesses, we can try to work on them, right?' He sounded stern.

'I guess so.'

A voice cut in. 'Blaze and Bravura, before you go, can we have a quick interview?'

Blaze glanced at her. She shrugged.

He said, 'Sure.'

A new avatar appeared – a woman in a smart suit, holding a microphone, who looked out of place in the fantasy landscape. 'So, Blaze and Bravura, you finished the challenge. How do you feel?' She pointed her mic at Sam.

'Exhilarated,' Sam said. Other people didn't need to know how bad she felt. 'It's such a privilege to be in this game. Even if we get knocked out in this round … although I hope we don't, obviously. It's been an honour to play alongside Blaze.' She turned to him. 'An honour. Honestly.'

He gave an exaggerated bow. He straightened up and smiled at the interviewer. 'Seriously, though. It's been a ton of fun. I always thought sloths were cute, but not any more.'

Sam forced a laugh. 'Yeah. Now all I'm going to be able to think about are murder sloths.'

The interviewer turned back to Blaze. 'What do you think your chances are?'

'I don't know. This is an untested game for us all and all the teams are very good. So your guess is as good as mine.' His voice was even and calm. He didn't think they'd made it. Sam could tell.

'Fair enough. Bravura? What do you think?'

She had not been expecting to be asked for a comment. 'I … er … I don't mind either way. I mean, just being here is amazing. Even if we get kicked out after this round, I'll be happy.' She caught Blaze's frown. 'Of course, I would love it if we won.'

'Like I said,' Blaze interrupted. 'Our chances are as good as anyone else's.'

Right. He didn't even look at her when he said it. What happened to 'it's just a game'?

Sam produced a smile too, because after all, the world was watching.

Luke took off his headset and pushed his chair away from his console. Phew. That was … difficult. He made a note of their time on the notepad that lived on the shelf at his elbow. He also wrote down the actual time. Nearly eleven o'clock. According to Syren's rules, everyone started playing at 8 p.m. The streams weren't broadcast until after the winners were announced. No one knew how well anyone else was doing. The top eight teams would go to the next round. Fifteen minutes after the top eight had gone through, the teams would be notified that the round was over. Those who were still playing could carry on if they wanted to finish the round.

So, if fifteen minutes passed and he wasn't notified that the round was over, then he could be pretty sure he was in the next one. He pushed his hair off his face. What could he do for fifteen minutes? He had recorded his gameplay, so that he could stitch together some highlights and do some commentary to go on his YouTube channel. It was probably best to wait before he did the commentary. Right now, he was still annoyed with Bravura. She was so very slow.

For Luke it was a matter of pride that his channel was mostly positive in its outlook. He had to be careful that he didn't ruin that in a moment of annoyance. He thought back through what he'd said in the interview at the end. He was fairly sure he hadn't been nasty. Hopefully, his voice hadn't given away too much.

He closed his eyes and took a couple of deep breaths. Blaze was where he went to get away from his real life. Needing money to buy his company was a Luke problem. He could not let it affect him as Blaze. For Blaze, this gig had to be just a bit of fun.

He opened his eyes and started making notes about what to

say in his recap for his followers. A few minutes later, he was interrupted by a notification on his phone. The contest was over. His gaze flew to the clock. It had been fifteen minutes. Did that mean they were in? Or they'd finished just after the eighth team got through.

A message came through.

> Bravura: *Did we make it?*
> Blaze: *Not sure. We came close, at least.*

Another message.

> Flick: *Yess! I think I'm in to the next round. We finished a good half hour before the game end. How about you?*
> Blaze: *Dunno. The game end notification went out about 15 minutes after we finished. So we could be the last ones in, or we could be 9th by a few seconds. Can't tell yet. I'm going back in.*

He put his headset back on. The game dropped him back into the training environment. The interviewer from before was projected on the sky, announcing the winning teams and their times.

He looked around as Bravura appeared next to him. They nodded to each other and turned back to the presenter.

Phil_the_Vicar and his partner had come first. Not hugely surprising. Phil was Flick's husband (in real life) and he was a very, very good gamer – and his teammate was a good amateur. There were a few others Luke recognised, including Flick. The team in seventh place had finished in two hours and forty-three minutes.

Luke thought of their two hours and forty-six minutes. Three whole minutes. His heart sank. That was too wide a margin.

'And team number eight … this was very, very close, folks.

64

There is only a difference of thirty seconds between this team and the one after it ...'

He glanced at Bravura. She was chewing her lip, eyes fixed on the presentation. She looked like she was going to cry. He felt bad for snapping at her.

'Before I announce this last team, can I just say how brilliantly everyone played. Yes, even the ones who ended the game by losing a player. We're very proud of our game and we didn't want to make it too easy for you, so rest assured, you did a great job. And remember, we will be releasing each new scenario in *SyrenQuest* as we finish each round. You can still play, even if you're no longer in the competition.'

Get on with it. Get on with it!

'So ... the final team to go into round two are ... Blaze and Bravura, with two hours and forty-six minutes. Congratulations, guys!'

Luke punched the air. 'Yes! Come ON!'

Bravura had her hands over her mouth. Her eyes shone.

He put out his hand. 'Well done, partner.'

They shook hands.

'I can't believe it,' Bravura said, her voice a choked whisper. 'I'm—'

He shot her a warning glance and flicked his eyes towards the presenter to remind her that she was being recorded. If she was about to go on about how much of a fan she was, she should at least know that she was on record. Her eyes widened when she got the message. Luke extracted his hand from her grip.

'Good job,' he said, quickly. 'We did great. We'll do even better in round two, right?'

'Er ... yes. Onwards and upwards.'

The presenter started talking again and the spotlight moved off them. Luke was fairly sure all this was being recorded anyway, so he said, 'I'm going to log off now, Bravura. I'll catch you later.'

She nodded. He switched his headset off and removed it.

A few seconds later, a message came in on the chat app.

Bravura: *I know I wasn't the best. I promise I'll practise my moves between now and the next game.*

Hah. She had said the same thing last time he'd spoken to her. Another wave of irritation washed through him. It was a miracle they'd survived the first attack. Why did he have to get the nice-but-rubbish newbie? It wasn't her fault she was a crap fighter. It was just his rotten luck. Still, they *had* made it into the second round. Maybe that would be the push she needed.

Blaze: *That would be great. I think the challenges will get harder. You need to react quicker. The character is fast, but the reflexes are all yours.*
Bravura: *Thank you. I'll work on it.*

He remembered what Flick said to him about how this was more to the newbies than it was to them.

Blaze: *Well done for today. We live to play another round.*

When Sam took her headset off, Niro was standing next to her, bouncing up and down.

'You did it! You made it into the next round!' Niro threw her arms around Sam.

'I know! I really didn't expect that. I was so rubbish.'

They jumped up and down a bit more until Sam stopped to pack up the headset.

'What if you win the big prize?' asked Niro.

'I won't.' Sam carefully put the headset back in its box. 'We just got lucky and squeaked in at number eight.' She sat down and stared at the Syren3 box. 'I'm glad we did, because I'd have felt terrible if I'd let Blaze down.'

Niro sniffed. 'He wasn't very nice to you, was he? Bit snappy, I thought.'

'Can you blame him? I was awful. I nearly got killed in the first fight with the sloths. I was so slow responding. If he hadn't pulled me out, I'd have been a goner. We both would. And then the one time when I could have rescued him, I missed. He rescued the situation, but I still missed.'

'But if you hadn't grabbed the tablecloth, you'd still be stuck on that monolith.' Niro put her hands on her hips. 'He didn't even acknowledge that. I don't think this guy is as nice as you seem to think he is.'

'No. He's lovely,' said Sam, firmly. She reopened the box and removed the headset.

'What are you doing?'

'I'm sorry, Niro. I hope you don't mind, but I'm going to get some practice in. I said I would. So I must.'

Niro shrugged. 'Fine by me. Netflix still works on my laptop.'

'Thanks. You're wonderful.' Sam lowered the headset and took herself to the training ground. The second round was the following Monday. She had four days to level up. She was damned well not going to hold Blaze back next time.

Chapter 7

It was still dark when Luke chained his bike in the racks by the side of The Nest. Since his nights were taken up with *SyrenQuest*, coming into work early was the only way he was going to get everything done. He unclipped his bike helmet and went to the side gate. The main doors didn't open until eight. It wasn't quite seven yet.

He swiped himself into the building, dropped his bag off in the office, and went down to the showers. There were two, one at each end of the building. After a stern memo a few years ago, people had stopped leaving their own shampoo and soap in there. These days, Luke kept his stuff in the office where annoyed cleaners couldn't chuck it out.

The regular cleaner, Darota, was pushing her trolley down the corridor. Luke flattened himself against the wall to let her pass.

'You're in early,' Darota said.

'Work to do.'

She paused and turned. 'You're not sleeping in your office again, are you?'

'Oh come on, I only did that once.' Luke peeled himself away from the wall. 'I'm sure I'm not the only person who's ever done that.'

Darota grinned. 'You'd be amazed at the things that I see in this place.'

'I bet,' said Luke. He gave her a wave and carried on towards the showers.

After, he managed almost an hour's work before his stomach reminded him that he needed breakfast. He went down to the cafeteria and bought a big bowl of porridge and coffee. Spotting Sam sitting by herself, reading something on her phone, he went over.

'Mind if I join you?' he asked.

She looked tired and, the way she was sitting hunched over her coffee, dejected.

'Are you okay?'

Sam nodded and put her phone facedown on the table. 'Yes. I'm fine. Just a bit tired.'

'Working late?'

She covered a yawn with the back of her hand. 'Something like that.' She glanced over at his breakfast. 'Oh my god, that smells amazing. Is that porridge with golden syrup?'

'It certainly is.' He gave it a stir. Thick and creamy, just the way he liked it. 'It's my favourite thing.'

'I haven't had porridge in ages. I've just had a granola bar. I feel deprived of hot comfort food now.' She took another sip of her coffee.

'I could get you a bowl, if you want …'

She shook her head. 'No. I'll be fine. I've had breakfast, even if it was just a granola bar. But I might treat myself to that tomorrow.'

They sat together, eating and drinking in silence, for a few minutes. It was surprisingly relaxed. Luke mentally patted himself on the back for not jumping in and filling the silence with something stupid.

'Do you always come in this early?' Sam asked him.

'Not always, but I needed to get my head down today,' he said.

'In fact, I've been here an hour already. I only came downstairs because I was starving.'

'Really? Me too.'

'Well, I'll be coming in at half seven this whole week, so if you want to join me for a porridge fest tomorrow morning, you're more than welcome.'

She glanced at her watch and sighed. 'I'd better get back to work.'

'Working on your pitches?'

Sam nodded, wearily. 'Plus, I'm still putting together my slides for my presentation in two weeks' time. I keep moving stuff around.'

'I'd be happy to take a look at it for you, if it would help,' he said.

'That's very kind, but you're doing so much already. I couldn't possibly—'

'I don't mind,' said Luke.

'But you just said you were busy enough that you had to come in early.'

Damn. He stared at her, frantically thinking of a way out. 'It would … be nice to think about something else from time to time, just for a change.'

Her expression changed for a second; she looked worried. 'Yes,' she said. 'I can see that.'

When Luke got back to the office, Pete was there. To Luke's surprise, he could see a *SyrenQuest* gameplay on the screen. Pete seemed to be watching one of last night's games at triple speed. He leaned forward to see which team it was. Pete noticed him, started, and closed the browser.

'Sorry, boss. I was just checking how my guys were doing on *SyrenQuest*.'

Luke noticed that his satchel, which he'd thrown under his desk when he came in, had flopped open. The post, which he'd shoved into it on the way out of his apartment, was peeping out.

He reached down and flipped the bag shut before he sat down. 'Your guys?'

'From the sweepstake.' Pete gestured in the direction of the office opposite.

'Oh yes. The sweepstake.' Luke himself had drawn FlickNife's team in the sweepstake. Flick had been highly amused when he told her. 'I should see how my team is getting on, too.'

The recordings had gone up on Syren's website last night as soon as all the players finished. He had meant to look at a few of the other people's plays to see if he could learn something that would be tactically useful, but by the time he'd done a short commentary for his YouTube channel, he had been too exhausted to do anything but collapse into bed and dream of murder sloths.

'Who'd you get in the sweepstake again?' asked Pete.

'FlickNife. Who did you get?' Flick's newbie partner was 19 and very good. It was no surprise that they had got through with one of the shorter times.

'Blaze and Bravura,' said Pete.

Luke had to work hard not to let anything show on his face. 'Was that them you're watching?'

'No. I watched them last night. This is KingDangerous. I wanted to see how different they were.'

This was what he had been planning to do – though for other reasons. 'Found anything?'

Pete made a face. 'As far I can tell,' he said, 'the world starts off roughly the same, but different decisions give the teams different obstacles. They're all looking for this key and no one knows whether they're close to it or far away.'

Luke nodded. He'd wondered about that last night. 'That's interesting. Some sort of branching that changes components as it builds …'

They both looked longingly at Pete's screen, where the browser window had been.

'We could check out some of the replays at lunchtime?' said Pete.

That was a good idea. He had to eat. May as well watch something while he did. He would just have to be careful not to reveal how much he knew about the game. But if he were able to watch some plays with Pete, it would speed things up a bit. He had chatted to a few of his gaming friends. They didn't have anything new to say about the game, apart from observing that each team seemed to be playing a slightly different version.

'Lunchtime, yes. That's a good idea,' he said. 'In the meantime, we have work to do.'

Sam's stomach rumbled. She looked at the clock on her computer screen. Lunchtime. Since she'd had breakfast extra early, she was famished. Her back felt stiff. It was probably time to take a break anyway. She stood up and stretched.

It had been a pretty productive morning. All the information and photos that she needed for her presentation for Boutique Belvoir were in one place. She'd written out what she wanted to say. Now she needed to put it into slides. She had two weeks before the presentation, but she was going to the SyrenCon the weekend before, so she wanted to be sure that everything was ready in good time.

She grabbed her bag and headed down to the cafeteria.

Kim was at her desk. 'Afternoon, Sam,' she said. 'What's the bag today?'

Sam removed the small, underarm bag and showed it to Kim.

'Late Nineties Calvin Klein?' said Kim. She turned it round in her hands. 'Doesn't hold an awful lot, does it?'

'Not really,' said Sam. 'Just the basics. I wanted to check if the insert works with them. It does.' She opened the bag and showed her the inner bag, which contained her purse, phone, lipstick, tissues, and a pack of paracetamol. The contents of the Shanthi bag were slightly mushed together, but it still fit.

Kim nodded, thoughtfully. 'How many bags do you have?'

'Sixty. Mostly my mum's – hence the Nineties-heavy collection. That was when she had the most money and the most inclination to spend on bags.'

'I think it's lovely that you're keeping her collection in circulation.' Kim zipped the bag up and turned it over in her hands again. 'Didn't see you come in today, Sam,' she said, her tone overly casual.

'I came in early.'

'Hmm.' Kim passed the bag back. 'You know who else came in early? Luke.'

'I know,' Sam said, without thinking.

Kim's eyebrows shot up. 'Seriously, what's going on with you two? You're both keeping weird hours. You both look exhausted …'

'I saw him in the breakfast queue. Nothing is going on,' said Sam. 'Stop stirring.'

'He obviously likes you.'

Sam shook her head. 'I won't even ask why you think that. You're going to say something stupid like, "It's obvious".'

'It is though.'

'I think he's just shy. He seems like a nice guy.'

'A nice guy … who likes you.'

Sam sighed. 'I hope not, because that would be awkward. He's really not my type.' She tucked her bag back under the arm. 'I'm off to get some lunch. Do you need anything?'

Kim made a face. 'No. I brought soup from home. It's a low-calorie day.'

While she was standing in the lunch queue, Sam's phone beeped. It was an email from Niro to say that she'd taken some more photos of the bags. She'd sent a link to a shared Dropbox folder. Brilliant. She could choose a few of these and send them to Luke to add to the crowdfunding site.

A follow-up message popped up from Niro.

I also found some photos of the full handbag collection that we took for fun. Useful for social media?

Sam typed back a message to say thank you. Sandwich in hand, she went back upstairs. As she turned to go into her office, it occurred to her that she should speak to Luke in person rather than simply emailing him photos and demanding that he do stuff for her. He was doing her a huge favour after all.

Luke found Phil_the_Vicar's video from *SyrenQuest*. It was still pretty long, but not the whole two hours. He set the playback to quadruple speed and kept his finger on the speed selector so that he could slow it down when something interesting happened.

He had just started watching when Pete came back with his lunch in hand and Kyle from the office opposite in tow.

'I told Kyle we were watching the playback and he wanted to join. Is that okay?' asked Pete.

'Sure. Pull up a chair.'

Pretty soon, the three of them were sitting round Luke's computer absorbed in the gameplay. The game started off exactly the same as it had for Blaze and Bravura. Phil_the_Vicar's team did the most cursory sweep of the ransacked hall before heading outside. When they came to the fork in the road, they chose the right one.

'We— The one I watched chose the other path,' Luke said.

'The one I was watching did too,' said Pete. 'They got attacked by these weird creatures with goofy faces and long claws.'

'Murder sloths,' Luke muttered.

'Ha! Yes. That's a great name for them,' said Pete.

He hadn't thought of it. Bravura had. In his mind, Luke tipped his hat to his blue elf companion.

He leaned forward, watching keenly to spot the differences. Part of him was studying the game as a player, the other part was trying to work out how they did it as a programmer. He was so engrossed that he didn't even realise that they had company until Pete said, 'Oh, hi, Sam.'

Luke whipped his head round so fast that he almost cricked his neck. 'Sam.'

She was standing by the door, looking awkward. 'Er. Hi. I see you're busy—'

He stood up. 'No, no, it's fine. We're just watching the replays of *SyrenQuest*.'

'It's this computer game competition that's going on right now,' Kyle said. 'It's a time trial elimination with—'

Annoyance flickered across Sam's expression. 'I know,' she said. 'You told me when we all watched the announcement.'

'Oh right, yeah,' said Kyle.

'Do you want to join us?' asked Pete.

Luke shot Pete a warning glance. He would have to have words with his assistant about stirring. Again. He looked towards Sam, torn between wishing she would stay, so that he could hang out with her, and wishing she'd go, so that he could concentrate.

'Oh. I …' Sam hesitated, her eyes were on the screen.

'I think—' Luke began.

'Go on,' said Pete. 'It'll be better than having lunch alone in your office, right? You might enjoy it. Move up a bit, Luke.'

'Oh, what the hell,' said Sam. 'As you say, I might enjoy it.'

Luke fetched the last chair in the office and set it next to his own. He shot Pete a glare. Pete merely grinned back.

'Here you go,' Luke said to Sam. 'Don't feel you have to stay, but you're more than welcome.'

He returned to his seat and skipped the video back a few seconds to catch up. When he sat back, he was all too aware of Sam next to him. She was close enough that he could feel the movement when she brought her sandwich up to take a bite. He stared fiercely at the screen and tried to focus.

'So, the object of the game is to get a key,' said Kyle. 'It's a quest.'

Luke risked a glance at Sam and saw her roll her eyes, her mouth too full of sandwich to respond. 'I don't think you need to explain it, Kyle,' he said.

'But Sam doesn't play. How does she know what's going on?' said Kyle. 'I'm just trying to be helpful.'

Luke looked back at Sam, who put her hand on his arm briefly and shook her head. He couldn't have spoken anyway. Any thoughts he had were drowned out by the sensation of her fingertips on his forearm.

Sam swallowed her mouthful. 'I know what a quest is. But thanks.' The look she gave Kyle was cold. She nodded to Luke. 'Shall we watch? If I have any questions, I'll be sure to ask.'

They turned back to the screen. Soon they were all engrossed. Phil_the_Vicar and his partner found what looked like ponies. A shortcut! Damn. If they had gone that way, Blaze and Bravura would have saved all that time they'd spent fighting murder sloths.

'That's so unfair,' said Pete.

Which was exactly how Luke felt. He reminded himself that he was Luke right now, not Blaze. But dammit. It was so unfair!

'You're just sore because Blaze didn't get that,' said Kyle.

Luke startled. His knee must have bumped Sam, because she jumped too. 'Sorry,' he said.

She waved his apology away.

'Pete got Blaze in the office sweepstake,' Kyle said, looking directly at Sam. 'So he's got a vested interest.'

'Right,' said Sam, faintly. 'He's the … pirate one?'

'That's Blaze,' said Pete. 'The pirate one. My housemate thinks he's cute.'

Luke didn't dare look at Sam to see if she thought Blaze was cute. That would be too weird. He tried to focus on the gameplay. The players were ambushed by a pack of wolves. Next to him, Sam gasped. Luke risked a quick glance and saw her staring at the game, eyes wide. She was getting into it.

He smiled and turned back to the screen. Phil_the_Vicar and his partner were making short work of the wolves. Both of them whirled around the screen.

'Huh. Lucky Phil_the_Vicar,' said Pete. 'He gets a newbie who can actually fight.'

'Yeah, Blaze's partner is awful. Lucky Blaze is good or they'd have been out of the competition already. One of the other newbies died and it was game over for both of them,' said Kyle. 'I can't believe Blaze and that girl made it into the second round, to be honest. There's no justice in the world.'

Luke clenched his jaw. Must not respond. Must. Not. Respond.

Pete gave a little sigh. 'They got lucky,' he said. 'Long may it continue.'

'It's such a waste that they picked someone like that. She is spectacularly shit,' Kyle continued. 'I suppose that's always a risk with lotteries. You're always going to get a few chancers in the pool and you never know when you'll pick one of them.'

Luke tried to tune him out and concentrate on watching the game. What a pain that Pete had drawn Blaze in the sweepstake. It was so difficult to sit here and listen to them discussing him and Bravura. He glanced across at Sam, who was looking down at her sandwich, frowning a little. He hoped she wasn't getting bored.

Sam finished her sandwich in silence, only half watching the action on screen. The guys had no idea that she was Bravura, of course. They were simply discussing a stranger, as far as they knew. And they hated her. She was dragging their hero, Blaze, down. She knew that, really. But it was different hearing someone else say it. She knew that there was a lot of discussion about her incompetent playing online already. She had quickly scrolled through some comments on the videos that morning and the hatred towards her was frightening. She had closed the browser and hadn't looked at Blaze's YouTube channel or the hashtags on Twitter since.

Privately, she didn't disagree with their assessment. She was bad at the game and very clearly hadn't done any practice. What was she even doing in *SyrenQuest*? Wasting everyone's time, that was what.

When Pete had initially suggested she join them, her first thought was that this was a good way to actually watch the gameplay. She had hoped to get ahead a bit, maybe pick up some interesting things to say when she next spoke to Blaze. But instead, she'd found out just how shit they thought she was. Somehow hearing it from people she knew, rather than faceless people off the internet was much, much worse.

'Oh, that's interesting,' Luke said. 'They've come to another fork in the road. Do you think this branches out again? Or does it loop back?'

They started talking about algorithms. Luke looked over his shoulder and gave her a small smile. She smiled back. He was checking on her. That was kind of him. She listened to him talking about techie things. He sounded different now, when he was getting into the weeds, talking faster than he normally did. There was something soothing about his voice.

Sam sat back and watched Luke for a moment. There was something in the way his strands of dark hair seemed to drop haphazardly onto his forehead and the way he was constantly fiddling with his glasses that made him look slightly bewildered all the time. But if you smoothed the hair down and put him in something that wasn't a fleece with the company logo on it, he might actually be quite handsome.

It was funny how personality affected how someone was perceived. Luke was shy, so you tended not to even register much about him when you first met him. Kyle was annoying but confident, so he was more noticeable. Pete was charming, so you could speak to him for hours and afterwards remember mostly that he was delightful company and therefore probably quite attractive.

What did Blaze look like in real life? Was he anything like his avatar? Did it matter? No. It didn't matter because she was going to get herself killed and get both of them thrown out of the game.

She sighed.

Luke turned. His expression plainly said, 'Are you okay?'

Now would be a good time to get out of there. 'I should go,' she said.

Without turning away, Luke hit pause on the video. 'Oh, sure.'

She stood up and he did too. It seemed he was going to see her out. 'Thanks for the … game viewing,' she said to the others. 'I'll see you guys around.'

As Luke walked the few steps to the door, he asked, 'Did you want to see me about something?'

'Pardon?'

'When you came up. Before we made you watch *SyrenQuest*. Did you need something?'

Of course. The whole reason for coming up there in the first place. She had completely forgotten about it. 'Oh, yes. I have some photos to add to the crowdfunding site.'

'Just email them to me and I'll take a look after work this evening. I'll get back to you about it all tomorrow.'

As she turned to go, he said, 'Are you coming in early tomorrow, too?'

She was going to have to come in early for the next couple of weeks. 'I am.'

'Do you fancy another breakfast meeting?'

She hesitated. What with Kim's teasing, she didn't want to encourage him.

'Um … I'm not sure what I'll be up to tomorrow. How about we see how it goes?'

79

He nodded more vigorously than needed. 'Oh sure. Sure. Of course.'

She hurried down the corridor. As she turned the corner to go to the stairs, she looked back. He was still standing there. Horrified, he quickly ducked into the office. He was so awkward, bless him.

Chapter 8

'Thanks for the photos,' Sam said to Niro. 'Luke's going to put them up tomorrow morning.' They were in the kitchen, getting dinner ready – or rather, Sam was. Niro was stacking the dishwasher with all the stuff she'd used during the day. 'I was in his office at lunchtime. They were watching some replays of *SyrenQuest*.'

'You're spending a lot of time with this Luke, aren't you?'

'Oh, don't you start,' Sam said. 'I have enough crap from Kim in reception. I am not interested in the guy.'

'You said you saw him at breakfast … and at lunchtime … You're potentially seeing him tomorrow morning for breakfast …' Niro closed the dishwasher and leaned against it. 'That's a lot of Luke, is all I'm saying.'

'Shut up and listen, will you?' said Sam. 'They were watching a replay of *SyrenQuest*. Phil_the_Vicar's one. And they were talking. They hate me. They think I'm useless.'

'Do you mean they hate Bravura?'

'Her, me. Same thing. The point is, all Blaze's fans think that Bravura is going to make him lose.' She tipped tinned tomatoes on top of the mince and stirred it. 'If the guys at work are annoyed, just imagine how bad the commenters on Blaze's actual feed are going to be.'

'Let's have a look.' Niro pulled out her phone and started typing with her thumbs. After a few seconds she gave a low whistle. 'Ouch. They really do hate you.'

'The worst thing is, I can't say I blame them. If I wasn't me, I'd be annoyed at her too.'

Niro kept reading her phone. 'Yeah. I'd stay away from the bottom half of the internet for a few days if I were you. Some of these are nasty.' She recoiled. 'Yikes. Sexist much?'

'Is it that bad? Let me see.'

Niro held the phone away from her. 'I wouldn't. It'll put you off your game.' She retreated to the other side of the room and resumed reading. 'Ew. I'm reporting that.'

Sam shook her head. 'Not helping, Niro.'

'Sorry, sorry.' Niro put her phone away. 'So what are you going to do about it?'

Sam put a lid on the pan and leaned against the worktop. 'I'm going to have to practise more. I don't know when, though. I mean, it'll have to be at night. I have to work during the day.'

'How's the crowdfunding target going?'

'Still nowhere near.'

'Maybe you could—'

Whatever Niro was going to say was cut off by the landline ringing. 'I'll get it. It'll be your parents. They're the only people who call this line.' Niro grabbed the handset. 'Hello, Lokuamma, it's Nirosha.'

Sam and Niro weren't actually related by blood. Niro was Sam's stepmother's niece. That was too complicated to explain, so they just said they were cousins.

While Niro made small talk Sam washed and dried her hands. 'Here she is,' said Niro.

Sam took the phone and walked into the living room. 'Hi. How're you?' There was always the awkward start of the conversation. She didn't like calling her stepmother 'Amma', but 'Aunty' was far too formal for this woman who had kept the family from falling apart and been every inch a second mother. One of her brothers had coined the term 'Aunty-amma'. It still wasn't perfect though, so Sam tried not to call her anything.

'Samadhi, how are you, darling? We haven't heard from you in ages.' Her stepmother's voice was warm.

'I'm fine. Doing really well,' said Sam. 'How are you and Thatha?'

She listened to her stepmother's update. Busy, busy, busy was the gist of it. No change there then.

'Your father's here. Let me put him on.'

Before Sam could reply, her father's voice came down the phone. 'Samadhi.'

'Hello, Thatha, how are you?'

'I'm well. You?'

'I'm fine.'

The pause that followed was painful. Their mother's passing had broken something between them. Even though Aunty-amma had helped each of them manage their grief individually, the link between Thatha and Sam was still awkward.

'So,' he said, 'how is your work going?'

Work was normally a nice, neutral subject. She could ask for advice and he loved helping with that. Work and money management were good topics for Thatha. Everything else was her stepmother's domain. But they thought she still worked for the management consulting firm. She hadn't told them about being made redundant, or about Shanthi Bags. 'It's er … fine,' she said. 'Same as always.'

'Good, good. I spoke to Gihan a couple of days ago.'

Her middle brother was the one who kept in touch the most. 'Yes. I saw the picture of his new car.'

Thatha gave a small chuckle. 'He's very pleased with it, it seems.'

'Yes.'

With that topic exhausted, there was another uncomfortable

83

silence. Guilt gnawed at Sam. She should tell them about what she'd done. But she was in a fragile position right now and the resulting backlash could finish off Shanthi Bags before she'd given it a chance.

'I'll give the phone back to Aunty-amma.'

'Bye, Thatha.' She wanted to add, 'I love you', but he wasn't the sort of person who went around saying things like that. Not anymore.

Her stepmother was back, all breathless enthusiasm. 'Listen, darling, we're coming down to London in a couple of weeks. It would be good to see you.'

'That would be lovely,' she said, even though it scared the living daylights out of her. She would have to do so much fast talking to make sure her parents didn't get wind of what she was doing. 'We should meet up for lunch or something. I can come to you.'

'How about dinner? We could get string hoppers from the place in Cricklewood. I'll email you nearer the time with details.'

They talked a bit longer, until Sam had to go and turn the hob off. She hung up and let out a long breath.

Niro was eating a packet of peanuts. 'Seriously, dude, you have to tell them.' She flicked a peanut into her mouth.

Sam hung her head. 'I can't. You know I can't. They'll be horrified that I'm not looking for another job.'

'You can tell them about the business. You have a cushion, financially, from the redundancy pay. You're not doing anything too wild.'

She shook her head. 'They'll be dismissive about it and … it's all too fragile. I was going to tell them when I reached my crowdfunding goal, but not enough people have pledged yet. I can't tell them when I know I'm failing!'

'You have to tell them at some point, though, Sam. They're going to find out.' Niro pulled out her phone. 'Especially if you get any press coverage.'

'If I do well enough to get press coverage,' said Sam, 'I'll tell them.' She put the handset back in its cradle and returned to the stove. 'Now, can we change the subject?'

She turned her attention back to the food she was cooking. She stirred it violently. If she was being honest with herself, she knew that she could weather the criticism about careers from her father. It would be hard, but she'd cope. No. The real reason she hadn't told anyone about Shanthi Bags was that when she'd started the business, naming it after her mother had been the most obvious decision she'd made. It was a tribute to her mother. She was making a difference in the world, by giving the world more of something Amma loved. There was no other name she could have used.

Her father rarely talked about Amma anymore, apart from when it was one of their birthdays or every year on the anniversary of her death, when they all went to the temple and made a donation to charity in her name. If Sam were to present him with a failing business emblazoned with the name Shanthi, she wasn't sure she could cope with his pain.

Chapter 9

Breakfast meeting. Sam smiled. It was such a formal way to describe meeting for coffee before work. It was also, weirdly, very Luke. When she arrived, he was already there, laptop on the table, scrolling through her pictures while he ate his porridge. It seemed that he'd taken her 'we'll see' to be a definite yes.

'Morning.' She slid into the seat opposite him.

'Hey. How are you today?'

'Ah. Same old, same old,' she said.

'Just let me finish my breakfast and we'll get your page sorted.' He pushed the laptop across to her. 'Do you want to point out which ones are your favourite?'

She turned the laptop so that they could both see it. 'Straight to work, huh?'

Luke flushed. 'I'm … not so great at small talk, or so I'm told. Sorry.'

She smiled. 'I didn't mean to make you feel uncomfortable.'

'Ha. Please. Uncomfortable is my basic state of existence. Don't worry about it.' He flashed her a smile. 'But seriously …' He nodded towards the computer.

'Okay.' She shrank the files back to thumbnails. 'I like this one, this one and … this one.'

She selected three of her mum's favourite bags.

'Hmm,' said Luke. 'None of those photos have you in them, still.'

'But the bags are the important thing.'

'Sam, we talked about this. For this page, you need a story. You need to give people a reason to invest in you.' He put down his spoon. 'Think about it. When you're crowdfunding, you're asking people to pay for a new, untested product. If the crowdfund is unsuccessful, the product won't even exist. If it *is* successful, the product will probably be available in a few years at a higher quality … and for less than they paid for it. You're not appealing to their head.' He tapped his chest. 'You're appealing to their hearts. So we need *you*. And we need your story.'

Sam resisted the urge to snap and withdraw. She looked down and picked at her nail varnish. 'I don't think so.'

Luke gave a little sigh. 'Sam, is there a reason you don't want to be identified with your product?'

'I don't …' What did he mean she didn't want to be identified with her product? She made the first prototypes by hand. She was a part of them.

'Do you think that you're not going all in because you're secretly afraid of it taking off?'

'No. Why would I be afraid of it going well? That's ridiculous.'

'There is such a thing as fear of success, you know. We see it all the time here.' He made a gesture that encompassed The Nest, then he went back to his coffee. 'Think about it. I'll wait.'

Sam drank her coffee too, trying not to scowl. How dare he suggest she wasn't trying? 'I do my best,' she said.

'I think you're trying very hard. But is it really your best?'

She frowned. He raised an eyebrow. Suddenly, she liked him a little less. 'You're very judgemental, you know that?' she said.

'I can let it go, if you want,' he said. 'But it won't help you. This is your one shot at making this company work. If you don't give it your all, it will fail. So, I would be a terrible mentor if I don't help you work out what's holding you back.'

'You're my mentor now? And here I was thinking you were just helping me with the crowdfunding pages.'

He moved back from her anger. She immediately felt bad.

'I'm sorry. I know you're just trying to help. I shouldn't have snapped.' She passed a hand over her tired eyes. 'I'm tired. But that's my problem. I shouldn't take it out on you.'

His expression changed. 'You're right. It's not ideal to take out your frustrations on someone else. Especially someone who is just trying to help,' he said thoughtfully.

Was that a dig at her? Well, she deserved it.

He leaned forward. 'Listen. I'm sorry if I pushed too far. But please, think about it. You would make a great face for the brand. If you don't want to, then that's okay. But think about why and who you'd like to use instead. People buy from people, so you have to have someone in the "about us" page.' He looked at his phone. 'I should get to work. I'll see you later.'

She watched him gather his stuff. 'Luke,' she said. 'Thank you ... for doing all of this.'

He looked up at her and smiled. The light fell on his face so that she could see his eyes crinkle behind his glasses. 'Like I said. Mentoring smaller companies is part of the deal when you've been here a while. It's my pleasure.'

He slung his satchel on his shoulder. 'We're watching a few more *SyrenQuest* replays from round one today, if you want to come join us at lunchtime.'

Oh. That could be useful. It would mean she could watch the replays with intelligent commentary in her lunch hour so that she could keep up when Blaze talked about it. On the other hand, she didn't particularly want to spend even more time with Luke if he was going to give her a hard time about her website photos. On top of all that, it was just so weird hearing people talk about her like that.

She was taking too long to answer; Luke looked worried.

'I'll think about it,' she said. 'I'm not sure what time I'll break for lunch today.'

'Well, we'll be there from half past twelve until half past one, if you fancy it.' A flash of his transformative smile, and he left.

Sam watched him go, noting how he greeted people as he went past. Kim was right. For someone who seemed to spend his time avoiding the limelight, he did seem to know a lot of people. They all treated him with a sort of respectful fondness.

She turned back to her coffee and breathed in the smell. She felt slightly raw. As though she'd somehow exposed more of herself than she had intended.

Did he have a point? Was she afraid of success? She couldn't think about this without a decent sugar hit. There wasn't a queue at the counter, so she went and got herself an almond croissant to eat while she thought.

Logically, what did success mean? It would mean getting a steady supply of orders for her bags. But for that to happen, she would need more people to know about her product, which meant more exposure … which would increase the chances of someone she knew finding out, so she would *have* to tell her parents. There was an alarming twist in her stomach. Sam lowered the last piece of almond croissant. Her heart rate sped up and her mouth felt dry. That wasn't indigestion. That was panic. Holy crap. Luke was right. She *was* afraid of success, sort of. Because then her father would find out.

When lunchtime came round, Kyle and one of the other guys from the office opposite came in. In unspoken agreement, Luke and Pete stopped work.

'Er … guys, could we leave a seat free? I told Sam we'd be watching, she said she might come.'

'Why leave her a spare seat if we're not sure?' said Kyle.

Pete rolled his eyes. 'Oh, leave him alone. He has hope.'

'Oh. You have a personal interest in the lovely Sam?' said Kyle, grinning.

Luke wanted to smack him. 'She's a friend,' he said, tightly.

'A friend you'd like some benefits with,' said Kyle, waggling his eyebrows.

'You know what, forget it. Take the chair. If she comes in, she can have my chair.'

There was a chorus of 'oohs' from the other guys.

'Shut up, Kyle.'

There was further teasing, until Pete put FlickNife's game up on the screen. A few minutes after the start, there was a quiet knock on the door. Luke's heart gave a little flip. Sam!

He stood up from his chair. In his haste, he caught his foot on the strap of his bag, tipping everything out onto the floor. He kicked it all back under the desk and offered her his chair. Behind Sam, Pete rolled his eyes heavenward and shook his head.

Sam gave him a sheepish little smile and sat down. 'Who are we watching?' she asked.

'FlickNife and her newb,' said Kyle, before anyone else could speak. 'FlickNife is actually a woman. Not some guy in a female avatar. And in real life, she's married to Phil_the_Vicar. So if they both get through to the final it'll be husband against wife—'

'Yes, thank you, Kyle. I read the Wikipedia entry too,' said Sam.

Luke wanted to cheer. He was now a tiny bit more in love with Sam than before.

Kyle scowled. 'Let's just finish watching the video.'

They watched, with the guys occasionally commenting. It was clear to Luke that their hunch about there being shortcuts at various points was correct. That was interesting to know. Was there a pattern to when the shortcuts occurred? They wouldn't make it random, would they?

When they got to the end of Team FlickNife's game, Pete searched for another game.

'Who are you supporting, Sam?' Pete asked.

Luke wished he could be so laid-back around her. When he gave up his chair, he had perched against the meeting table. He leaned forward to hear her answer.

'I'm not sure, really,' she said. 'I guess FlickNife or Bravura, since they're the only women.'

'FlickNife is the only woman pro-gamer involved in *SyrenQuest*,' said Kyle. 'In case you were wondering.'

Luke rolled his eyes. Sam spotted it and smiled at him. The conspiratorial nature of it gave him a warm glow behind his sternum.

'I should go,' said Sam. She pushed the chair back.

'Come join us tomorrow?' said Pete.

'Sure.' She flushed slightly, pink creeping beneath the brown on her cheeks. 'After talking to you guys, I'm getting into it … a bit.'

The sheepish expression on her face did strange things to Luke's chest. He knew that look. That was someone who was falling in love with gaming and didn't want to admit it. He saw her to the door and waved her off. When Kyle left too, Luke closed the door and stood there, staring into space. For a wild moment, he contemplated the idea of having a girlfriend who understood his gaming obsession. There had been a few in the past, but not many. The last time he'd had a girlfriend was at university. Once he'd started working, between getting the company started and keeping up the YouTube channel so that he could pay the rent, there hadn't been much time for dating.

In the office, Pete was tidying up. 'Man, I wish you'd hang your bag up like a normal person,' he said. 'It's a health and safety hazard stuffed under your desk like that. Look. All your paperwork has fallen out. Seriously, Luke. You should—'

The sudden silence got Luke's attention. Pete straightened up, slowly, holding a thick envelope. The contents were half out of it. Right on the top was a compliments slip. From Syren.

Pete stared at the *SyrenQuest* logo. 'Luke. Why do you have a parcel from Syren?'

Luke thought fast. 'It's just some information about the new headset. I thought I'd check it out after seeing the gameplays ...'

The look Pete gave him was pure scepticism. He pulled the compliments slip out. 'That's a great excuse, except on here it says, "Hi Luke. More fan mail for you this week. Michelle."' He looked down at the handful of still sealed envelopes. 'They're addressed to Blaze.' He stared down at them, as though he didn't believe what he was seeing.

Damn. How could Luke explain that? 'I ... erm ... know him. So I was taking the fan mail to ... give to him.'

Pete's expression had taken on an almost pleading quality. Luke sighed. He didn't like lying. Hiding his alternate identity was fine. But lying outright felt very wrong. 'I'm sorry,' he said. 'I have no good explanation.'

'That still isn't helping, Luke. Why are you getting fan mail sent to *SyrenQuest*? And addressed to Blaze?' He looked down at the envelopes and shifted them in his hands.

Luke reached forward and took the envelopes from him. 'Would you believe I was his manager?'

Pete frowned. 'I cannot imagine that, no. Besides, it still says "for you". Not for your client.'

Luke stuffed everything back into the envelope. 'You can't imagine that I could possibly be Blaze?' Hopefully, that sounded too unbelievable that Pete would just laugh at him.

A range of expressions passed across Pete's features in quick succession. Surprise, confusion, amazement, confusion again. He stared at Luke for a moment, eyes narrowed. 'Actually. Yes. I can. I mean, you'd have to be a hell of an actor, but ... we never see him.' He pointed to the envelope. 'And it would explain that.'

Luke picked up his bag and stuffed the offending envelope inside. This time he hung the bag up on the hook below his coat, partly to buy himself some time. He could tell Pete another lie, but Pete would always suspect. He would have to second-guess everything Pete said after that. He spent so much time with Pete that it would be exhausting. Besides, he could trust Pete, he was pretty sure of it. Bradley had known for years and never sold him out. And he was the sort who had his price.

He came to a decision. 'Okay.' He turned around. 'Can you keep a secret?'

'Of course.'

'You caught me. I am Blaze.'

Pete stared at him for what felt like ages. 'You're not messing around?'

Luke shook his head. 'As if I'd do that with you.'

'Bloody hell, Luke.' Pete sank down into his chair. 'Bloody hell.'

'To be fair,' Luke said, to no one in particular, 'most of the fan stuff comes in by email. I just blitz through it and reply in the evenings. But with *SyrenQuest*, some people have started writing in. Not a lot. Usually drawings done by kids and stuff. They told me to hold the things up to the light before I opened them, just in case there's a nutter sending weird things, but it's all been pretty harmless so far.'

Pete was staring at him, mouth slightly open. 'But how?'

'What do you mean, how?' Luke sat in his chair and, trying not to think about how it was still warm from Sam's body heat, rolled it over to Pete. 'The usual way. I play games at night and load them onto my channel.'

'I thought YouTubers were full-time or something. Blaze has a huge following. How do you find the time? Do you actually have a manager?'

'I wish,' said Luke. 'No. It's just me. There was a time when I could have gone full-time on it. That's part of the reason I did so badly in college. YouTube was paying me quite well, so I didn't have to try too hard to get a job, if you see what I mean. Then the algorithm changed and earnings dropped.' He shrugged. 'I could have doubled down or played it safe and got a regular job. In the end I did neither and started up a business.' He grinned, weakly.

Pete was still looking at him with big eyes.

'It's not that big a deal,' said Luke.

'It … sorta is.'

'Seriously, don't tell anyone. I don't want people to know.'

'But how is this possible?' said Pete. 'I mean, look at Blaze. He's cool and confident and awesome and … no offence, but you're you.'

'See, this is why I don't want people to know.' Luke leaned forward and clasped his hands together. 'Please, Pete. Swear to me that you won't tell anyone.'

'Does anyone else know?'

'Not many. Bradley knows. He used to play too. A few old friends from uni … that's about it. I've tried very hard to keep the two lives separate.'

'Why? Why the secrecy? If I was a famous YouTuber, I'd want everyone to know about it.'

Luke sat back and pushed his fingers through his hair. 'Blaze is … a persona. I can do and say things as Blaze that I really can't do when I'm me. I like that. I get to step outside of all this.' He waved a hand to indicate the office. 'The work, the worrying about money, the way my brain disowns my mouth when I try to talk to a woman I like. All of that just goes away when I'm Blaze. All I have to do is hit things and run around and make wisecracks, which are weirdly easier when I'm him.'

Pete gave him a funny look. 'Can you talk to girls when you're Blaze?'

'I can talk to girls,' said Luke, affronted. 'It's just when it's someone I like that I have a problem.'

'Why don't you talk to Sam as Blaze? Then it would be easy.'

That was a stupid suggestion. Luke gave him a glare that, he hoped, conveyed the depth of stupidity. 'For a start, it would be difficult to get in and out of costume at work. Besides, what would I do? Go up to her as Blaze and say, "My mate Luke fancies you"? Don't be daft.'

Pete threw his hands heavenwards. 'Oh my god, Luke! I don't mean like that. I mean inside.' He mimed putting something to his ribs. 'Put your Blaze confidence on and then go talk to her as you. Jesus.'

Luke considered it. The thought was weird. When he was Blaze, he was a hundred per cent Blaze. He spoke differently, he walked differently. 'No,' he said. 'It honestly doesn't work like that. Nice thought though, Pete.' He pushed with his feet so that his chair wheeled back to his computer. 'Now, can we please forget about all of this?'

Pete opened his mouth.

'Please,' Luke said again.

Pete nodded.

'And you can't tell anyone.'

Another nod. 'Fine.'

'Great. Let's get back to work.'

For the next few minutes, there was no sound but the clicking of keys. Then Pete said, 'Luke?'

'Mmm?'

'Can I come and watch you play on Monday?'

Luke looked up. He hadn't had someone with him when he played for years. It might be fun. 'Sure.'

Sam opened the handbag wardrobe to take out the bag that went with tomorrow's outfit and thought of Luke and his insistence that she should be the face of her brand. Should she take that seriously? He had been right about her being afraid of success. Could he be right about the other things too?

Sam removed the Shanthi bag from the bag she'd used that day and put it back in its place. Instead of taking out the next day's pick, she reached to the back of the wardrobe and pulled out a slightly grubby denim shoulder-bag. This one was not part of the collection. It was the one that Amma had kept her stuff in during those final days in hospital. The cancer she'd beaten when Sam was a toddler had returned so stealthily that by the time they found out, it was already too late.

She unzipped the bag, her nose close to it. The smell was chiefly of her mother's perfume – Sam had sprayed it into the bag at one point, the half-empty bottle was still in the bottom of the bag – but there was also a hint of hospital. The only way to get rid of the antiseptic smell would have been to wash the bag and she still wasn't ready to do that. With the smell came the overpowering memory of the fury and the helplessness of sitting by a hospital bed. Her heart constricted painfully. She zipped the bag shut again and shoved it back into its corner. This was not how she wanted to remember her mother. The pressure of tears hurt her eyes. She sat down on the floor and put her face in her hands, the tears dampening her fingertips.

If she used Amma's name and image on the Shanthi Bags website, that was how she would be remembered – a woman who loved handbags. But she was so much more than that. No one was just one thing. Or even merely a collection of all the things that they loved. There was nothing that could capture Amma completely. But the handbags captured Amma for *her*. She could use the website to talk about her and outline something of what made her special. A public tribute to her, rather than a tribute in her heart. Sam sighed and looked up. Her brothers might understand that. Her father … might not.

He would hate everything about it. The fact that Samadhi had left an apparently 'stable' job to strike out in the risky world of a start-up business. The fact that she was using her mother's bags. The fact that she'd kept it quiet for so long. Sam stood up and brushed off her knees. She'd had no choice but to keep it quiet. Otherwise, there would have been all kinds of pressure to find a new job. Thatha was old fashioned in many ways. He had started work with one company and had stayed there. The idea of a portfolio career was alien to him. Her brothers had moved out of the country to get on with their careers. She almost wished she'd done the same.

She looked at the clothes she'd hung on the back of the door for tomorrow. Blue. Inside the Shanthi bag on the floor, her phone buzzed. She chose a handbag that matched and closed the wardrobe, before she checked her phone. It was a message from Blaze, about more shortcuts in the game.

She sat on the bed to reply. He hadn't been his usual genial self when they played in round one and she was a little bit hurt at how gruff he'd been. She knew she deserved it, at some level, but there was no need for him to be rude. He'd known she was a rookie right from the start. She didn't have to take that.

On the other hand, she didn't want to antagonise him even more. Stick to the facts, she decided. They were stuck together for the next round anyway, so she would be entirely professional and not let her feelings get in the way.

Bravura: *I noticed those too, but I still can't see the pattern to it. I guess we'll have to see what we come across in round 2.*

Three flashing dots appeared that suggested he was typing. They stopped. Then started again and stopped again. Sam drummed her fingers on her leg in frustration.

The message finally appeared.

Blaze: *I'm sorry I was so rude when we played in round 1. Winning is important to me. But I shouldn't have taken it out on you.*

Sam sniffed. No, he bloody well shouldn't have. She typed back: *What happened to 'it's just a game'?*

Blaze: *I may as well tell you. Something happened in real life. I suddenly find myself in need of money. Winning this*

97

tournament would be the easiest way to get what I need in the time frame that I need it. So my attitude went from not caring much about winning to it being very important. But, as I say, that is not your problem. You were doing your best. I'm sorry for snapping at you.

Sam read the message twice. That sounded ominous, like there were goons waiting to break his legs if he didn't pay up.

Bravura: *Are you okay? Are you in danger?*
Blaze: *Not in danger. Lol. I suppose it does sound like that from my message. No. I just need to invest in something that's important to me or risk losing it. Real life can be a drag sometimes.*
Bravura: *Can't it just!*
Blaze: *So. A truce? You do your best. I'll do mine.*
Bravura: *A truce. I will practise as much as I can though.*
Blaze: *And I'll try and think about what's going on with the game.*

Sam went downstairs feeling much better about life because Blaze wasn't an asshat and she had managed to talk to him without coming across as a massive fangirl.

She could feel the connection forming between them. He obviously felt comfortable enough to tell her something about his personal life – something he rarely did. He needed to win. He hadn't shared the fact that he had financial troubles on YouTube. He had entrusted her with a secret. Maybe he saw her as a friend. She hoped so. To her, he already was a trusted friend.

Of course, now it became even more important that she didn't screw things up in *SyrenQuest*. If Blaze needed to win, she would do her best to help him. Even if it meant practising late into the night. She would not let him down.

Chapter 10

Much to Sam's relief, round two of the game seemed more of a test of agility than fighting skills. Once again, they were looking for a key. She and Blaze were making good time. The first hurdle involved crossing a swollen river by jumping on the debris that was floating past. She watched it for a few seconds, counting under her breath. If she fell, she would either drown, or get swept off until she was miles away from Blaze.

'I'm going for it.' Blaze took a run-up and jumped, landing on a tree that was hurtling past. He landed and by the time he'd regained his balance, was quite a way downstream.

'Head upstream.' Sam took a few steps back, ran, and jumped. She landed on a log. She righted herself and leapt to the next one. She kept an eye on where Blaze was and headed towards him, so that they didn't get separated.

'This is like …' Blaze jumped again. 'That *Crossy Road* game on steroids.'

Sam was actually enjoying it. She was finally better at something than he was. She was already nearer the opposite shore than he was. One final leap and she landed a little short of the shore. But the river was shallower at the edge, so she waded out and clambered onto the grassy bank. Blaze took a massive leap and landed with a splash. He lost his footing and got carried downriver a short way before he got up and waded to the shore. Sam walked down to meet him.

'Phew,' he said. 'That was fun.'

'Where to next?'

They both looked up at the wayfinder, which was leading towards the trees that were not far from the river's edge.

'Deep, dark woods,' said Blaze. 'Come on, you.'

His tone was friendlier than it had been last time. That was good. If he was joking around with her, he must like her. Right? Sam kept pace with him, jogging along, sword in hand, her senses on high alert. She had spent most of the evenings between rounds practising. If they got attacked, she really, really hoped she didn't need to be rescued by him again. The field they were running through had knee-high grass and little yellow flowers. There were birds overhead.

'This is nice,' she said.

'Nothing's trying to kill us,' Blaze said in return. 'That's weird.'

He had a good point. The wayfinder led them to a wood. The meadow ended abruptly where the trees began. The contrast between the two made the woods look even darker.

'Okay. *Now* something is going to try to kill us.' Blaze took out his cutlass.

Sam tightened her grip on her sword. 'There's no path. I guess we just wade in?'

'Sounds as good a plan as any. Come on then.' He plunged in.

The glow of the wayfinder was still visible, even through the trees, but there was no path. Everything was quiet, apart from the whispering of the trees and the odd burst of birdsong. They waded on.

Sam's health bar was always there, at the top of her visual field. Was it her imagination or was the bar creeping lower? She glanced across at Blaze. His was creeping downwards too.

'Blaze. Why is our health declining?'

He stopped, frowning. 'You're right. But why?' He looked down at his legs.

Sam did the same. They were walking through what appeared to be tall grass, but the blades had a strange sticky quality to them. She picked a leaf and brought it up closer to her eyes. The leaf was covered in small glistening stalks.

'Carnivorous plants?' she said.

Blaze turned around. There were no visible means of escape. 'We have to go through. There isn't another way.'

Sam was just raising her head to look up when something whipped out of the underbrush and wrapped itself around her, trapping her arms against her body. She wriggled. All her fighting practice was useless when she couldn't move her arms. Blaze leapt forward and cut her loose.

'Argh.' Two separate vines had appeared and wrapped around Blaze's legs. Sam hacked one vine off while Blaze tackled the other. The vines, once cut, turned brown and looked almost like rope. Without stopping to think, she grabbed a couple and put them into her inventory.

More and more vines were appearing. They hacked and chopped their way through, but both of them were suffering from the stinging grass as well. All the while, their health slowly declined.

'We can't keep doing this,' Sam gasped. A vine got her by the wrist. 'Blaze!'

He cut her loose. 'How the hell are we supposed to get through? The entire ground is trying to eat us and the rest of it is trying to throttle us AND eat us at the same time.'

Sam struck out at another vine. 'There must be something.' She looked up. Trees. 'We could try climbing the trees.'

'How do we know they're not poisonous?' Blaze was dancing around, slashing vines.

She had a hint of an idea. It was so hard to concentrate when

101

things were trying to kill you. 'Birdsong.' That was the thought that was trying to get her attention.

'What?'

'Can't you hear it? There are birds in this forest. The trees must be safe or they'd be dead.' She ran for the nearest tree and scaled it. A vine caught her ankle, but she cut it quickly. When she hauled herself onto the lowest branch, her health bar stopped dropping. She turned to look for Blaze. He was caught in a tangle of vines now, a short distance away from the base of the tree.

She looked along the branch she was sitting on. It wasn't particularly thick. The end of it was just above where Blaze was trapped.

She ran along the branch and lay down at the end. Her character was light, but she still had enough weight to bend the branch. 'Grab it,' she said.

Blaze managed to cut loose from the vines that were holding him. He put the cutlass between his teeth and jumped up. Once he had hold of the branch, Sam scooted backwards. Blaze hauled himself up and made his way towards the trunk. The vines, unable to reach that high, waved around below them.

Blaze lay facedown on the branch, panting. 'That was terrifying.'

Her health bar was quite low now, but Blaze's was worse. It was in the red.

'Fix your health,' she said.

'Can't. I have no potion left.'

She only had a small one. She was sure she'd had more at the end of the last round. She looked at Blaze's health bar. If he died, she died too. 'Here.' She tossed the potion to him. He caught it. She couldn't read the expression on his face – somewhere between annoyed and impressed. At least he didn't argue. He swigged it and his health went back up to nearly two-thirds.

He pushed himself up to a sitting position. His green eyes met hers. 'Thanks.'

Heat flashed through her. He was seeing her as an equal,

someone worthy of attention, for the first time. She had to be cool about this. She shrugged. 'If you die, it's game over for me too.'

'True. But still.'

They both stood up, balancing on the branch. 'I guess we go from tree to tree,' said Sam.

Blaze looked upwards and pointed at the wayfinder. 'That way.'

It was mostly a pathfinding puzzle now. Blaze kept up his normal patter as they went. They made good time until they arrived at an extremely tall tree. The wayfinder was directly above it.

'I guess we go up?' Sam said. She was feeling less intimidated by Blaze now that *she'd* saved *him* for a change. This was the Blaze she knew and loved. He was cheerful and friendly ... and she was playing alongside him! They were actually a team.

'I guess we do,' he said amiably.

They climbed. It was a long way up. Sam couldn't help wondering if there was some sort of shortcut they'd missed. Maybe one that let them fly to the top or something. They would have to look for it in the replays.

The key was in a nest at the top of the tree. Whatever had made the nest was not there.

'I bet the minute we step in the nest the owner of it will come back,' Blaze said.

'I could run and get it. I might make it back out in time.' She wasn't confident she would.

Blaze looked round. They were high enough that they could see over the tree canopy to where the woods ended. 'I can't see anything that might be useful for getting us down. But I guess we'll cross that bridge when we get to it.' He pulled out his cutlass. 'Okay. You run and grab. I'll fight whatever it is. Aim to get out of the nest and under it.'

'Okay. On three.' She counted down and sprang into the nest. Sure enough, a screech rang out from somewhere. She ignored it, grabbed the key, and ran back to the side of the nest. The next screech was accompanied by a hellscape of claws and feathers. Blaze was next to her, blade whirling. Sam reached the edge of the nest and scrambled over the side. She clung to the twigs and crawled until she could drop onto the branch underneath. Her health was dangerously low now, flashing red.

Blaze appeared, still fighting. He spun round, dropped over the side, throwing his sword at the claw that was coming for him. Right at the last minute, he grabbed onto the nest and swung under it. The move was so beautifully executed, Sam nearly applauded. The sword disappeared down towards the ground. Blaze hung from the bottom of the nest as an enormous beak tried to peck him. Sam reached forward, grabbed his belt, and tugged, swinging him to safety.

The minute Blaze landed on the branch next to her, the tree, the bird, and the nest all disappeared. They landed in a heap back at the training grounds.

They untangled themselves and both flopped back onto the ground. Sam's heart was pounding and adrenaline zinged through her and not just because of their close escape.

'Phew,' she said, panting.

'We made it.' Blaze sat up. 'Good job back there.'

'Well, you too.' She sat up too. 'Obviously.'

'It was pretty close for a minute there,' he said. 'I thought one of us was going to run out of health for sure. As challenges go, that was tight.' He wasn't looking at her.

Sam realised he was talking to his followers, not her.

There was a soft whoosh and the interviewer's avatar appeared. Blaze got to his feet. He held out a hand to help Sam up. She stared at it for a millisecond. He was giving her his hand? She took it and he pulled her to her feet. She was holding Blaze's hand. *She was holding his hand.*

He looked down at where she was gripping his hand. Oh. Right. She let go, hot with embarrassment now.

'Blaze! Bravura! How was that?'

'Brutal,' said Blaze. 'But we made it. Right, Bravura?' He clapped her on the shoulder. 'You have to hand it to Bravura. She was the real star of the quest.'

Sam glowed. She nodded, too overcome to speak.

'How did you think you did?'

'We made it to the end and in pretty good time, so we might be in with a chance.'

'Possibly, possibly. I can't tell you that. But I can tell you that we lost three teams to the health potion trap.'

'That was a low blow,' said Blaze. 'If Bravura hadn't given me her last small health potion, I'd have died.'

Sam's heart raced anew. She had saved him. He had noticed her and, for once, not because she was terrible at the game. The people commenting on his videos would have to stop hating her now.

Their time came up on the display above them. Less than an hour. Surely, that was good.

'Well, good luck.' The interviewer beamed and disappeared.

'I'm going to take a small break,' Blaze said to her. 'Well played, Bravura.'

'Thank you. You too. You were amazing.'

He gave a theatrical shrug. 'All in a day's work.'

Sam took her headset off and made sure the mic was not on before she let out the squeal that had been building up inside her.

Niro grinned at her.

'Did you see that? He gave me his hand. Did you see?' said Sam.

Niro looked surprised. 'I … yes, yes he did.'

'You must have noticed.'

'Well, yes. He helped you up. In a friendly kind of way. That was such a ridiculously fast-paced round, I'm just surprised that was the main thing you took from it.'

Sam waved a hand. 'Oh, yeah, yeah. I didn't get to try out

my fighting skills. But I wasn't crap. And I think I'm making progress getting to know him. He was all friendly and he said nice things about me.'

'He said nice things about your playing ...' Niro said, carefully.

'Same thing.' Why was Niro being such a downer? 'Things are finally going right,' Sam said. 'Can't you be happy for me?'

'I am. I am. I just think ... you know, you shouldn't read too much into—'

Sam frowned. 'I don't think I am. Anyway. I'm going to go grab a drink and then go back in to see if we made it into round three.'

Luke took his headset off and swivelled his chair round to look at Pete. 'And that, mate, is how it's done,' he said, still in character.

'Wow,' Pete said. 'I mean, actually ... wow. That was such a tense round.'

Luke nodded. 'Wasn't it just? Bravura might be a rubbish fighter, but she's got agility and thinking nailed.'

'You were being very nice to her, I noticed,' Pete said.

'She was doing a good job. Credit where credit's due.' He was still feeling bad about how he'd behaved in the last round. To start with, he had been trying to make amends. But Bravura really had done well this time. 'And she gave me her last health potion, even though she could have done with it herself. That's ...' He frowned. It meant something.

'Teamwork?' said Pete. 'Is that the word you're looking for?'

Luke smiled. 'Yeah. That'll be it.' He reached for the bottle of water he kept on the shelf – far back, so that he didn't accidentally knock it over. It was thirsty business keeping up a running commentary the whole time. As he drank, he considered how strange it felt to be part of a team. He didn't object to it.

'Besides,' he said. 'If I'm being friendly towards her, maybe it'll tone down some of the nastier elements I've seen in the comments.'

Pete grimaced. 'I saw that. I also saw you'd been wielding your moderating powers on your channel.'

'Damn right. I'm not having that kind of toxic nonsense on my patch.'

'Good. I hope Bravura isn't too upset by it. Is she?'

'She's not mentioned it.' Mind you, he hadn't asked. 'She doesn't seem to have any social media presence, apart from a few comments on my videos. But I guess that just means she isn't using the name Bravura. I didn't want to bring it up in case that made things worse.'

'Fair enough, I suppose.'

Luke had some more water and put the lid back on the bottle.

'Can I ask you something?' Pete broke into his thoughts.

Luke swallowed his last sip of water. 'Sure.'

'Why do you have such a strong Northern accent when you're Blaze? You don't sound like that now. Which one is real?'

'They both are, I guess. When I was 16 … when I started the channel, I grew up in Sheffield. We moved down south a couple of months later.' He almost winced at the memory. His Yorkshire accent had stood out in Surrey. It had singled him out as different and made him terribly self-conscious. 'I sort of smoothed out the accent over time. But Blaze has still got it. It just comes back as I relax into his character.'

He turned back to his console. Losing his accent had involved anger and tears and elocution lessons, but it had helped, he supposed. Or had it? He picked up his headset and looked at it for a moment. Perhaps that's why Blaze was so different to him. When he was a teenager, Blaze was all the things he wanted to be. The inner boy that he could never fully unleash in real life. Cocky, confident … and much more Northern. No wonder he felt like they were different people.

A notification came up on his game screen. He put his headset back on.

Sam stood next to Blaze and they watched the announcement. So far, Phil_the_Vicar and FlickNife's teams had made it to the third round.

'And in third place … we have Team Blaze!'

Beside her Blaze punched the air. 'Yes!' He turned and high-fived her. 'Nice one, Bravura.'

'One step closer,' she said, her throat tight.

'Yes indeed.'

The last team of contenders were announced. Fireworks went off in the sky. 'These four teams are now in the semi-finals,' the announcer said. 'They will compete against each other to get the final key. The two teams that are the fastest will face each other LIVE on stage at SyrenCon this weekend.'

Sam could barely breathe from excitement. She had made it into the semi-finals. She hadn't even expected to make it past the first round. She turned to look at Blaze.

He was talking to his YouTube people again. 'So all we have to do is come in the top two in the next round. Easy as, right, Bravura?'

'Er … right. Yeah.'

'So, don't forget to tune in on Thursday night, folks. I'll see you there.' He grinned at her. 'And I'll see you on Thursday too, Brav.'

She squeaked out, 'Bye.' In her mind, she was screaming, *he called me Brav!*

When she took her headset off, she could barely contain her elation. 'He called me Brav. He had a nickname for me!'

Niro put her hands over her ears. 'Well, he's certainly got over his moody phase.'

Sam took a deep breath. 'Sorry. I'm just a bit excited.'

'No, really?' Sarcasm dripped from Niro's voice. 'I'd never have guessed.'

'This is a big deal for me,' said Sam. 'I'm playing next to Blaze. And we're winning. It'd be like you having dinner with Chris Evans.'

'Hey. Leave Captain America out of this.'

'You know what I mean.' She gathered up the headset and started to pack it away. 'Do you think he might like me? We could be … I dunno … friends, at least.'

'I'm sure you could,' said Niro. 'Anyway, you get to find out when you meet him for real at the convention next weekend.'

'Oh.' Holy crap. She had almost forgotten about that. 'I'm going to meet him … in real life.' She looked at the screen, where the *SyrenQuest* logo was rotating in silence. 'I'm going to meet Blaze.' She was suddenly burning hot. Her breath shortened. She had, for years, wondered what it would be like to meet Blaze in real life. To look into those green eyes. To be on the receiving end of his smile. And now she had the chance to do it. 'Oh my god, Niro. I can't do it. What if he's not like that at all in real life? What if it's all fake and he's really a horrible old man with nasty breath.'

'Have you googled him? He's been seen in real life before. Stop being mad, Sam.'

Sam took a deep breath and let it out. Niro had a point. And yes, she had googled him. He looked tall and slim and he *sounded* young. She could only imagine that he looked like his avatar. Beard, pirate outfit, green eyes, cheeky smile. And she was going to meet him.

Another bolt of panic. 'My costume.' She turned to Niro.

'You have your costume. We sorted it out already, remember?'

'Yes, but is it good enough? I have to look like my avatar. I'm going to have to do make-up and paint myself blue and—'

'Woah.' Niro held up her hands. 'Calm down. Tell you what, let's go and look at the costume and try it on, okay? I'll help you with the make-up. I've still got the make-up brushes and stuff from when I did theatre. We'll order the body paints and you have until the weekend to practise getting your face right. You're going to be fine.'

'I don't want anyone to recognise me,' said Sam.

'So what if they do? You're awesome. You made it into the semi-final round of *SyrenQuest*. You should be proud.' Niro stood up. 'Come on, daaahling, let's get you to make-up.'

When Luke took his headset off, Pete was saying something.

'Pardon?' he asked.

'I said, have you got the costume already?'

'Oh yes,' Luke said. 'Wanna see?'

'Like you have to ask.'

The costume had evolved a little over the years, but was basically the same pirate-inspired coat, boots, and trousers that he'd chosen when he was building his avatar years ago. Different games had different skins, but he always chose something that nodded to this core outfit.

'The *SyrenQuest* guys added a long coat with rolled-up sleeves as one of the options,' said Luke. 'One of the newbies has the same coat, but the rest of his outfit makes him look like a space cowboy.'

Pete picked up the tattoo sleeves. 'These are cool.'

'They are. The tats on the avatar don't match these, but otherwise, it's fine. I just have to make sure I wear these to cover up the ends.' He pulled out a bag containing some leather bracelets and woven bands. 'You know how I sometimes get fan stuff?' He pulled out a couple of friendship bracelets, each about one and a half inches wide. 'These are from fans.' He picked out one that had 'BLAZE' weaved into it. He handed it to Pete. It felt strange, sharing this stuff with someone. It made him realise just how long he'd kept Blaze a guilty secret. 'Some of them are pretty impressive. I like to wear them to conventions and hold my arms up so that they get photographed. People love it if they spot something they sent.' And it also meant that his face was obscured in most of the photos of him.

'What's the weirdest thing a fan sent you?'

He didn't have to think about that. 'Someone sent me underpants. I did not keep those.' He smiled. 'I did have someone give me a cardigan they'd knitted once. I put it on and had my photo taken with him. It was a good cardigan too. Very cosy.'

Pete was looking at the tat sleeves again. 'Aren't you ever tempted to get real tattoos?'

Luke laughed. 'I'd love to. I tried. But I threw up and the guy had to stop.' He pushed back his sleeve and showed Pete his forearm. 'I was supposed to be getting the name of my girlfriend at the time on my arm. But he only got this far before I gave up.'

Pete looked at the small L on his skin. 'At least you got her initial.'

'Nope.' Luke pulled his sleeve back down. 'Her name was Emily. That's not an L. It's half an E. She wasn't impressed.'

'This is so unbelievable,' said Pete. 'And very cool.' He started typing into his phone.

'What are you doing?' Luke asked, alarmed. 'I hope you're not telling anyone any of this. I told you, it's a secret.' He had been so sure he could trust Pete.

'No. I'm trying to see if I can get a ticket to the con this weekend. I wasn't planning on going, but now that I've had a peek behind the curtain, I really want to see more.'

Luke relaxed. 'You know that I will blank you if I see you, right?' He didn't want any clues linking Blaze back to his real life.

Pete raised his hands. 'Of course. I completely understand that.'

'In that case, I hope you get a ticket.'

While Pete was scowling at his screen, Luke got down the hatbox that contained his wig. It was a little dusty, but nothing that wouldn't brush out. Walking over to the chest of drawers that he used as a dumping ground for everything, he found the parcel containing the new glue-on beard that he'd bought.

'Yes! I'm in.' Pete put his phone away. He looked at all the clothes and accessories that Luke had laid out on the bed. 'This is quite a lot of stuff.'

'Well, I do have to transform into a whole other person.'

'Your eyes are a different colour to his. How do you do that?'

'Coloured contacts. I have a regular set and a green set. But I hate wearing them, so in real life, I tend to live in glasses instead.'

'I'm impressed with your dedication.'

Luke shrugged, but he was quite pleased. He *was* dedicated to being Blaze. He showed it mostly through the hours he put into playing, but the dressing-up side was important too. It allowed him to go to conventions and network with other YouTubers without compromising his anonymity. Besides, it was part of the fun.

Pete was picking everything up, looking at it reverentially, and putting it back down. 'I don't understand why you go to all this effort, though,' he said. 'Why the secrecy?'

Luke paused in the middle of choosing which cuffs to use. 'Because Blaze isn't real. He's not me.'

Pete's expression was blank. He shook his head.

Luke tried again to explain. 'It's like I step into a different body and I can say and do things I wouldn't *dream* of doing in real life.' He hadn't articulated this to anyone before. 'So I need him to be a separate person. I know he's not real. Does that make sense?'

'I guess so,' said Pete. 'But I still can't get my head around the fact that you're Blaze. If I hadn't actually seen you play, I might have thought I'd imagined it all.' He picked up the wig and stroked it. 'I'm glad I got hold of a ticket.' He put the wig on and looked in the mirror. He looked different with long blond hair. 'I will be there to see you win *SyrenQuest*.'

'I might not win.' Luke picked up the hanger with the costume on it and hung it up on the curtain rail. He hadn't expected to get to the semi-finals, if he was being honest.

'You will.' Pete took off the wig and stroked the stray hairs down.

Luke sat on the bed. 'It would be really handy. I need the money right now.'

Pete looked puzzled. 'You do?'

Luke sighed. He hadn't told Pete about the conversation with Bradley. 'It's to do with work,' he said. 'Bradley wants to sell his share of the company and I want to buy it.'

Pete's eyes went wide. 'Oh wow. That's … major.'

'If I have the money, I would also like to hire you on a permanent contract to be our sales and customer service guy. I think we're a good team.'

Pete slowly put down the wig he was holding.

'Of course, I know you'll be looking for jobs now and if I win, I can offer the contract to you before you decide to leave. Assuming you want to stay, obviously.'

'Mate, I'd love that,' said Pete. 'You're a great boss and I am having so much fun in this job.'

'But I can't do any of that without a substantial amount of money.' Luke put the wig back in its box. 'So I'd better win.'

'I believe in you,' said Pete. 'And Bravura. I believe in her too.'

'She's come along quite a lot, since that first round,' said Luke. 'She can do more of the moves without pausing to think about them now. And she's a bloody genius with puzzles.'

Pete grinned. 'You've thawed towards her a lot. As we saw earlier with the mildly flirtatious banter.'

Luke shook his head. 'No. The game stuff … it's not real.'

'But you have been flirting with her.'

'I don't think so.'

'That's not what matters though, is it?' said Pete. 'What matters is, does *she* think so.'

Sam sat cross-legged in front of the handbag collection. 'Which one should I take to the con?'

Niro was on the floor next to her and surveyed the collection. 'Something blue? To go with your body paint?'

'Or the silver backpack purse?' She pulled it out. 'It would leave my hands free.'

'Even better idea.'

Sam opened the bag and breathed in, just to see if it held any leftover memories. No. This one was too new. Sam herself had used it more often than her mother had. The thought reminded her of Luke, for some reason. She turned around to Niro. 'You know what Luke said? He said I was afraid of the business succeeding and I was pulling my punches. I'm starting to wonder if he's right.'

Niro stretched her legs out and shifted position so that she was leaning against the bed. 'Okay. How so?'

'I think …' Sam said quietly. 'I'm afraid of two things. One is that I'll let my mum down somehow if I fail and the other is that my dad will be upset with me when he finds out I left my "safe" job to do this.' She paused. That wasn't the whole story, was it? 'And that I used Amma's name for the bags.'

'He might not be.' Niro got her phone out and started tapping.

Sam rolled her eyes. 'Of course he will be. All my life it's been "study hard, Samadhi; get a stable job, Samadhi; work hard, Samadhi". Starting my own craft-based small business is pretty much as far from getting a stable job as you can get.'

'Yes, but—'

'*And* I named it after Amma.'

Niro wrinkled her nose. 'Okay. I can see how that would play badly. Does he still not talk about her?'

Sam shook her head. 'Only on the anniversary of her death. When we go to the temple.'

Niro clicked her tongue. 'You're going to have to tell him at some point.'

'I know. But I want it to be when the company is successful.' She tipped her head back. 'Which it won't be, at the rate things are going.'

'How about your brothers? What did they say?'

114

She hadn't told them either. She looked at her feet.

'Oh, Sam. You have to tell them. They might be able to help bring your dad round.' Niro shook her head. 'You know, I think I see where this Luke guy was coming from. It's almost like you're hoping you don't make it so that you don't have to tell them and have the awkward conversation.'

Which, when Sam heard it said out loud, sounded so stupid. 'Luke is right, isn't he? I'm not giving it my all because success scares me almost as much as failure. Oh crap.'

'I don't know about pulling your punches, but if you mean you have to come clean to your family and face the music, then yes. He's right.'

Sam looked back up at the handbags. 'I guess I need to own this. If I don't give it my all, I'll regret it. This is my tribute to Amma. I'm going to use it as my memorial to her. But it's also about me giving myself a chance to do something I think is worthwhile. I'm tired of working myself to the bone for other people.'

'But you're going to have to tell your dad.'

Sam nodded. 'I will. I'm seeing them next week – after the convention, and after my presentation on Monday morning. Hopefully, by then, I'll have worked out a good way to explain it to them. If I could get the crowdfunding to work, then it would be so much easier because I could show them how many people want the product.'

Niro pulled earbuds out of her pocket and popped one in her ear. 'Uh-huh.'

Sam turned. 'Are you even listening to me?'

Niro waved a hand at her, eyes down on the phone. 'Just a second. Oh, wow. That was fast.'

'What?'

Niro shushed her. 'Just a sec.' Her eyes widened. 'Oh, boy.'

'What?' Sam scrambled over to her cousin and peered at the screen, just in time to see a YouTube clip come to an end.

'Here.' Niro put the sound on and played it back.

The title screen appeared. 'Blaze and Bravura flirting for two minutes straight.' Oh.

The clip was culled from Blaze's gameplay videos and it swept through their friendship – Bravura looking starstruck on day one, Blaze being annoyed at how slow she was, his giving her an amused smile, her hauling him up onto the monolith, the two of them holding each other steady at the top of the monolith, his saving her from the vines, her giving him her health potion. A romantic soundtrack had been added, making it look every bit a love story.

'Oh no. How embarrassing.' Sam stared at the comments underneath as Niro scrolled through them. 'Still, it's better than the "she's rubbish, she deserves to die" stuff I've been seeing lately.'

'Definitely.'

Niro put 'Blaze and Bravura' into the search bar.

'It's not the only one.' Niro showed her the other titles: 'Blaze and Bravura, a love story', 'Bravura being in love with Blaze', '#Blazevura'. 'I hate to say this, but it looks like you guys are a Thing.'

'We're not. I mean, he … he doesn't know me. He's going to be so annoyed.' She pulled her knees up and hugged them to her. She didn't know how she felt. Part of her was delighted. She had loved Blaze from afar for so long. Just meeting him online had been a source of delight to her, but … she had never dared contemplate that he might return those feelings.

'Hey, you okay, Sam?'

She shook her head. 'I don't know. Do you think Blaze feels anything for me? I mean … he's definitely mellowed towards me since our first game.'

Niro gave her a sly grin. 'You did save him. He's bound to be impressed.'

'And he gave me his hand to help me up. Even though it was just our avatars and it was a pointless thing to do …' She knew she shouldn't get her hopes up, but she couldn't help it.

Niro laughed. 'I wish I was coming to the con with you next weekend! I'd love to see what happens when you meet in real life!'

'We won't really meet as we are, will we? I'll be Bravura. I'll look different.'

'So? You're still you. I mean Bravura looks a little more … out there. But essentially, you're still the same person. It's not like you've invented a whole different personality to be online. He's probably exactly the same.' She gestured to the screen. 'According to half of YouTube, you guys have chemistry together online – so who knows what will happen when you meet in the flesh.'

'If he really looks like his avatar, I'll just die of happiness,' Sam said. 'I'm pretty much in love with him already, regardless of what he looks like.'

Niro rolled her eyes.

Sam squeezed her knees to her chest and tried not to grin. She was going to meet him at the Syren Convention. Who knew, maybe their developing friendship online would translate into something in real life.

'It's all to play for,' she said happily.

Chapter 11

The moment she walked into the building, Sam scanned the cafeteria for Luke. Ah, there he was. He was sitting at their usual table, watching something on his laptop while eating his porridge. She had composed her email about Shanti Bags while sitting on the Underground, but she still wasn't sure she wanted to send it to him. She got her coffee and, feeling the need for extra sustenance, a croissant.

When she walked over, Luke spotted her and closed his laptop.

'Morning,' he said, smiling. His hair flopped over onto his forehead and he pushed it back. 'How are you today?'

'Good, thank you.' She wanted to scream, *I'm going to be in the* SyrenQuest *semi-final with Blaze*, but of course, she couldn't. So she just had to be upbeat for no reason instead. 'You?'

'Wonderful,' he said. He did look happy. There was something about the sparkle in his eyes. He looked … bigger somehow. As though something constraining him had been released. It must be the day for good news.

Sam took a deep breath. She had snapped at Luke when he had made a helpful suggestion. Now it was time to be humble and admit he was right. 'I thought about what you said … about being afraid to succeed. And I think you're right. If I'm going to do this, I have to give it my all. So, I've rewritten the story of the brand to centre me and my mum and …' She pulled out her phone, found the draft email she'd written on the Tube, and hit send. 'I've just sent it over to you.'

His phone pinged. 'Let's have a look.' He theatrically rolled up his sleeves and picked up his device.

Sam blew on her coffee and watched his face as he read it. The smile and twinkling eyes were replaced by a frown of concentration. She watched his eyes move behind his glasses. What was different about him today? Luke gave off this vibe of being slightly worried all the time, like he was trying not to take up much space. This disappeared when he was working. Now, he was so focused, so intense, that you couldn't help but notice him. Sure he dressed like a student and needed a haircut, but he wasn't as small or forgettable as he seemed to want you to think. She studied his face. Good cheekbones, strong jawline. Behind his glasses, he had kind, light brown eyes. He was attractive if you looked at him properly. And people loved him. So far, everyone in The Nest seemed to know Luke and no one had a bad word to say about him. That was nice too.

'This is excellent.' Luke looked up.

Sam hastily dropped her gaze. It would be weird to get caught staring at him.

'You named your company after your mum?' he asked, softly.

'Yes. She liked handbags.'

'She died when you were so young. I'm sorry that happened to you.'

She shrugged. It was what it was.

He studied her face solemnly for a moment. 'I think I understand now.' He looked back at the email. 'The connection makes it so much more poignant.'

Poignant was one way to put it. Painful was another. The idea of putting Amma's picture on the website – one with her carrying one of her favourite bags – alongside a photo of Sam carrying the same bag had come in a flash of inspiration. Seeing it made her heart squeeze, but she had decided she was going to give it her all and give it her all was exactly what she was going to do.

Luke looked back at the email and frowned. 'Are you sure you want to share this much?' he said.

'You were the one saying I should tell people more.'

'That was before I understood quite how personal and painful it might be.' He chewed his lip thoughtfully. 'You could just stick to the "times I left things in the wrong bag" stories. It wouldn't tug at the heartstrings as much, but it would work okay.'

He was giving her a way out. For a second she was tempted to take it. But no. This was her tribute to Amma. It wouldn't be a real tribute if it didn't mention her. 'No. I'm sure I want this to go on the website. If I'm going to use her name, I may as well do it properly.' She added, 'Thank you for thinking of that, though. It was kind of you.'

He looked at her without saying anything for a few seconds. He seemed to come to some sort of a conclusion. 'In that case, I think this should go up on your website as soon as possible.' He scrolled through the email again. 'It's clear, it's heartfelt. Put it alongside those photos and you've got a great compelling story. It's perfect.'

His praise made her feel warm inside. It had taken a lot for her to confront her feelings about her mother and put them down on paper. She hoped her description had done Amma justice.

'Thank you,' she said. 'I'm glad you like it. I'll have to work out how to update the site. I know I made some notes on how to do it when I set it up in the first place.'

'Oh, it won't take too long. It's mostly just cutting and pasting.'

'Hah. Easy for you, maybe. It's going to take me a day or two.'

He looked down at his breakfast. 'Why don't we make a start now? I don't have any meetings this morning. If you have an hour or so, I'll swap it out for you.'

'Seriously? That would be awesome! Are you sure? You really don't have to do this.'

'Positive.' He cleared his stuff from the space next to him, so that the table was clear. 'Come on.'

She moved over, so that she was sitting next to him. He opened his laptop and passed it over to her. 'Can you log in, please?'

She logged into the backend of her crowdfunding site and passed the laptop back to him. He adjusted his glasses and started to work.

There was nothing for Sam to do apart from answer the odd question and watch. Once he got going, Luke worked incredibly fast. He had nice forearms, she noticed. One of them had what looked like a tattoo of the letter L on it. She watched as his fingers flew over the keyboard, moving text around, resizing images and positioning them on the page. He seemed to know exactly what he was doing, and it was weirdly hot. He was working without a mouse as well, just a touchpad and one of those little bud things. What was it called? Like a nipple. Oh. She wished she hadn't thought that. A flood of images of what else those fingers could tease, pinch, and move popped unbidden into her head. She quickly turned away and focused on her coffee. *Entirely inappropriate. Try to think of something else.*

Looking up, she saw Kim buying her coffee before she went up to open the reception desk. Kim made an 'ooh' face and fluttered her fingers in a wave as she headed off to the lifts. Sam waved back. Oh great. Kim had seen them together and Sam's face was burning. There would be questions later.

She checked on Luke again; he was leaning forward, fiercely intent on what he was doing. He had his bottom lip between his teeth. His hair had flopped forward onto his forehead again. He gave an impatient flick of his head, which did nothing to move the hair.

That must be distracting. Sam unclipped one of her hair grips, reached across, and pinned the errant curl to the rest of his hair.

Luke turned. She got the impression that he was surfacing from a great depth. She also realised what an incredibly intimate thing she'd just done. She moved her hand away quickly. 'I just— Your hair was annoying you so I pinned it.'

He stared at her for a second, lips slightly parted. Then he said, 'Thank you. Good call.' He turned back to his work, but his fingers, poised above the touchpad, didn't move. She must have broken his concentration.

Sam slid out of her seat and gathered up the used crockery. 'I'll just tidy up,' she said, not making eye contact. 'Back in a minute.'

The trolley for trays of used things was at the other side of the cafeteria. Sam slid the tray in and then stood there for a minute and wrestled down the sudden rush of feelings. What was she thinking? She shouldn't be having inappropriate thoughts about Luke. Sure, he was hot when he was concentrating, but she was in love with Blaze. A few weeks ago, it would have just been a celebrity crush, but Blaze was real to her now. She was going to meet him in … gosh, five days! This was no time to be thirsting after someone else. She looked back at Luke, who was busily working again. She definitely shouldn't be thirsting after Luke of all people. He was a friend and a lovely bloke who didn't need her leading him on by fiddling with his hair.

She had to pull herself together and focus. There were only two things she should be thinking about right now. Getting more funding for her business and winning *SyrenQuest* so that she could impress Blaze.

Luke was still in a daze when he went back up the stairs to his office. Sam had been delighted with the revamped fundraising page. It hadn't taken him long to do. He had done enough of those pages for clients. When he and Bradley were starting out, they'd worked with a lot of small festivals that had to raise funding before they could even think about having an event. Bradley had arranged things so that Luke would make their fundraising pages for them on the understanding that they'd be paid when the target was raised. For the most part, it had worked. Many of those small festivals came back every year. Luke always fitted them in, even if it meant working through the night. Loyalty, he felt, should be rewarded.

Would Sam come back when she needed to revamp her website? Probably. Hopefully.

From the minute she had reached up and gently pushed his hair back, his concentration had been shot to bits. It had taken a massive effort to get his head back in the right place to finish the page. Thank goodness she'd gone off to clear the plates.

He reached the first floor. Sam was standing by the reception desk talking to Kim. Luke tried to walk past unnoticed.

'Oh, Luke. I like the hair accessory,' said Kim, peering round Sam.

Damn. He'd forgotten it was still in his hair. Well, not forgotten exactly. He reached up and unclipped it. 'Sorry. I forgot I still had it.' He handed the clip to Sam. His fingertips grazed her palm and he felt the thrill of contact all over again.

'Luke's hair was falling into his eyes, so I lent him my clip,' Sam said. It obviously meant nothing to her. 'Thanks again for sorting out my crowdfunding page,' she said to him.

'Not a problem. I'll see you guys later.' He fled the reception area and ran up the stairs. Kim was giving him a look that he knew only too well. She was going to tease him mercilessly about this. He normally let her teasing bounce straight off him, but he wasn't sure he could do that right now. He got into the office and leaned against the door.

Pete was at his desk, his attention focused on his computer screen.

Luke carefully hung up his coat and bag. He pulled himself together. 'Morning, Pete.'

Pete looked up. 'Have you seen the thing on YouTube?'

'The "Blaze and Bravura" thing?' said Luke. 'Sure. I saw that last night. People do that sort of thing all the time. That's not serious.'

'Are you sure about that?' said Pete. He pointed to the screen. 'Look at the number of views.'

Luke peered over Pete's shoulder. 'Nearly two million views? It was only a couple of hundred when I saw it.'

'And it's not the only one. There's a #Blazevura thing on Twitter.'

Luke winced. 'They're not being cruel to her, are they?'

Pete gave him a strange look. 'You're not worried about yourself?'

'I've been doing this long enough to let it slide off me, but Bravura is new. Plus, she's a woman and gamer trolls are horrible to women.' He got his phone out and opened Twitter. Sure enough, there was #Blazevura, one of the top trending topics. He scrolled through. A few 'look at your man like Bravura looks at Blaze' things were okay. A few true nasties. He spent the next minutes reporting and blocking. 'Some people are the worst.'

'So what does this mean, then?' said Pete. He was still staring at the YouTube numbers, which were slowly ticking upwards. 'You've gone viral. This must mean something.'

Luke sat down and pushed his hair off his forehead. 'Well, the increased YouTube views means money for me, so that's good. The increased interest means more people checking out *SyrenQuest*, which is probably good too, since the whole point was to get eyes on the Syren3 headset … Apart from that … not much.'

Pete made a face. 'Oh come on, going viral must have some advantages.'

'Nothing compared to showing up consistently for twelve years,' said Luke. 'I've been there before. It is useful for profile, but it fades pretty fast.' He realised what he must sound like. 'I'm sorry to spoil the dream.'

Pete shook his head. 'I can't believe that I'm working with someone famous.'

'I'm not famous. Neither is Blaze. Now, we should get to work, I think.'

'Oh. Right. Speaking of, where were you? You're normally in hours before me.'

'I was helping Sam with her crowdfunding site. It looks good now.'

'Sam, eh?' said Pete. 'No wonder Bravura doesn't get a look-in. You only have eyes for the lovely Sam. How's that going?'

'It's okay.' He touched the spot on his forehead where her fingers had skimmed across his skin. He had been so engrossed in what he was doing that it had taken a few seconds to register and when it did, she was so close to him, he could feel her breath moving the air by his cheek. Close enough to kiss. For a second there, he thought she might have felt the same frisson. There was hope. 'Yeah,' he said. 'It's going okay.'

Sam drummed her nails on the side of her coffee mug. As always, whenever she took a break, her thoughts turned to *SyrenQuest*. She had a niggling feeling that there was something really obvious she was missing. Watching more games might finally let it drop into place, but she wasn't sure watching gameplays with the guys upstairs was such a good idea right now.

Her response towards Luke was bothering her. She was noticing him in a different way right now and that was weird. She wasn't the sort of person who fell for more than one guy at a time. What was wrong with her? It wasn't just that she was noticing him. She'd actually been flirting with him, hadn't she? Like pinning his hair for him. It was such a flirty thing to do. It was bound to have given him the wrong impression.

Ha! The wrong impression. As if she hadn't been seeing him in a whole new thirsty light about thirty seconds before that. She was only days away from meeting Blaze. Maybe her subconscious was trying to redirect her because she had no chance with him. Yeah. That must be it. Stupid subconscious.

She took a sip of coffee and unlocked her computer again. She could stay here and have her lunch quietly, by herself. In fact, it would be better that way. There was no chance of her saying the wrong thing and letting slip that she was Bravura. Except it wasn't nearly as much fun. The conversation among the guys made her notice things she wouldn't have picked up if she'd watched it by herself.

It would be fine. Now that she knew what her subconscious was up to, she could trust herself not to do anything stupid around Luke again.

Her phone beeped. She picked it up, expecting another message from Niro, who, bless her, had been keeping an eye on Twitter for her, so that she didn't have to see some of the terrible stuff that people were saying about Bravura. It turned out that, as much as people hated an incompetent Bravura, they hated the competent Bravura even more. There was no logic to it. People were insane.

But the message was from Gihan. The one who had got her interested in watching Blaze play on his YouTube channel.

Sam. Isn't this your handle? Is this YOU? Tell me it's you. That would be mind-blowing! There was a link, which led to one of the many #Blazevura compilation clips.

She wondered about lying, but what was the point? Gihan would know her voice if he was expecting to hear it.

She messaged him back. *I thought you didn't play anymore.*

I still watch Blaze though, when I'm bored or a bit down. I'm at home with the flu right now so I thought I'd watch some of his new stuff and bam! There you are. It is you, isn't it? I can't believe you get to play alongside Blaze. You lucky cow.

Yes, it's me. Please don't tell Dad.

Obviously, I won't tell Dad. Though he might be impressed. You know, you're holding down a job and playing games in your spare time, just like he always told us to do.

Ah. Right. Yeah. About that …

There was a pause and her phone rang. It was Gihan. He never phoned her.

126

'What's going on?' he asked, instead of a greeting. His voice sounded muffled and heavy with cold.

'Hi, Aiya. Nice to speak to you, too.'

He coughed. 'Oh. Yes. Hi. I'm not fine. Sounds like you're not either. What's going on?'

Sam sighed and looked at the ceiling. 'Where to start,' she said. 'I ... got made redundant three months ago. Well, not made redundant. I took voluntary redundancy.'

'Okay. That's not so bad. You got a decent settlement, right?'

'Yes. I did. About a year's worth of salary.'

'So, what's the problem? Dad would be impressed that you got a settlement and found a new job.'

When she didn't respond, he said, 'Looking for a new job?'

Sam sat up straight. If she wanted this thing to succeed, she had to go all in. Telling her dad was a scary step, but Gihan ... well, he might understand. At least she could sound him out without being too worried that he'd explode. Probably.

'Listen. Aiya. You have to promise not to go off on one until I've finished speaking. Deal?'

'What have you done?'

'Deal?'

'Fine. Fine. Deal. Now what's going on?'

'I started a business making handbag inserts. It's called Shanthi Bags. I'm using Amma's handbag collection to show-case them—'

'What?' His exclamation was full of hurt.

'Are you ... not okay with that?' She braced herself.

'You're using Amma's memory to advertise your thing? No. I'm not okay with that.'

'But it's not like that,' she said. 'And you promised you'd listen.'

Gihan gave what sounded like a grunt. She took that to mean 'go ahead'.

'As you know Amma left me those bags. I think she wanted me to use them. She was proud of them and I'm proud to carry them.'

'So? How does that tie up with using Amma's memory for financial gain?'

'First of all, I think of her every time I use those bags. I was so much younger than you when she died. My memories are fleeting and they're triggered by smells and things. When I close my eyes, I can't see her without help.'

'You think I can?' His voice cracked. She couldn't tell if it was because he was coughing or crying.

'I don't know. All I know is that every time I use one of her bags, I think of her. And I can't change bags as regularly as I do without my insert bags. I want other people to have that too. I think Amma would approve.'

Her brother was quiet for so long that she asked, 'Are you still there?'

'I am,' he said. 'I don't like it. But you're right. She would approve, wouldn't she?' He made a small noise – half laugh, half sniff. 'She loved her bags. I remember when Thatha got her that wardrobe for them. We helped her put the bags in. You were really tiny then.' Another sniff. 'It still feels weird, though, Sam.'

'I know what you mean.' She rubbed her forehead. 'I thought all those thoughts too, you know. About whether I was sullying her memory and all that. But then I remembered what Thatha said when he got engaged to Aunty-amma. He said that the only way we could taint Amma's memory was if we forgot her. Every time I look at my website, I think of her. Every time someone buys a bag, I'll think of her. And because she's on the website, other people will know about her.'

'Hmm. So a tribute, of sorts?' He coughed.

'Yes. Something like that. Do you understand?'

Another long pause, before he said, 'I think I do. But Thatha might not. Although, to be honest, he'll probably be more freaked out by the fact that you've done something as risky as starting your own business.'

'But if it doesn't work out, I'll at least have tried. Anyway, my qualifications haven't died. If it all goes wrong, I'll just go back to being a project manager.'

'That's a very good point.' He broke off for a long coughing fit. 'Listen, I'm going back to bed. Good luck with *SyrenQuest* at the weekend. I'll probably still be off, so I'll be watching.'

'Aw. Get well soon. Have you got enough herbal stuff?'

He rattled out a laugh. 'Yes. I stocked up on the sachets from the last time we went to Sri Lanka. Don't worry.'

'Get well soon, Aiya.'

'I will. You have a great time playing *SyrenQuest* with Blaze. Win!'

'I think we were lucky to make it to the semi-finals. I don't think we'll get through on Thursday night's round.'

'Pfft. You get to go to SyrenCon with your head held high, though. And you get a free headset. You lucky, lucky cow.'

'That's true.' A few weeks ago, she wouldn't have dreamed of having a direct line to chat with Blaze. Or him calling her 'Brav'. Or holding his hand, albeit virtually.

Just as she was about to hang up, Gihan said, 'Oh, Sam.'

'Yes?'

'Can you get me Blaze's autograph?'

He sounded so sheepish that she had to laugh. She wasn't the only one who found comfort in watching Blaze. 'Sure,' she said. 'I'll do that for you.'

'And I'll drop some hints to Thatha about how there isn't such a thing as a steady job these days. I mean, I've changed where I work and how I work so many times now.'

'Thank you.'

Once she hung up, she felt a little better. Of her two brothers, Gihan was the sentimental one. They had held each other up through the difficult times and if he was okay with her talking about Amma, then her more stoic brother would be too.

She stared into space for a bit, thinking over what she'd just said to Gihan. In trying to articulate how she felt, things had somehow fallen into place a little better in her mind.

She looked at the presentation she'd drafted. No. That wouldn't do. Luke was right about putting more of herself into it. If she was going to do this, it was worth doing it right.

She scrapped it and started again from the beginning.

At lunchtime, Sam went upstairs to Luke's office to find that there were more guys in there than before. Luke stood up and offered her his seat. 'The club's grown,' he said.

'You're still following the game, Sam?' said Kyle.

Sam shrugged. 'It's interesting.'

'I suppose the possible romance isn't hurting,' Kyle said.

Sam frowned. 'What romance?' If they started talking about the whole #Blazevura thing, there was a chance she would say or do something to give herself away. Coming up here to watch the game suddenly seemed like a stupid idea.

Luke said, 'Shut up, Kyle,' at the same time Pete said, 'Just ignore him.'

Sam looked from one to the other and decided the wisest thing to do would be to not say anything. She sat down and unwrapped her sandwich. Pete pulled up the Syren website.

'Not that one,' said one of the new guys. 'Let's watch the Blaze and Bravura one.'

Sam felt a jolt of horror. No. She couldn't watch herself and Blaze. Not in company. What if someone recognised her voice?

'Already seen it,' said Pete. 'We saw it last night.'

Sam relaxed.

'We?' asked Kyle.

Pete looked up and glanced at Luke.

Luke made a face. 'Pete came over to mine and we watched it together,' he said.

'I can't believe you guys had a watch party and you didn't invite me,' said Kyle.

'It wasn't a planned thing,' said Luke, firmly. 'We met up after work and ended up watching. I don't particularly want to see it again. I'd rather watch FlickNife or Phil_the_Vicar.'

Sam privately agreed. She didn't want to see her own game again; she wanted to see someone else's. She had a theory about the hidden rules.

'Well, I'm going to go watch the Blaze game on my computer, then.' One of the other guys stood up and made for the door. 'That's the one everyone's talking about.'

Everyone was talking about it? Was that because of the whole #Blazevura thing? Sam quietly took out her phone and checked Blaze's YouTube channel. Holy hellfire! That was a lot of views to have had in one night!

'Everyone else okay with FlickNife's game? Good.' Pete hit play.

They watched it at double speed. For the most part, FlickNife and her partner made similar choices to the ones Blaze and Bravura had made. They did slightly better in the carnivorous forest, because they were better fighters, but they still ended up in the trees, both low on health and only one small health potion between them. The health potion was with the newbie.

That was interesting. The game was forcing them to choose who should have the most health. For Sam, it had been an easy choice. Blaze's health had been lower than hers. But for Flick and her partner, the decision was more nuanced. Flick had less health, but she was the better fighter. The newbie took the potion. When they reached the nest, the bird returned almost immediately. It was only because they were both such good fighters that they managed to get through the round without dying.

Sam frowned. She and Blaze had been given a few extra seconds to get the key, presumably because she'd given him the health potion. 'Does this game have a morality component?'

She didn't realise she'd said it out loud until the men all turned to look at her.

'That seems very unlikely.' Kyle's voice was extra patronising. 'There's clearly a—'

'How do you mean?' Luke interrupted, his expression intense.

'I … watched the Blaze game last night,' she said.

'For the romance,' Kyle scoffed.

Sam ignored him. 'And Bravura gave her potion to Blaze. That was the only real difference between the two sets of plays. And they had a bit more time to get the key.'

'Coincidence,' said Kyle.

'No. Hang on. That's a good point,' Luke said, frowning. 'It makes sense,' he continued, thoughtfully. 'They're promoting this game for children. Quite clever really. The hardcore gamers are going to be interested in the tech and the kids are going to be interested in the game. If they get the kids talking about it and wanting it, the parents will get sucked in too – and that's where the money is. I know this is a soft launch, but they've chosen popular YouTubers rather than full-on e-athletes. The thing that … they … all have in common is that they have a large proportion of younger viewers.'

'How do you know that?' The question slipped out before Sam had a chance to censor it.

'I looked it up,' said Luke. 'All the pro-gamers here are popular with tweens and teens … and adults too, obviously, but they're the sort of channels that parents let their kids watch.'

In that case, the morality stuff and the lack of gore made total sense.

'That's a very astute observation, Sam.' Luke looked impressed.

'I … just noticed, that's all,' she said, not meeting his eye. She had to be careful what she said in front of these guys. They thought she was casually into this. She couldn't let on how invested she was.

Besides, she needed to talk to Blaze. Sam made a show of looking at her watch. 'I should get back to work,' she said.

'How's your presentation going?' Luke asked.

She stood up quickly. 'Not too bad. I'm nearly done, I think.'

'Great. Let me know if you want to run it past someone for practice.'

'Sure. I'll do that. Thanks for letting me watch the thing, guys.' She gave them a quick wave and practically ran back to her office.

Later that day, she got a message from Blaze.

Blaze: *The game might be rewarding ethical behaviour. I was watching the other gameplays with friends and it seems that when the newbie gave their health potion to the pro, they got a bit of extra time. I've watched a few games and this checks out.*

Sam stared at the message. Damn. She had been hoping to impress him with that titbit of knowledge that evening.

Bravura: *I was about to message you to say that very thing.*
Blaze: *Great minds etc.*

He thought they were alike! She felt a warm glow thinking about that.

Bravura: *This game is as much about strategy as skill, I think.*
Blaze: *Well, that's why we make a great team.*

Her face heated up. A great team! She fanned herself. He was flirting with her, wasn't he? Oh wow.

133

Blaze: *I'd best go do stuff. See you Thursday night for the semi-final. Keep me posted on any other insights that occur to you.*

Bravura: *You too.*

Sam stared at the phone, grinning for a moment before she pulled herself together. She had a list of tasks to do. When she opened up the file she was working on, she was still grinning.

Chapter 12

'How on earth are we going to get that down?' Blaze said, his hands on his hips. It was Thursday night and they were in the middle of round three, the semi-final of *SyrenQuest*.

Sam frowned. They had been through worse just to get here. Her fighting skills were still bad, it turned out. The wall in front of them was high – if she fell off that, she'd die, and her health bar was only just above halfway full.

Blaze walked up to the wall and tested it. 'It's too slippery to climb,' he said.

She looked around. This place was a ruin that had been taken over by the jungle. A few tall walls, covered in lichen, still stood with trees growing through window openings and roots breaking through the floor. Everything had a green sheen to it. She watched Blaze trying to fit a knife into the gaps between the stones. No. That wouldn't be it. They had already used knives to climb a wall once before. This game didn't seem the kind to reward the same behaviour twice. Carefully, she picked her way to the end of the clearing. Before turning back round, she checked that the vegetation was just regular plants, not something that could eat her. From this distance, she could see that there were other ways to get higher. That pile of rocks made an erratic ramp. From there you could get to that tree and run along it to … there … which put you roughly in line with the ledge with the key on it. But how to get from the tree to the ledge? It was a sizeable gap.

'Blaze!'

He wasn't listening. He continued with his futile attempts to climb.

Sam sighed and said louder, 'Hey! Blaze. I think I might have something.'

To his credit he didn't argue like he would have done a few days ago. He came running up, pirate coat flapping. 'You have a plan?' As he got nearer, she could see his expression. Hope. He trusted her now. This gave her a little thrill, but she shut that thought down. She had to focus on the task at hand.

She pointed out the route she'd spotted. 'The only difficulty is getting from the branch to the ledge. Maybe I could jump it.' She walked closer until she was below the branch, Blaze following behind her.

'No. That's too far to jump,' he said.

'I could do it,' she said. Her character was lighter and more agile than his.

'And how would you get down? The game doesn't end until we're both together with the key. I can't get up there. So you'd have to get it and come back down.'

'A good point.'

They looked around again. Blaze narrated what he was seeing. 'This jungle is very thick. We're in a clearing but even here, there are roots curling up from the ground and trees and ferns. The only thing missing are the canopy and the vines …'

'Vines.' They both said it simultaneously.

'If we tie a vine to me as a rope. I can brace myself on the ledge and you can climb up,' Sam said.

It took them a few minutes to go back into the forest and get a long length of vine.

'Remember, we're racing against the clock,' said Blaze. 'It's first, second, or nothing.'

'Like I could forget,' Sam muttered. She threaded the rope through her belt and secured it. Blaze tied a small stone to the other end, so that she could pull it up and throw it with more control. She looped it across her body tightly.

'Right. Off we go.' She took a run-up and jumped onto the pile of rubble. A short scramble later, she made it to the top.

'I'll just stand here and try to look useful,' Blaze said, talking to his viewers. 'This is why it's an advantage to have players with different skill sets on the team. I would probably be too heavy for that branch, but Bravura's an elf, so she's nice and light. I definitely wouldn't have been able to make that jump.'

'I might not be able to either,' said Sam. She lined herself up so that she was facing the branch and mentally ran through the combination of commands she'd need. This needed a spring upwards, rather than a flying leap. 'Only one way to find out.'

She ran along the top of the rubble and leapt. When she landed, the branch bounced a little, so that she had to crouch to regain her balance. 'That was the easy bit,' she said. This talking to the audience thing was getting a little more comfortable.

'Okay, so now all you have to do is take a death-defying flying leap onto a shallow ledge, grab the key, find something to brace against, and pull me up. Easy as, right?' His tone was light, but she could hear the worried undercurrent in his voice. He didn't think she could do it. Well, stuff that. She could do it. And if she failed – the drop would kill her and they'd both be out of the game. And he'd never need to speak to her again.

She ran along the branch to the middle of the tree, carefully manoeuvred around the trunk to get to the other branch, then aligned herself as best she could, so that she could take a long leap to the ledge.

'Okay. Here goes,' she said.

'Don't die.'

'I'm not planning to.' She ran as fast as she could and leapt at the last possible minute. She flew through the air, blue arms stretched out in front of her, fingers splayed. *No, no, no, no, no.* She was going to fall short. Panic burned through her. Oh no. She crashed into the edge of the ledge. In her ear, Blaze gasped. She had one forearm on the ledge, her legs dangling below. In real life, she'd be dead. But this wasn't real life. Her character had muscles. She hauled herself up until most of her upper body was wedged precariously onto the ledge. Her questing fingers found a handhold, a misaligned brick. She swung first one leg, then the other, and pulled herself up until she was lying, panting, facedown on the ledge.

'You did it!' Blaze's voice was triumphant. Ha! He didn't think she was a deadweight anymore. *Take that, YouTube commenters.*

'Yes.' She got onto her hands and knees to stand up. Suddenly, a roar echoed through the forest and Blaze gave a surprised shout. She struggled upright in time to see something that looked like a giant green lizard charge Blaze. He ducked out of the way just in time. It turned back to have another go.

Shit. What now? She got to her feet. Her main job was to get this key. So, key first. Everything else second. Blaze was more than capable of fighting off a giant lizard. She stood up and reached for the key. When she picked it up, nothing changed, apart from a third key appearing in her inventory. She turned back to check the scene below.

The lizard was coming at Blaze with teeth and claws. He raised his sword. The lizard circled, so its tail was now behind him. If Blaze didn't move, he was going to get sideswiped. 'Blaze, look out. The tail looks dangerous.'

'Bit busy watching those claws right now.'

She glanced up. Far away, something was circling in the sky. As it turned, the silhouette was unmistakable. Dragon. She looked down at the creature fighting Blaze. That must be a dragon, too. The thought that it was smaller than she'd have expected went through her mind, but she didn't have time to consider that now.

She looked around at her small perch. Without a run-up, she couldn't make it back to the tree. There was nothing else on this ledge, apart from the protruding rock she'd pulled herself up on. She unhitched the rope and secured it as best she could. It wasn't terribly safe, but it only needed to hold a little while. She dropped the rope and shimmied down it. Below her the dragon's tail swiped at Blaze. He ducked out of the way.

She was almost to the ground when the tail whipped past and caught the rope a few feet above her head. The rope came away from its mooring. Luckily, she didn't have far to fall. She rolled out of the way, the rope wrapping itself around her.

'The rope,' said Blaze. 'See if you can get it round that back leg.' He jumped onto the creature's head and hit it hard between the eyes. In the few seconds it took to recover, Blaze had slid down and slipped the free end of the rope around its front leg. Sam did the same with the back.

'Grab the rope and follow me.'

They both took hold of the middle of the rope. Blaze leapt over the creature's back, past what looked like stubby wings. Sam followed, jumping more easily than her partner. The lizard twisted around itself trying to catch them.

'We have to pull it over. Pull.'

She pulled. The lizard overbalanced and fell onto its back. For a moment, it flailed and then went still.

'What happened? Is it dead?'

'No. It's going to play dead for a minute while it figures out what happened.' Blaze raised his blade. 'Long enough for me to kill it.'

He started walking towards the creature, which lay there still, apart from the occasional twitch.

'Wait!' said Sam.

He turned. 'What?'

'We don't have to kill it.' It was lying there, panting. Sam stared at the wings that were spread out under it. They looked somehow half formed. She moved closer. There was a certain softness about the creature, despite the claws and fangs.

'Is that … a dragon?' said Blaze, who was staring at the wings too. 'Why didn't it just flame me?'

'I think … it's a baby dragon.'

'I'd have expected it to be cuter.'

'I imagine it's cute to its mother …' She looked up. 'I think we should definitely not kill it … and maybe we should get out of this clearing as soon as we can.'

Blaze gave her a long stare. He seemed to come to a conclusion. He sheathed his sword. 'You got the key?'

'Yes.'

'Then let's go.' They went back into the woods. Just as they were leaving the clearing, a massive shadow fell across the forest canopy. The dragon on its back let out a roar, loud and higher pitched than before. The replying rumble made the ground tremble.

Blaze said, 'Run!'

They sprinted through the forest, thankfully only made of non-carnivorous trees now, half expecting to be chased by something enormous any second. They burst out into a clearing. And they were back in the training ground.

'We did it,' said Sam. She was suddenly exhausted. Her character sank down to sit on the ground. 'We got the last key.'

Blade sat down beside her. 'I hope we did the right thing by not killing the dragon.'

'We're here, aren't we? We completed the level. It can't have been the *wrong* thing. Besides, imagine if we'd killed it and then realised it was a baby. I'd have felt awful.'

Blaze laughed. 'I would have, too. Thanks for spotting that before I did anything stupid.'

She shrugged with exaggerated nonchalance. 'We're a team, aren't we?'

He grinned at her. 'We are.'

Happiness bloomed warm and vibrant inside her. A few weeks ago, he hadn't known she existed. Now he was looking at her like they were equals.

A show presenter materialised in front of them, a man this time. Sam recognised him. He was a well-known vlogger and games commentator called Lance. 'Blaze and Bravura! You found the key and completed level three. Congratulations!'

Blade got back onto his feet and turned to give Bravura a hand up. She put her hand in his. It was amazing how realistic the avatars felt. She could barely tell where the real her ended and the avatar began, but it didn't matter, because all the versions of her had registered the change in how Blaze was treating her. He was treating her like a friend now.

She stood, resisting the urge to jump up and down, still high from the adrenaline rush.

'How did you find that round?'

'Terrifying,' said Sam.

'Flesh-eating plants, dragons,' said Blaze. 'I dread to think what you've got planned next.'

'Well, we wouldn't want to make it too easy for you.'

'Oh, you didn't,' said Blaze. 'It's fiendish. If it wasn't for me being bigger and stronger, we would never have got through round one. Bravura's problem solving to get through round two. And if she hadn't been small and light, we could never have got through this round. I dread to think what you'd have done to two players with the same skill sets.'

'Ah, now. You're not the only ones to complete the round. There's always a solution no matter what size or shape you are.'

Sam was about to respond when the comment fully registered. They weren't the only ones to complete the round. Only the two fastest teams could go into the final. How many others had got through?

She and Blaze exchanged a glance. He was thinking the same thing.

'Your time in the semi-final round was …' Lance waved his arm. The timer came up behind her. 01:27:43. Just under an hour and a half.

That wasn't bad. It depended on how quickly the others had got through.

'What do you think? Pleased with that?'

Blaze shifted position. 'Yeah. Not bad, eh Bravura?'

Delighted to be included, she said, 'It's pretty good.'

'Do you think it was good enough, though?' This time the microphone was pointed at her.

She glanced up at Blaze, who gave her an encouraging nod.

'I'd … like to think so. But then, we're competing against amazing players like FlickNife and Jimothy and Phil_the_Vicar, so … who knows.'

'So, are you going to tell us?' asked Blaze. He raised his eyebrows.

Lance beamed. 'Okay then, let's see who's on the leaderboard, shall we?'

Behind him the screen came up. 'In first place, is … Phil_the_Vicar and GodlessJeff, with one hour, six minutes, and six seconds.'

Her heart sank. That was a significant lead over their time. A whole twenty-one minutes. Someone else was bound to have got through before they did.

'And … hang on, I'm just getting confirmation.' Lance made a play of listening to the voice in his headpiece. 'Ah, we have confirmation that second place is … Blaze and Bravura! Well done, guys! You're into the final.'

Sam's hands flew to her mouth. 'Oh my god. We did it.'

She turned to Blaze, who was grinning wildly and punching the air. Carried away with the excitement, she threw her arms around him and hugged him. 'We did it.' She pulled back slightly to look at him. 'We did it.'

His face was very close. Her gaze locked with his. 'Yes,' he said, softly. 'We did.'

Time slowed down. She looked at his lips. What was it like to kiss in this game? Was he going to kiss her? She drew a deep breath and so did he. His eyes never left hers.

He seemed to shake himself. 'We did,' he said again, firmly. He moved away and turned to look at Lance. 'Look out, Phil – we're coming for you.'

She felt like she'd been dropped into ice. Of course. People were watching. 'Yeah,' Sam said, weakly. 'Team Blaze.'

'That's fantastic! We'll see you guys at the final.' Lance disappeared. Sam looked shyly up at Blaze. Was his feed still on? Would he cut out what had just happened? They should talk about it.

She drew a breath. 'About—'

'It was an excellent game. Bit intense though,' Blaze said, speaking fast. 'I really need a break. We'll catch up later, yeah? Good game.' He held out a fist.

'Sure.' She gave him a half-hearted fist bump and held in her sigh until she had turned her mic off.

She took off her headset and turned to find Niro sitting next to her with her mouth in a big O.

'What just happened? There was a moment there, right? Between you.' She flapped her hands at the screen. 'There was a real moment.'

Sam turned the headset over in her hands and said nothing. Yes, there had been a real moment. She didn't know if it was even possible to kiss someone in the game, but she would have been willing to find out. But he clearly wasn't interested in kissing her.

Niro poked her in the arm. 'Come on. Tell me I didn't imagine it!'

Sam shook her head. 'No. You didn't imagine it. There was something. But … It was a mistake. He backed off so fast.'

'Of course he backed off. Everyone was watching. He was flirting with you, just a tiny bit, but the whole way through.' Niro was practically bouncing with excitement.

Sam stared at her, hope starting to rise again. 'He was a bit, wasn't he?' And there had definitely been a moment. 'I mean, he *had* to take a step back. Like you say, everyone was watching.' Her heart rate picked up. 'Besides, we were still inside the game. No wonder he was all flustered and embarrassed.'

'And this weekend, you're going to meet him in real life!'

Sam thought her heart was going to burst. 'I am!' Maybe all those daydreams of hanging out with Blaze were not just empty dreams after all. Maybe that moment could happen again, but in real life. She would find out in just a few days. 'Oh my.'

Luke put his headset on the table. He saved the recording, methodically going through his usual steps, keeping his head down. He wished he hadn't said Pete could come over and watch him play now. Pete would want to discuss it and he didn't know how he felt about it yet.

He wasn't even sure what had happened. There had been a moment there when he'd forgotten he was in the game. He had looked into Bravura's eyes and, for some reason, all he could think about was Sam.

'So ... what just happened?' said Pete. 'I honestly thought you were going to kiss Bravura just then. Or she was going to kiss you. Can you even kiss people in the game? I know the facial recognition is pretty good, but ...'

'Don't be ridiculous,' said Luke, not looking at him. He took a swig of water. 'No software is that good.'

'But something just happened.' Pete was clearly not letting this go.

Luke tipped his head back until it hit the headrest of his chair. He spent a lot of time sitting in this room, so a few years ago he'd invested in a decent chair. His 'gaming room' was essentially the box room. It doubled as his office when he was working from home. Right now, with both him and Pete in it, it felt dreadfully snug and too hot.

He rubbed the spot on his head where the headset rested. 'I

don't know what happened. Something she said made me think of Sam and … I dunno. I lost focus for a bit.'

Pete stared at him for a minute. 'So, you stopped being Blaze and became the real you? That's what happened?'

'Essentially, yes.' He pushed his hair back. He really needed to get a haircut before the convention.

Pete shook his head. 'No wonder you keep your two personalities separate.'

'Exactly.' Luke set the files to backup and stood up. 'Time for a break.' He stretched.

Pete opened the door and shuffled out of the office. 'You're going to SyrenCon,' he said.

Luke followed him out. 'I was going anyway. The pros and the people who won the newbie lottery all got an invitation right at the start. But I'm also going to play in the final.' The news hit him properly for the first time. Phil_the_Vicar and GodlessJeff were very good. They'd finished well ahead of him and Bravura. But, the game was unpredictable. The small decisions you made at the start affected what happened later, which meant that if he and Bravura got lucky, they were in with a chance.

He glanced at Pete. If he won, he could buy Bradley out and have a bit left over to make some changes in the company. For the first time in a long time, he felt genuinely hopeful.

'We should celebrate,' said Pete. 'Fancy the pub for a quick pint?'

He had work to do, but what the heck. He was going to be in the final of *SyrenQuest*. 'Why the hell not? Let's go.'

Chapter 13

The next morning, Sam arrived at The Nest and scanned the cafeteria as usual. Luke wasn't there. Okay. Perhaps he was running late. She got herself some breakfast and a coffee and sat down to go through her emails. By the time she'd finished, there was still no Luke. How odd.

She wasn't entirely sure why she was looking for him. It wasn't like she could tell him that she would be playing in the final of *SyrenQuest*. She didn't need to see him for anything else. Deciding she was only looking for him out of habit, she gathered her stuff and went upstairs. Kim was just firing up her computer.

'Morning, Sam. What have we got today?'

Sam put her bag on the counter for Kim to look at.

'Ooh,' Kim said. 'Is that ... an original Kate Spade, "The Sam"?'

'It is. Mum used to joke that she'd named me after it.'

Kim picked it up and turned it back and forth reverentially. 'It's a classic.'

'Yes. I have another one in red, a later edition. My mum got it for a bargain on eBay.' She had a sudden memory of her father saying fondly, 'This new site you've found will bankrupt us all, Shanthi', and them both laughing. Sam smiled. 'She loved eBay.'

She picked up the pen to sign in. 'Um ... Luke hasn't come in, has he?' She scanned the list of signatures. Luke's wasn't there. She didn't want to think about why she noticed his signature every day. He was just a friend. This whole business with Blaze was confusing her. She was in love with Blaze. That's all there was to it.

'So what exactly is going on with you and Luke?' Kim sat in her chair and leaned her elbows on the desk. 'You two are spending an awful lot of time together.'

'Still nothing,' said Sam. 'Seriously. I'm not interested.'

'Not even a teeny bit?' asked Kim. 'Although, I've seen him in his cycling shorts. It's not a teeny bit, if you take my meaning.'

'Kim!'

'Just making an observation.' She sat back. 'He scrubs up nicely too. Not that you see him in a suit that often. It used to be Bradley that did the suit part.'

Sam paused in the act of picking up her handbag. 'What happened there? I've never seen Bradley around. It's always only Luke and Pete.'

'Ah now. It's a bit hard to tell for sure,' said Kim. 'But I'm guessing the guys fell out. Bradley stopped showing up and Luke started to look more and more harassed. I thought Pete starting would make Luke a little less stressed, but …' Kim leaned closer and said in a lower voice, 'I have a few theories about what they fell out about—'

Whatever her theories were, Sam wouldn't find out, because Kim stopped short and stared straight behind Sam.

Sam turned. A man had just arrived and was standing at the top of the stairs, his head bent as he rubbed his glasses with a cloth. He had dark hair, cut very short, and was wearing a jacket over a shirt and jeans. The man finished what he was doing and looked up.

'Luke?' Sam stared too. He looked different. With the curls gone, his face was more noticeable.

'Oh, hi,' he said. He put his glasses back on and blinked. 'Ah, that's better. It's drizzling out and my glasses fogged over when I got in.' He smiled and Sam felt an unexpected tug in her stomach.

Kim was right. He did scrub up nice. Without the shapeless fleece, he had wide shoulders and a tapered waist. This was a man who kept fit, after all. And that smile. It looked even better without all the hair surrounding it. Luke was hot in a very stealthy kind of way. She hastily looked down, pretending to search for her door pass. Which was in the side pocket of the Shanthi bag – it always was. That was the whole point of the Shanthi bags.

'How come you're all dressed up today, Luke?' said Kim. 'Got a date?'

'Meeting with the bank later today.' Luke pulled a face. 'It's not going to be pretty.' He came up to the desk, leaned on one hand, and signed in with the other.

Sam stopped staring and turned to leave.

'Sam, are you joining us at lunchtime today?' Luke said.

'What's happening at lunchtime?' Kim asked.

'We're watching one of the *SyrenQuest* gameplays. We've been working our way through them. It started because of the … erm … sweepstake. But we've all become invested now,' said Luke.

'Oh. Is this the #Blazevura thing?'

Both Sam and Luke looked at her in surprise. 'You don't normally care about video games, Kim,' Luke said.

'Oh, I don't care about the game,' said Kim. 'I really want to know if she gets the guy. She's so obviously into him and he's probably into her, but doesn't realise it yet.'

'I have to go,' said Sam and fled. #Blazevura was still going strong. Everyone had an opinion and most people agreed that Bravura was completely and unsubtly smitten with Blaze. They were also equally sure that Blaze had no idea how she felt. A lot of the comments that she'd seen – the ones that didn't want to make her claw her own eyes out – had been along the lines of 'Wake up, man! Chick likes you' and 'Get your head out of your ass and look at the girl properly'.

It was embarrassing that her feelings were so transparent on the screen. At least she wasn't using her real name. No one knew it was her. There was no need to cringe every time someone mentioned it.

The trouble was that Blaze would have seen all the same commentary. What did he think of it? After that awkward moment in the game, their conversations in the chat had been more formal than before. It had all been confined to talking about the game and trying to work out patterns. He hadn't mentioned the social media furore. Neither had she. He hadn't called her 'Brav' again either. She supposed they would have to talk about it when they met.

She felt a little frisson at the thought. This weekend, they would meet face-to-face. If anything was going to come of it, it would happen on the Saturday – the night before the game. That was tomorrow. For today, she needed to get her presentation sorted out and make sure everything was in order for her pitch meeting on Monday morning. That way she could give *SyrenQuest*, and Blaze, her full attention without worrying about the pitch meeting.

By the time Luke got into the office at least two other people had done a double-take and commented on how smart he looked. Was he really that scruffy normally? He let himself into the office and shrugged off his jacket. Pete glanced up. 'You look smart.'

'You're the fourth person who's said that since I walked in. It's getting a little insulting.' His work fleece was hanging on the back of his chair. He put it on.

'And now you look more like you normally do,' said Pete.

Luke studied his fleece. 'Is this … not a good look?'

Pete shrugged. 'You look like an IT nerd.'

'Which is what I am.' Luke pulled his laptop out of his satchel and plugged it into the docking station.

'Yes, but you don't have to look like one.' Pete pushed his chair back, away from his keyboard and studied him. 'I don't get it,' he said. 'How can you be him? He's so cool and you're so … you.'

'He's a persona. It would be impossible to be that controlled for more than a couple of hours. Trust me. I should know. Whenever I go to cons, it's exhausting. I have to go sit in my room afterwards and stare at a wall for a bit sometimes, just to decompress.'

Pete shook his head. 'Still can't get my head around it.' He grinned. 'I can't wait to see you in action this weekend.'

Luke linked his fingers and stretched his arms out, trying to work some of the tension out of his shoulders. 'Yup. It'll be nice to be someone else for a bit, I think.'

'Are you going to talk to Bravura about what's going on?'

Luke sighed. 'I should, I guess. I've been avoiding it. I like her. She's nice and all that, but … none of that stuff is real. Blaze is a character and I'm sure Bravura is too. Neither of us is going to be the same in the real world.'

'But she's a fan. She said so right at the start. She knows you. You can't tell me that someone could listen to you wittering on about games for years and not get to know you.'

'A version of me,' he said. 'Not the real me.'

'What if she comes on to you?'

'I'll just have to turn her down. Tell her I'm in love with someone else.'

Pete gave a low whistle. 'The L word!'

'Oh. You know what I mean.' He logged in and scrolled through his emails, but his mind wasn't fully on the task. What *did* he mean? He liked Sam. They got on well and she already knew more about him than anyone else around here. But love? That was a bit of a stretch. Maybe the foundations for love. Or the first steps or something. He glanced across at Pete, who was drinking coffee, still watching Luke with a thoughtful expression on his face.

Luke looked away. He should talk to Sam. He was slowly falling into this fantasy that he meant anything to her, just because she meant something to him. He was as badly deluded as Bravura. Almost. At least he'd spoken to the object of his affections in real life. There was only one way to find out if Sam felt anything at all for him. He should ask her out the next opportunity he got.

Sam finished her last slide and saved the file. The presentation was much better now. She was still talking about her product, but she also had a bit about herself and adding the examples of times she'd left stuff in the wrong bag injected a much needed shot of humour to it early on. A quick break and she would run through it again, just to make sure she'd covered everything.

Maybe she should ask Luke to look at it. It would be good to get a second opinion.

She stretched and rolled her shoulders. First, she needed a drink.

Rather than go downstairs to get a fancy coffee, she decided on tea instead. There was a kettle in the kitchen. As she waited for the kettle to boil, she hummed the *SyrenQuest* theme song. Something niggled at her. Something about the words in the song.

She started pouring hot water over her teabag and hummed the song again.

Welcome to the Quest my friend
Be the fastest to the end
The paths depend on which you choose
When one dies, you both lose

Choose the right, not the wrong
Spare the young, heed the song
One last thing you have to know
Where one goes, you both go
Where one goes, you both go

She paused mid-pour and lowered the kettle. The first verse of the song was just the rules of the game – *be the fastest to the end; when one dies you both lose*. But the second verse seemed more random.

Choose the right … in the first round, they had chosen the left fork in the road. If they were supposed to choose the right, then they'd chosen wrong. Which made sense. They had missed the shortcut.

Spare the young … that just *had* to be about the baby dragon. What about *heed the song*? Was that about noticing the birdsong in the carnivorous forest? Or was it about the theme song itself? Had they left clues in a place so obvious that no one had noticed.

She pulled up the game chat app and messaged Blaze.

Bravura: *I think the theme song has clues in it. Think about it.*

Blaze: *What? Like giving you clues to where the shortcuts are?*

Bravura: *Yes. I haven't fully worked it out yet, but I think 'spare the young' was telling us not to kill the baby dragon. Everyone who killed the baby dragon got turned into toast. That's why we got through even though we were slower than the others.*

Blaze: *That is unexpectedly devious. I can't believe you spotted that.*

Bravura: *I think I just got lucky.*

Blaze: *Talk about hiding in plain sight. The song is so cheesy. Let me have a think about that. Thank you. That's a really useful insight.*

Bravura: *You're welcome. See. I'm not totally useless.*

Blaze: *Never said you were. You're practically a pro. You're keeping up with some pros already, remember?*

Sam smiled at her phone. He was being nice to her. He thought she was practically a pro. Practically one of his group. She read the conversation back. When he said 'hiding in plain sight' did he mean the clues? Or her? What if it was her? Her face felt hot.

Chapter 14

Luke yawned. It was late afternoon and he was struggling to concentrate. SyrenCon was tomorrow. All he could think about was the competition … and the occasional drift to Sam.

Pete had gone out to meet a potential new client and he was alone in the office. He glanced at the pile of paperwork he'd prepared to take to the bank. Fat lot of good that had done him. Even if he pulled out all the savings he had, which he couldn't do in a week, he wouldn't have enough to be able to buy Bradley out. The bank had refused him a loan. So there was only one thing to do. He had to pin all his hopes on winning *SyrenQuest*.

Ugh. He leaned back, pushed his hand into his hair and was momentarily surprised to find short fuzz instead of tangles. Judging by everyone's reaction, it was high time he'd cut his hair, even if he hadn't needed to wear a wig at the weekend. He rubbed his hand over his head. It was a little too short, but it would grow back soon enough.

Would Sam prefer his hair short or long? He sighed. Realistically, she wouldn't care. He thought of her gently pinning his hair to keep it out of his eyes. Or maybe she would.

She had that big pitch on Monday. He probably wasn't going to see her before then, so he should go and wish her luck. He didn't have the focus to do any more work anyway. He stood up. Yes. That's what he would do. He'd be a good friend and wish Sam luck.

He paused at the door. His smart jacket was hanging on the coat stand. He shrugged off his fleece and put on the jacket. It couldn't hurt to look smart.

When he got to her office, Sam was frowning at her computer. She raised her eyes when he knocked.

'Hi.' She smiled like she was pleased to see him. He felt a flutter in his chest.

'I just popped round to say good luck for Monday. I might not see you before your pitch.'

'Thank you.' She looked at the computer and back at him. 'Luke, do you have a moment? Can I run through the pitch for Boutique Belvoir with you? I redid my slides this afternoon.'

'Sure. Of course.' He came in and shut the door behind him.

This office was small. He stood there and glanced around, feeling huge and out of place.

Sam pulled out a chair for him. 'You sit here. I'll stand. I present better that way.' She pushed her own chair back and picked up the wireless mouse. 'Right. Let me just …'

Luke sat down, self-consciously clamping his knees together. Sam got the presentation up on the screen and started to talk, clicking through the slides as she went. He had heard an approximation of what she was telling him before. Her mother, the inspiration, the product, and how it gave her the ability to showcase the bag collection. The difference now was Sam. She spoke about the product with passion. When she talked about her mother and how using the bags every day was a tiny reminder of the woman whose memory was fading with time, there was such pain in her voice that Luke felt his eyes prickle with tears. This was what he'd been pushing her towards. If he'd had any money, he would have invested in her in ten seconds flat.

When she finished talking, he applauded. Sam beamed at him,

her eyes sparkling. If he'd thought he had liked her before, that was nothing compared to how he felt now. Right now, he was willing to die for her. Or at least risk major injury.

'That was amazing,' he said. 'Do that on Monday and they won't be able to resist.'

'Really?'

'Yes. You were brilliant. The presentation is brilliant. It's all great.'

She gave a funny little giggle. 'It's all coming together,' she whispered.

'It is. You've done an amazing job.'

She leaned forward and put her hand on his arm. 'Thank you so much, Luke. I couldn't have done this without you and all your help.'

Her eyes looked wet. She was too close. Luke's heartbeat rocketed as her gaze locked with his. The whole world whooshed down until there was just him and her, breathing the same air. He could kiss her. Right now.

A tear rolled down Sam's cheek. She removed her hand from his arm so that she could wipe it away.

'I'm sorry,' she said.

He had to do something. Now. Before the moment passed. 'Sam, I really like you,' he said. It came out all wrong. He sounded like he was 12. But he had to keep going. 'When you've finished your pitch. Could I … take you out for dinner? Or … a drink …' He lost momentum. 'Or something.'

Sam's expression was sad. She was going to say no. He died a hundred deaths in the next two seconds.

She shook her head. 'I'm so sorry. You're a really nice person and I'm … sorry.' She moved her hands around as though trying to describe something with them. 'I'm flattered, but I don't really see you that way.'

He didn't know what to say.

She looked down. 'Anyway, there's this other guy—'

'Oh. Sure. Of course.' There was another guy. Of course there was another guy. He stood up. 'Just forget I said anything. It was—'

'I'm sorry.'

'No. No. Don't worry about it. It was nothing.' He opened the door and backed out of the tiny office. 'Good luck with the presentation on Monday. Have a great weekend.'

He legged it down the corridor and up the stairs. He burst into his office and flattened himself against the wall by the door, in case Sam came and looked in.

Pete, back in his seat, stared at him. 'What is going on?'

Luke looked to the side, listening intently. She hadn't followed him. Obviously she hadn't followed him. Why would she? He was the weirdo who had asked her out because she was friendly and he'd misunderstood the signs. He let his head thump against the wall and groaned.

Pete walked to the door and stuck his head out. 'No one there,' he said helpfully. He closed the door. 'So, what's going on?'

Luke thumped his head against the wall again. 'I asked Sam out.'

'And?'

'She said no. She doesn't see me that way. And she's seeing someone else.'

'Aw, mate,' said Pete. 'I'm sorry.'

Luke breathed out. His heart rate descended to normal. 'I feel like such an idiot. Of course she's seeing someone. She's beautiful, smart, and nice. I don't know why I thought she was single. I should have asked.' Had she actually said she was seeing someone? She'd said there was another guy … oh, what did it matter. Whoever the guy was, it wasn't him and that was all that mattered.

'To be fair,' said Pete. 'I thought she was single too.'

'She was very nice about it,' Luke said. 'So … that's good.' No. It wasn't good. It was embarrassing. He stared ahead of him for a moment, then banged his head backwards on the wall again.

'Stop that,' said Pete. 'You can't give yourself a concussion. We need you to win this thing on Sunday. We need you in top form.' He clapped his hands together. 'In fact, come on. We're going out for a drink. My meeting went really well. I think we may have a new client soon. So. Let's go celebrate ... and commiserate.' He handed Luke his coat. 'Come on. You're dressed for a night out anyway. Let's go make the most of it.'

Luke opened his mouth to object because of the amount of work he had to do, then shut it again. Sod it. He needed a night off. 'Good idea. Let's go.'

Blaze: *Evening! I've thought about your theory about the song. I think you might be right. Best to keep it between us, in case there are more clues that we can use in the final.*

Bravura: *They tend to only make sense at the time. I only spotted the last one by mistake. At least we're aware now.*

Blaze: *Yes. I'll be poring over the lyrics this evening.*

Bravura: *We can compare notes tomorrow. In real life. Argh. I'm so nervous.*

Blaze: *About the competition?*

Bravura: *That too, but mainly about meeting people. Syren just told me that I have to be on a panel. I've never been on a panel before. There's going to be people watching.*

Blaze: *Just remember that Bravura isn't really you – unless you want her to be. You get to choose how much of the real you comes out. If you wanted to, you could be a whole different person. Your avatar doesn't have to be you. Once you're in costume, you can be whoever you want to be.*

Bravura: *I hadn't thought of it like that.*

Blaze: *I often have to remind myself that Blaze isn't the real me. I find it helps to make things less stressful. Cons aren't like real life. They're manic. Be prepared to be accosted by fans.*

Bravura: *I'm not famous. They won't want to talk to me.*

Blaze: *You'd be surprised. At least you get to hang out in the VIP area, which will give you somewhere to escape to.*

157

Bravura: *Okay, properly scared now.*

Blaze: *Don't be. Most of us are friends. We'll look after you.*

Blaze: *Hey Flick, can I ask a favour?*

FlickNife: *For you, sweetie, anything.*

Blaze: *You're going to be in the VIP area at the weekend, right? Can you keep an eye on Bravura for me? She's quite new to the scene and it might be a little overwhelming for her.*

FlickNife: *Aren't you sweet, worrying about your friend. Do I sense a little something between you?*

Blaze: *Not from me. She's really nice, but I've been … distracted elsewhere.*

FlickNife: *Oh my god. Seriously? Who is this girl? (Or boy.) Give me deets.*

Blaze: *Girl. Well, woman. She's someone from where I work. Really smart, pretty, friendly.*

FlickNife: *How long have you been dating? Is it serious?*

Blaze: *Alas, not dating. It's not going well. But the point is, I can't really think about anyone else right now. She's special.*

FlickNife: *You're going to have to tell me everything tomorrow night. Drinks with me and Phil after 'work'? And let poor Bravura down gently, will you?*

Blaze: *Yeah. I'll work out how to tell her. If she's even interested. And yes, drinks with you and Phil would be great. Looking forward to seeing you.*

FlickNife: *It's been far too long. See you on Saturday, love.*

Chapter 15

'You friend-zoned him?' Niro was making dinner. She had put the chicken pilau in the rice cooker, which was steaming away on the worksurface, filling the kitchen with the smell of cooking basmati. 'Poor Luke.'

Sam nodded miserably. 'I felt so bad for him. He looked so upset.' She swirled her wine in her glass. 'When I left, I saw him and Pete going to the pub. Hopefully Pete can cheer him up.'

Niro paused in the act of washing up the pan she'd fried the ingredients in and gave Sam a thoughtful look. 'I thought you liked him.'

'I do. He's nice and sweet. He's a good friend.'

'Oh yes, that was it. Cute aww, not cute phwoar.' Niro popped the pan on the draining board and dried her hands.

Sam briefly thought about Luke in his smart jeans and jacket before she caught herself. What was she doing? 'He's grown on me a bit. Under different circumstances, I might have thought about it.'

'Different circumstances?'

Sam poured her cousin a glass of wine and handed it to her. 'There's Blaze …'

'Blaze.' Niro clicked her tongue. 'I can't believe you turned down a perfectly good real-life date because of a computer avatar. Blaze may or may not be a good guy in real life.'

'Oh, he is. I know him, remember. I've followed his channel for years. I know that he would love to get a tattoo but doesn't like needles. I know his birthday is in June. I know his favourite breakfast is porridge. I know him.'

'That's just a bunch of facts about him. Being a fan is not the same as knowing him,' Niro pointed out. 'I'm a big fan of Meatloaf. I don't actually know him.'

'But I've spoken to him by DM. We've played on a team together. I think I can claim to know him at least a bit. And I'll meet him properly this weekend.' She took a sip. 'There's a chance that there won't be any spark when we meet … but what if there is?'

'I dunno. I guess it'll be good. But you will be careful, won't you? I still don't think that you really know him …'

'Well, I do. The feelings I have are bloody real to me. And Blaze … okay, he was standoffish at first. He didn't know anything about me. But we've become friends now and I think he might like me just a little. I don't think I'm imagining it. There must be something there if everyone is making memes about us getting together.'

Niro was quiet for a second. She idly twirled the lid of the rice cooker so that it spun around in the bubbling steam. 'I hope you're right. I really do.'

Sam looked down into her glass of red. She had loved Blaze's voice for years. Now she'd got to know him a little better, she'd seen nothing to persuade her that he wasn't just as amazing as she'd always thought he was. She smiled. Tomorrow, she would find out for sure. 'I hope so too.'

Luke went to the SyrenCon venue partly in costume. He was still in jeans, but the contacts, facial hair, and wig were in place, so that he looked like Blaze in casual clothes and didn't raise any eyebrows on the Tube. He was met at the door by one of the crew from Syren, who took him through to his room without him having to queue. A few people stared and pointed. He kept his sunglasses on and kept walking.

Blaze: *Are you guys here yet?*
FlickNife: *Are you kidding? Phil and I are in the VIP lounge, enjoying a cup of coffee and a flapjack without the children. We're the only ones here right now, apart from Syren people. Come join.*
Blaze: *Let me costume up. I'll be there in 20.*

The VIP lounge was a smallish room with a snack station and a screen that was showing snippets of gameplay. Luke walked in. He was a little later than planned because a few people had stopped him and asked for his autograph. There were other people dressed as him, which was always weird. He was set apart by the fact that his lanyard said VIP on it and his badge simply said 'BLAZE'.

There were a few people in the VIP lounge. Phil and Flick were sitting together. Phil's costume was mostly black with a navy-blue frock coat; he looked like he could just pop a white collar on and go to work. Flick had on what she called 'armour with floaty bits', which she wore over scale-patterned leggings and a long-sleeved top. It was a surprisingly convincing approximation of what her avatar wore. The main difference between Flick and her avatar was their size. The avatar was a svelte little thing. Flick was a plus-sized lady.

She waved to Blaze and shouted, 'Hello, you.'

When he went over, she gave him a big hug, before Phil did the same. Luke got himself a cup of coffee and sank down onto the sofa next to Phil to catch up. Phil and Flick had been around for a long time – longer than he had. They were a little older than he was and were all that was left of a much larger community. As people got older, they often drifted off and lost touch. Nowadays,

Luke was an oldie compared to the rest of the pros and Phil and Flick were practically grandparents.

'Your girl's not here yet,' said Flick, grinning at him.

'She's not my girl,' said Luke. 'Just a teammate.'

'Uh-huh. A team that me and mine are going to wipe the floor with,' said Phil, smugly.

'Granted,' said Luke. 'Your newb is pretty good.'

'Jeff. Yeah. He's fast, which is a good thing when you're against the clock. Good fighter too.'

Luke laughed. 'I can't believe you got paired with someone called GodlessJeff.'

'Oh, he changed his screen name specifically. He originally went by PeerlessJeff, but he thought it would be funny to change his name when he found out he was paired with me. If you look at the original video, you'll see he's got a different name.' Phil made a face. 'He has an interesting sense of humour.'

Luke thought of some of the comments he'd seen Jeff make. The guy was not someone he'd want to be friends with. 'At least he's keeping it clean.'

Flick leaned forward. 'Enough of this talking shop,' she said. 'Blaze. Tell me about this woman in your life. You said you'd tell me and you may as well do it now before there's a lot of people around to overhear.'

He shook his head. 'Yeah. That is not going well.'

Flick gestured with her hand for him to elaborate.

When he finished explaining, she said, 'Ouch. So what are you going to do? Accept and move on?'

'What else can I do? I really like her, you know. She works in the same building as me. Plus, we're friends, which makes things extra complicated.'

'Well,' said Flick. 'You're not the real you this weekend. You're Blaze. There's plenty of people here who would be more than happy to take your mind off things.'

'Okay,' said Phil. 'This is the point where I gracefully leave the conversation.' He patted Flick's knee. 'I'm going to go talk to that group of nervous-looking young people over there. I'll see you guys later.'

Flick craned her neck. 'They're all nervous-looking young people to me.'

'That's because you guys are ancient,' said Luke. 'I've aged a hundred years just sitting next to you.'

This was an old running joke.

'Experience will win out,' said Flick. She gestured towards her husband's retreating back. 'How do you rate your chances?'

Luke grinned. 'Oh, Phil will probably win, but I'm sure as hell going to give him a run for his money.' He took a sip of coffee. 'Besides, this game is so unpredictable in its consequences. I think Bravura and I are in with a chance.' Being in this environment, he was starting to feel more and more like Blaze with every passing minute. Which was just as well because soon he would have to go out into the main convention and by then he had to be a hundred per cent in character.

Sam finished her make-up and looked at herself in the hotel room mirror. She was practically unrecognisable, thanks to the blue body paint that Niro had got for her face and neck. She had pinned her hair back so that it was as close to her head as possible. Niro had shown her how to use tape to make her wig stay in place. It took her much longer to do it herself than when Niro had done it. The long blue hair and pointy ears combined with rest of the make-up, including the stick-on cheekbone-building stuff, had all worked, making her face look pointed and elfin.

Her costume wasn't exactly like her avatar, but it was close enough. She had sewn herself a set of armour from metallic fabric, which she wore over tight blue leggings and a top, and thin gloves that she'd dyed the same blue.

The rapier she'd got was plastic. She buckled that on too and checked the full effect in the mirror. All in all, pretty convincing. She struck a couple of the fighting poses. Oh yes!

Since she wanted her hands free, she'd opted for the small silver backpack purse. She threw a small tub of the blue paint in, dropped the Shanthi bag containing her usual purse essentials on top, and closed the bag. All good to go.

A message arrived.

> Blaze: *Hey. Where are you? I'm in the VIP room, but I can't see you here.*
> Bravura: *On my way down.*
> Blaze: *Cool. I'll let one of the staffers know. They were going to look for you.*

She was about to tuck her phone back in when another message pinged.

> Blaze: *Word of warning, you might get accosted by people wanting to talk to you. Tell them you're busy. And if they ask you to sign something, just don't sign any body parts.*

What? Why would anyone want her to sign stuff? She shook her head. She wasn't famous.

> Bravura: *Noted. Thanks. See you in a bit.*

According to the wall on the clock, she had about fifteen minutes to get down to the VIP room. She locked her room and walked out, her heart hammering in her ears. She was finally going to meet Blaze.

She got to the conference floor and a group of three teenagers came up and shyly asked her to sign their programmes. 'I think you're amazing,' one of them said. 'You were so bad at the start and then you got better and better.'

164

'I hope you and Blaze get together,' said another. 'He's so hot.'

She grinned nervously in response, and signed 'Bravura' on the papers they held out to her.

'Good luck,' they said to her. She wasn't sure if they meant with the game or with Blaze. She didn't mind. She would take all the luck she could get. It took her longer to get to the VIP room than she'd expected because more people spotted her VIP lanyard and badge and tried to talk to her. Someone asked her to sign their arm, which she declined.

When she got to the VIP room, it was full of people dressed as their avatars. The few people not in costume were in shirts with the Syren logo emblazoned on them. The few women, mostly Syren employees, stood out in the predominantly male crowd. For a moment, she was overwhelmed. People in costume were milling around, chatting awkwardly, holding drinks. It was like a surreal office party.

A woman in a Syren jacket said, 'Bravura. You're here. I'm Marsha. I'm here to look after you today.' Sam recognised her as the presenter in the earlier stages of the game.

She took hold of Sam's arm at the elbow and craned her neck searching round the room. 'Let's see if we can find Blaze ... Ah, there he is.'

There he was. He looked exactly like his avatar come to life. If Marsha hadn't been dragging her through the crowd, Sam would have stopped to pinch herself.

Blaze saw her and smiled his familiar half-smile. Sam almost stopped breathing. Wow. Just look at those green eyes! He had the best smile. She had seen it before, in the game, but the real thing was a thousand times better. For a second, Luke flashed through her mind. He had a nice smile too. She pushed the thought away. Luke didn't belong in this world. Right now, she was Bravura and her world was all about Blaze.

Luke smiled at Bravura. He'd had no idea what to expect, but it was still a surprise to see that she looked almost exactly like her avatar, only with more human proportions. She had gone to a lot of effort with her costume, which he appreciated. Dedication to the project at hand was a good thing. He always respected people who went all out in their cosplay. He put a lot of effort into making it look like he wasn't making an effort. He wanted people to believe he genuinely did have blond hair and green eyes.

'Hi!' he said, loud enough to be heard above the buzz in the room. 'Nice to meet you at last.' He leaned across and shook her hand. She was a little shorter than him, which felt strange because their avatars were the same height.

'Me too,' she said. 'I mean, it's nice to meet you in real life too. Oh my, this is so weird. I'm not used to hearing your voice coming out of your actual face.' Her eyes widened. 'That sounds so wrong. I'm sorry.'

He laughed. 'I know what you mean. I felt like that the first time I met people too. You get used to it after a bit. Isn't that right, Flick?' He tapped his friend on the shoulder. She turned around and beamed at Bravura.

'Hello, Bravura!' Flick said. 'It's so nice to meet you. I'm so glad you made it into the game, otherwise I'd have been the only woman there.' She shook the younger woman's hand vigorously.

Someone took a photo of them. Flick posed while Bravura stood there looking awkward. Poor kid. This must be her first con.

'Can I get you a drink?' Luke asked her.

She nodded.

He dropped his voice. 'Relax,' he said. 'You're doing great. You're a finalist. Be proud.'

She gave him a grateful grin. 'Thanks.'

'If you need anything, I'm here. So's Flick. So relax. Enjoy the moment. Okay?'

She looked at him with big eyes. Oh dear. Pete and everyone else was right. She did have a thing for him. He went over to the drinks table. The waiter was opening a fresh bottle of fizz, so he had to wait. He stared at the empty glasses and wondered how he felt about Bravura. She was nice enough. She'd upped her game after he told her how it was important to him to win and he appreciated that. But beyond healthy respect and maybe friendship, there was nothing else. He hadn't even considered it because he was so crazy about Sam. The cork popped and the waiter poured first one glass, then another.

Sam didn't want him. So what was stopping him?

He picked up the glasses and made his way back. Flick was introducing Bravura to three of the other pros, KingDangerous, Jimothy, and Rahuligan. She was looking completely stunned by the whole thing.

She was clearly overwhelmed. He loved his gaming community, but he had seen how bad things could go, especially for women. Bravura was too kind and naive to handle it.

And she had a celebrity crush on him. He liked her well enough, but his heart was with Sam. And *that* was what was stopping him. He had to be careful not to encourage Bravura's attentions because he wasn't a monster.

When he reached the group, he handed Bravura her glass and exchanged friendly greetings with the other pros. A man wearing a Syren lanyard approached them.

'Five of the pro-gamers in one place,' he said. 'And Bravura, too. Let me get some photos.' He gestured to the photographer who had been flitting around the room. 'Are you guys having a good time?'

Luke took his position next to Bravura. Flick was on the other side of her. Everyone leaned in. He remembered to do his trade-mark half-smile.

The man from Syren stepped a little closer and said, 'Blaze, can I have a word with you, please? In private.'

'Sure.' He followed the man to a quieter corner of the room. 'Is something wrong?' He looked at the man's ID badge. 'Erm … Harry.'

'Oh, no. Quite the opposite, in fact,' said Harry. 'I'm in charge of PR and marketing for this project. We've been keeping an eye on the social media channels and the thing that's getting the most attention is this rumoured romance between you and Bravura. In fact, it's almost eclipsing the chatter about the headset and the game.'

He could see why that would be a problem. 'I'm sorry,' he said. 'I can assure you that there's nothing like that going on. I can have a quick word with Bravura, if you like. I don't think she's actually aware that she's putting out any vibes. I didn't want to upset her before the final, but if it's a prob—'

'No. No, it's good. We're getting people coming in from demographics that we weren't expecting to hear from. Like mums watching the games with their kids for the romantic tension. You have a small cult following among mums of tweens, did you know?'

Luke did, in fact, know that. He smiled and said nothing.

'Anyway, talking to you, it's clear that the interest is one-sided – so I guess it's a good thing I haven't mentioned this to Bravura yet. But we'd like the speculation to continue a bit. I can't tell you what to do in your personal life, obviously ...'

'No. You can't.' Luke didn't like where this was going. It didn't matter to him, but how would Bravura feel if she realised they were capitalising on her crush? 'And you can't manipulate Bravura like that.'

Harry gave him an exasperated look. 'But we haven't manipulated her. It's all come from her.'

'But—'

'Look, just don't do anything to squash the rumours, okay? Just until tomorrow. We want a lot of people to watch the game final. No one cares whether you win or lose. We just want to see the drama play out.'

'I care.'

Harry's face gave an annoyed twitch. 'Of course. You care. But ... just *try* to keep things open. Okay? It's important. We hired you to be a brand ambassador. This is part of that deal. We're not asking you to do anything immoral. Just be seen with Bravura and don't let her ask you out, so you don't have to turn her down.' He paused and examined Luke's face. 'Unless, you don't want to turn her down. If you guys actually *are* going to get together, if you could do it after the final, that would be good.'

Luke shook his head. 'You'd never guess you were from marketing,' he said, sarcastically.

Harry shrugged. 'PR. It's the job. So, are we cool?'

No. He was not cool, but it looked like he didn't have much choice. He didn't have time, or the money, to argue about his contract with them. 'Fine. I mustn't turn Bravura down until after the final,' he said sulkily. 'I'll try and stay away from her.'

'No. Don't do that. You need to be seen together. Fuel the gossip.'

'Right. Whatever.' He had no idea how he was going to do this without upsetting Bravura. He needed time to think about how to tell her in the kindest way possible. In the meantime, he had to make sure he was never alone with her. He could probably rely on Flick to chaperone. 'Can I go back to my friends now?'

'Sure,' said Harry. He checked his watch. 'Actually, we need to get you guys up to the stage for the panel.'

Luke followed the man back to the group, pausing only to say hello to another YouTuber he recognised.

Sam tried to watch Blaze talking to the man from Syren, but people kept coming up to introduce themselves. It was weird how they knew her without her knowing them. It was flattering, but it made her feel exposed. She was struggling to remember who she'd spoken to – especially with more than one person dressed in the same costume. All the attention was overwhelming.

Flick showed up by her side and handed her a glass of orange juice. 'You okay?' she said. 'Is this your first convention?'

'It is and … it's a lot, right?' She put her empty wine glass down on a nearby table. Orange juice was probably a sensible option. She didn't want to get drunk and start babbling. She usually lost her internal filters when she was drunk.

Marsha from Syren came up to them. 'Guys. The panel is starting soon, so if we could come this way, please?' She ushered them to a door at the far end of the room. It turned out that the VIP room was just behind the auditorium.

Flick opened the door and peered through. She was shooed away by a stern-looking man. 'There's a good turnout,' she told Sam when she got back.

Sam's throat went dry. Even without a peek behind the door, she could hear the audience. She took a gulp of orange juice and her throat felt like sandpaper.

Flick's expression was sympathetic. 'Don't worry,' she said. 'You'll be great. Remember that you don't owe them anything. You're not paid to be here. This is meant to be just for fun.'

'It's not though,' Sam said. 'What if they hate me? I know most of them already do. I'm just a nobody who got lucky in a competition. I'm not even very good. There must be loads of people out there who are more qualified to be on the stage than I am.'

Flick frowned. 'So what if you got lucky in the draw? You're still good enough to have made it to the final. I mean, look at me and my rookie partner. I'm awesome and he was pretty good. We still lost. You beat us.' She fixed Sam with a stern glare. 'It doesn't matter how you got here. You're here now. You have been given an opportunity. You can choose to fritter it away or you can choose to make the most of it and enjoy it to the max. The outcome is entirely up to you, got it?'

Sam, pinned by the teacherly glare, nodded.

'Good. Now let's go.'

Flick dragged Sam over to Marsha, who was lining them up. Blaze was at the head of the queue. He said, 'Shouldn't Bravura sit next to me?'

Sam felt butterflies in her chest. He wanted her to sit next to him.

'We are part of the same team,' Blaze said.

'You're going to be introduced in the order that's on this list.' The woman pointed to her clipboard. 'Sorry,' she said to Sam.

'Oh no, it's fine,' said Sam. Blaze caught her eye and grimaced. She smiled back and shrugged.

She ended up near the back of the line behind Flick and in front of GodlessJeff. She stood trying to not fiddle with her costume.

'That's a great outfit,' said Jeff, looking her up and down. 'I see you went for Lycra to make yourself blue, rather than full body paint.'

'Yes,' she said, tersely. Jeff gave her the creeps.

They walked into the auditorium as they were announced. The fans of each pro-gamer cheered as their favourite came on. Sam and Jeff got polite applause. They were seated in a long row, facing out towards the audience. If she wanted to see Blaze, Sam had to lean forward to look past everyone else. She tried it and was rewarded with his familiar half-smile. She sat back, feeling a bit better.

There was a bottle of water and a glass in front of her. Sam poured herself a glass of water. It was harder than usual because her hands were shaking.

'Nervous?' asked Jeff, quietly.

'Aren't you?'

'Not especially,' he said. 'These are my people.'

'Ah. Right.' She peered out at the sea of faces. There genuinely was a variety of colours, since a lot of people were in costume. Were these her people too? She wasn't as into gaming as Jeff clearly was, but as Flick had pointed out, she was here, legitimately in the final. Best to make the most of it. She took a sip of water and put the glass down on the table. It gave her something to hold on to.

Lance, who was interviewing them, sat at a table set at an angle

171

to the rest of them, so that he could see them all. He introduced them, then started on his questions.

Sam took a deep breath. Here went nothing.

Most of the interview was aimed at the professionals, so Sam could relax and listen. Everyone handled the questions, mostly about the headset and the game itself, with good humour. Cameras snapped. A video camera captured everything for the live stream. Behind Lance, a few phones were out, recording.

'So, Flick. You must be here to support your husband, Phil_ the_Vicar, who is in the final.'

'Actually,' said Flick, with none of her usual warmth, 'I'm here because I was invited to participate, since I'm one of the pro-gamers taking part in the competition. Just like these guys.' She gestured to the other pros who were on the other side of her. They all nodded. 'In fact, unlike two of them, sorry, fellas, I made it to the semi-final before I got fried by that dragon. So, in answer to your question – I am here as a pro-gamer who is taking part in the promotion. And, while I'm here, I'll be supporting my husband, who is in the final.' She shot Lance an icy smile.

He didn't seem to notice. 'Bravura, this next one's for you.'

Sam stiffened.

'Your costume looks amazing. Did you make it or buy it?'

Really? Flick got asked if she was supporting her husband and she got asked about her costume?

'I … made it,' she said, her voice a little shaky. 'Most of it, anyway. And an artist friend helped me with the make-up.' Her hand fluttered up to her cheek. She caught herself and put it back down.

'You mean those aren't your actual cheekbones?' He grinned at her.

What the …? 'No,' she said. 'And these aren't my actual pointy ears either.'

This got a ripple of laughter from the audience and loud whoops from some women in the auditorium.

Sam smiled. She could do this.

Lance carried on. 'I notice that both of you ladies are wearing the same armour. There were several options of female armour and you, the only two contestants playing female characters who also identify as female themselves, chose the same armour. Isn't that a coincidence?'

Sam glanced at Flick, who had that same steely look in her eye again. She raised her eyebrows to ask if Flick wanted to take the question, but Flick waved her hand to let her go first. Damn.

May as well be honest. 'I knew I had to wear whatever armour I chose in real life as part of my costume,' she said. 'And this seemed to be the only one that you could wear in practice. I don't know why, but male body armour looks like it might actually provide some protection, but the female armour is mostly just shiny bits in strategic places.'

'Quite right,' said Flick. 'I chose this armour for the same reason. Trust me, you do not want to see me prancing around in two mince-pie cases and strategically placed tinfoil.'

There was a titter of nervous laughter.

Now Lance noticed the atmosphere. He looked from Flick to Bravura and back again. 'I see you ladies have made friends.'

'Flick's a famous YouTuber,' said Sam. 'I'm honoured to meet her.'

Flick leaned forward. 'And I'm delighted to meet Bravura. I'm also delighted not to be the only woman in the panel. For once.'

Lance said, 'Hmm', and moved on to some other questions. Sam noticed that he was careful to include Flick in any technical ones.

Finally, he said, 'And now to some questions submitted by viewers and visitors to the website. This was by far the most frequent question.' He turned to look at Blaze. 'Blaze and Bravura. I'm sure you've seen the romantic clip compilations that are going round. Are you two the hottest couple to come out of this competition?'

What? How on earth was she supposed to answer that? Sam's

mind whirred and she could feel the heat rising in her face. Oh no. Oh no. She didn't dare look at Blaze.

Thankfully, Blaze responded before she had to. He said, 'Oh, come on man, we've literally only just met in real life. We're online friends. That's all.'

Lips clamped together in panic, Sam nodded.

'So, the rumours that you're a couple are definitely not true?'

Behind the camera, a woman wearing a Syren T-shirt held her palms up and made stalling motions at Blaze. What was that all about?

Sam leaned forward and saw Blaze looking puzzled. 'Erm …' he said.

He wasn't denying it. What did that mean? Did he feel the same way about her? Sam's heart raced.

Blaze glanced at her and quickly turned away. 'Like I said, we're friends,' he said.

Lance was staring at her. She had to say something. She cleared her throat. 'Yes,' she said. 'Friends and teammates.'

Blaze grinned and bowed his head in her direction. She gave him a thumbs-up and smiled. A hundred camera phones clicked.

'I see,' said the interviewer. 'Okay then. This last question is for GodlessJeff and Bravura. Who do you think will win tomorrow?'

Jeff leaned forward. 'I think Phil and I will,' he said. 'We finished twenty-one minutes before those guys in the semis. We're faster, we're better fighters, we're both experienced players. It's no contest, really.'

'Bravura?'

She leaned forward. 'Well, as Jeff pointed out – only one of us is an experienced player. I'm a newbie and even though Blaze is awesome, our combined skills aren't as good as Team Phil's. In fact, even compared to the other teams, we're not the best, we're not the fastest and yet … here we are. At the final. We made it this far, so who knows, right?'

This got a round of applause from the room. Jeff looked annoyed. Phil was laughing.

'Same question to Phil and Blaze.'

Blaze opened his arms out. He looked totally relaxed, a born performer. 'I don't know who'll win,' he said. 'But I hope we'll have an entertaining game.'

Phil leaned forward. 'Exactly. The whole point of this competition is to have fun.' His gaze flicked to the staffer behind the camera, who was holding up a sign that read, 'Syren3'.

'And showcase the amazing Syren3 headset,' Phil said obediently. 'Isn't it incredible? The gameplay feels unbelievably real.'

There followed a spirited discussion about the merits of the headset. Most people loved it. One of the guys found that it distorted the voices of other players too much. Everyone agreed that yes, it was an issue, but it was still worth it.

'One last question,' said the interviewer. 'I think we'll take it from the audience.'

The microphone ended up with a woman who was dressed as a sorceress from another game. 'This is a question for Blaze. If you guys aren't together …' She gestured to him and Sam. 'Does that mean you're single?'

'Ah. Blaze, do you want to answer that?'

Blaze stared straight ahead. The whole room was silent. Sam held her breath. Time stretched. She turned to look at him. He seemed … sad.

Flick coughed.

That prompted him back to life. 'Can I just say … it's complicated.' He smiled at the questioner. 'Sorry. That's all I can say right now.'

'And, that's all we have time for.' Lance did the closing speech, mentioning everyone on the panel again, Syren did a very short promotional reminder for people to order their sets, and then the session wrapped up.

Sam felt shaky from the adrenaline crash. She let out a long breath and stood up, slowly.

'Hey, you okay, Bravura?' Flick said. 'You did so well. Was that your first panel?'

She nodded. 'I hope I didn't say anything wrong.'

'On the contrary, you were amazing.' Flick patted Sam on the shoulder. They both looked across at Blaze, who was still sitting at the table, leaning forward staring at his phone. He started typing furiously with his thumbs. The set of his shoulders was vaguely familiar. For some reason, it reminded Sam of working at The Nest. Weird.

She walked towards him, hoping to finally chat to him. They'd been in each other's company for over an hour now and she still hadn't managed to say more than a few words to him.

Blaze stood up, eyes still on his phone.

'Hi,' she said.

He turned his green eyes on her. 'Oh. Hey.' Another glance at his phone, where a notification light was flashing. 'Um … I'm really sorry, but something urgent has come up. A … er … real-life work thing. I have to go sort it out.'

'Oh.' She didn't bother trying to hide her disappointment.

'I'm sorry. I'll catch up with you guys later, okay?' He looked past her at Flick. 'You've met Flick already,' he said. 'I'm sure she'll introduce you to the rest of the gang properly. Right, Flick?'

'Of course. We'll be in the bar,' Flick said, warmly.

'Fab. I'll meet you there as soon as this gets sorted. Sorry.' He left quickly, already engrossed with his phone again.

Sam stared after him. This evening was not turning out the way she'd been expecting it to. Niro said that nothing was real until she'd met him in person. This was her one chance to do that and he kept being taken away. It was so unfair.

'Real life has a habit of getting in the way. The number of times I had to leave a convention to go and sort out a childcare crisis.' Flick shook her head. 'Come on. Let me buy you a drink.'

Sam nodded and followed the older woman. She ended up sitting at the bar with Flick and KingDangerous, Rahuligan, and Jimothy. They were all relaxed and friendly, completely at home in the convention environment. People kept coming up to them and asking to have selfies taken with them. A few even wanted their photos taken with Sam. Some bought her drinks. After the second or third drink, she was more relaxed. She had a long conversation with a woman dressed in Japanese-style armour about costume design and an even longer conversation with the pro-gamer guys about fusion cooking. She'd laughed at Flick's description of the school run as a zombie game. In general, she was having more fun than she'd had in ages. But all the while, she was keeping an eye out for Blaze. Tonight was the only time she would have to talk to him. Tomorrow, they would be straight into the final and after that, depending on whether they won or lost, she might never see him again.

Luke sat at his laptop, trying to fix the error message that his client's ticketing system was bringing up. Of course it had to go wrong on a Saturday. On the one Saturday when he wasn't at home. He had been troubleshooting for over an hour now and it was getting seriously annoying. He double-checked his settings and hit update. Please work. Please work. The connection was slow. He didn't trust the security on the hotel Wi-Fi, so he was burning through his own data.

While the site was updating, he checked his DMs and found a load of messages, some friendly ones from Bravura asking him if he was coming to the bar and some increasingly rude ones from Flick asking the same. He replied to them both. To Flick he mentioned what the PR man had said.

Flick: *You feel bad because Bravura likes you?*
Blaze: *Sort of. I would have been more distant, but Syren want me to keep the 'romantic tension' going. I like her well*

177

enough and, who knows, we might have got on in real life,
but now that the Syren guy has told me they need me to keep
that tension alive, I feel bad. Like everything I say that's mildly
encouraging is a lie. I hate it.

Flick: *Ouch. That is hard. Poor girl seems to really like*
you too.

Blaze: *I know. I think I should tell her that Syren is working*
a PR angle on us.

Flick: *Not in a message though. You'll have to get your arse*
down here and do it face-to-face.

Blaze: *Obviously. What do you take me for?*

He definitely had to get down to the bar and talk to Bravura.
He didn't want to give her the wrong idea by flirting with her. It
had been bad enough when he was forced to say 'it's complicated'
in front of her at the panel. It wasn't complicated. He had no
feelings for her. Even though Sam had rejected him, it was too raw
and too recent for him to move on. It was unkind to lead Bravura
on, especially when she had a fairly obvious fan-crush on Blaze.

He had to tell her about the PR plan. He wasn't sure how to
approach it, but it was better that she heard it from him than
anyone else. He could ask for her help, maybe.

Either way, he wasn't going to be able to do anything until
this wretched site was fixed. Hopefully, it wouldn't be too much
longer. He drummed his fingers on the table, irritated.

Finally! Yes! It worked. He sent a text to his client to say the
site was back up.

Before going out into the fray again, he checked his costume.
Beard still glued on. He had swapped his contact lenses for glasses
while he was working, so he swapped them back and blinked.
He rather liked the green eyes. He tied the eye mask back on.

The guy looking back at him from the mirror was a whole
different person. He drew a deep breath and reminded himself
that he wasn't Luke – slightly panicked computer guy. He was

Blaze – pro computer gamer, all round fun dude. When he left the room, he had already regained Blaze's swagger.

It took a while to get to the bar because he stopped to talk to people and pose for selfies. He didn't normally get this much attention. It must be because he'd made it to the final; he, Bravura, Phil_the_Vicar, and GodlessJeff were the stars of the show. No. The Syren3 headset was the star of the show. But the four of them were the key supporting cast.

He stepped into the bar. The entrance was a little higher than the main floor, so he could see across the room from there. He spotted Bravura sitting with the guys. She was pulling her phone out of her bag. He couldn't shake the feeling that she looked familiar. She reminded him of Sam. Which just went to show how much of a lost cause he was when every girl he saw reminded him of Sam.

He was about to go down the steps when he saw Flick point to Bravura's silver bag. Bravura grinned, opened the bag, and pulled out another, smaller cloth bag. Time slowed down. Luke stared. He knew that inner bag. It was a Shanthi bag. In fact, he had seen that exact bag just yesterday when Sam used it in the demo portion of her presentation. He looked at Bravura's face. Oh god. He was so blind. No wonder she reminded him of Sam. She *was* Sam.

Frozen to the spot, he clung to the railing in front of him. He felt sick. Bravura was Sam. What did this mean? If he went over there, would Bravura flirt with him again? But she was Sam. Who didn't want him. What if something happened between them? He'd have to tell her and then she'd be angry because … well, it was embarrassing. Flirting with the guy you'd just turned down because you didn't know it was the same guy. And if she didn't want him in real life, she couldn't really want him at all. Right?

As he stared, paralysed with indecision, she turned her head, caught his eye, and smiled. That smile. How had he not seen this before? She waved.

Luke couldn't breathe properly. He couldn't go over there. Nothing good would come of it. No way. He turned and walked back out into the foyer. It took all his self-control not to run.

Sam watched as Blaze looked at her … and fled without acknowledging her. What? He had definitely seen her. He had been staring at her with a weird expression on his face. Then she'd waved and he had just left.

'What's up?' Flick followed her gaze. 'Is that Blaze? He's leaving?'

'Yes. Apparently, he changed his mind about hanging out with us,' said Sam.

'Maybe his day job crisis called him back.' Flick picked up her phone. 'Let me ask.'

Sam got her own phone out, opened the app, and messaged him.

Bravura: *Hey. Not joining us then?*

No reply.

She and Flick both turned to their drinks.

'The look on his face was weird,' said Sam.

'How'd you mean?'

'Just … odd. Like he was worried or scared or something.' Sam gestured to herself and Flick. 'What is there to be scared of?'

Phil sniggered.

'What?' said Flick.

He raised his hands in surrender. 'Nothing, love.'

Sam watched them, not really focusing. When Blaze had been staring at her, he looked horrified. It was her that he was afraid of. But why? What did he think she'd do to him? She thought about his discomfort when asked about his love life. People thought they should be together. Everyone, *everyone* thought that she had a thing for him. It was *his* feelings people were unsure about. Maybe he'd been afraid that she'd jump on him.

She looked down at herself. Had she somehow given off a predatory man-eater vibe that she hadn't been aware of? She was wearing the same costume as she had done earlier in the evening, when he'd been perfectly nice to her. The only difference was that she wasn't sick with nerves. Was the idea of her so terrifying to him? Oh god, perhaps it wasn't fear she'd seen. He was just repulsed by her. Her mood, already precarious, plummeted. He would rather run away and miss seeing his friends than talk to her.

Marsha came up to the bar. 'Where's Blaze?'

'Not here,' said Flick. 'Silly boy.'

Marsha turned to Sam. 'Did he speak to you about the marketing plan – about what we need you to do?'

Sam had no idea what she was talking about. Flick was frowning and looking flustered. Something was going on.

'Yes,' she lied. 'But he wasn't entirely clear what the angle was.'

'Simple really,' said Marsha. She stepped closer and dropped her voice. 'Just keep the romantic "will-they-won't-they" between you going until after the final. We'll see what the reception is tomorrow afternoon and then we'll take it from th—'

Flick spilled her drink, making Marsha spring back, away from the bar. 'Bloody hell. I'm so sorry,' she said, mopping ineffectually with a tiny bar napkin.

'It's fine.' Marsha checked the radio unit clipped to her hip. 'It's not wet.' She looked back at Sam.

'I've got it,' Sam said. 'Thanks. Everything is much clearer now.'

It was. That's what he had meant when he said it was complicated. That was what that almost-kiss was about. A set-up. And she had fallen for it. No wonder he had been keeping away from her. Pretending to flirt with her online was one thing, but pretending to flirt with her when she was actually in front of him would have been much harder. Or maybe seeing her in real life had made the idea of flirting with her an appalling one. So much so that he'd run away. Confusion gave rise to anger. How dare he?

'Bravura, are you okay?' asked Flick.

181

'You knew,' she said, glaring at Flick. 'You knew about the marketing thing.'

She shook her head. 'Only for about an hour. He only just told me.' She gestured to her phone.

Oh, so while he was avoiding replying to her, he was talking to Flick.

She checked her phone. He'd read her messages and wasn't replying.

'I'm sorry,' Flick said. 'He didn't want to go along with it. I'm pretty sure Syren sprung it on him—'

Sam held up her hand. 'I don't want to hear his excuses from you. They have to come from him.'

'That's true. He was going to tell you when he came down.'

'But he chickened out. Right.' Sam stood up. 'It was nice to meet you. I have to go to bed now.'

'Oh, no. Stay for another drink. I'll try and find out what's going on.'

'No, thank you,' said Sam. 'I have to play tomorrow.'

Flick seemed to deflate. She nodded. 'Okay. You go get some rest. We'll see you at breakfast, yeah?'

'Hmm.' Faking a smile, she waved goodbye to the others and threaded her way out to the door. Several people stopped to wish her good luck for the next day, some of whom also wished her luck with Blaze. How embarrassing. She managed to smile and thank them, too.

Outside the bar, it was quiet. A few people, some in costume, some not, drifted around. Sam hurried to the lifts.

'Hey!' someone called.

She stopped and turned. A woman dressed as a sorceress – possibly the same woman as before – was bearing down on her. There was something mussed up about her. Perhaps she'd had too much to drink. 'Hey you. Bravura.' If she was wanting a selfie, this was not the way to go about it. Sam pulled on her smile. 'Hi. How can I help?'

182

The woman waved a phone at her. A selfie request. Sam sighed. It was easier to comply than argue. 'Sure.'

The woman held the phone in one hand, then stood next to her. Sam smiled at the camera awkwardly. Bravura smiled back on the selfie screen. The woman's face in the camera image contorted and suddenly, Sam was in a headlock. For a second, Sam froze, doubled up, with her head under this woman's sweaty arm, too stunned to move.

'He's mine,' the woman growled. 'I've seen the way you simper at him. He's not interested in you. Because he's mine, you understand. Mine.'

Sam recovered, grabbed the woman's arm, and pulled. Her nails dug into the fleshy arm. The woman screamed and let go. A female security guard came running up.

'She attacked me!' the woman screamed. 'Look, she's left a mark on my skin.'

The guard gave her a disdainful look. 'I saw what happened. Stand back please.' She turned to Sam. 'Are you okay, miss?'

Sam nodded.

'We'll escort this person out.'

'You've got it wrong! She attacked me!' The other woman was pointing to her arm, where the nail marks were already fading.

The guard calmly pointed at the security cameras. 'Are you sure you want to go there?'

Another guard came jogging round the corner. He led the woman away. As she left, she looked over her shoulder at Sam and said, 'This isn't over, Bravura. I'm watching you.'

'You're sure you're okay, miss?' the female guard asked.

'Yes. I'm fine.' Sam touched her neck. 'Her grip wasn't very tight. I'm more shocked than hurt.'

'You might want to touch up the … er … blue.' The guard indicated her neck.

'Oh yes. I will. Thanks.'

When she got to her room, she checked in the mirror and saw

that some of the blue paint had rubbed off from her neck. The paint was designed to stay on, but it wasn't meant to stick after an attack like that.

A shower made Sam feel much better. There were still hints of blue on her, but she was going to have to paint it all back on tomorrow anyway. She sat on her bed and checked her messages again.

There was still nothing from Blaze. Bloody cheek. She wrote a message to him.

So, Syren asked you to flirt with me as part of their marketing.

No. She couldn't say that. It made her sound weak and needy. She didn't need him to like her. Oh, who was she kidding? Of course she needed him to like her. He just didn't.

She flopped backwards on the bed and stared at the ceiling. He had looked weirdly at her and gone away. Why? But then again, why not? He didn't know her. He'd met her for real for the first time then decided he didn't like her. After all, what claim did she really have on him?

That woman who had assaulted her thought she had a claim on Blaze too. Who was to say that her claim was any less valid than Sam's? Oh god, was she just another crazy fan? No. That couldn't be right. She and Blaze were friends. But only because of the game. What if he was tolerating her because he was being paid to do it for *SyrenQuest* and she was blowing their supposed connection all out of proportion?

She groaned and picked up her phone and looked at the messages she'd sent him before.

Bravura: *Is everything okay?*
Bravura: *Blaze?*
Bravura: *I guess you're busy. I'll see you tomorrow. I'm meeting Flick at breakfast at 8. If you want to discuss strategy.*

Ugh. She sounded so keen. Was he ghosting her? But he'd have to see her tomorrow. Ah crap. She needed to talk to someone about this before she drove herself mad.

She called Niro.

'Hello, cuz! How is it going in wonderland?' Niro was somewhere loud. Given the tone of her voice, she'd been drinking.

'Niro. I need to talk to you. Blaze is being a complete arse.'

'No! What did he do? What did he do? Wait. Lemme get away from this noise so I can hear. Okay. Tell me. What does he look like in real life?'

'Very similar to his avatar actually.'

Niro whistled. 'Hot.'

'Yes, but not so friendly.'

'That's unexpected. What's going on?'

She explained what had happened. How all of Blaze's friendliness had been a ruse cooked up by him and Syren.

'No wonder his attitude changed between rounds one and two. They must have told him their plan in between the two. It was all just a marketing thing.'

'Bastard,' said Niro.

'I feel so humiliated.'

'Listen. Sam,' Niro said. 'You don't have to be there. You only went to meet the guy. Now you've met him and you don't like him, you can just leave.'

'But then we'd have to forfeit the game.'

'So? You don't actually care about the game, do you? Just the guy.'

'I …' Sam frowned. Yes. In theory, she hadn't cared about the game. She had only practised so that she didn't let Blaze down. He needed to win. At first the prize money hadn't felt real, because her chances of winning were so tiny, but now … Now, anything was possible and the prize money would make her life so much easier. 'I do care about the game. I'm so close now I can't not play. I've met the other people now and me throwing the game would make a mockery of all their hard work. I can't do that to them. Besides,' she added as a sudden afterthought, 'I think I'm contractually obliged.'

'So there's your answer then. Play. Then get out. If he's playing silly buggers, you blank him right back.' There was a cheer from somewhere in the background. Niro, muffled – as though she'd put a hand over the phone – said, 'One minute.'

'You should get back to your party. Thanks for chatting to me, Niro.'

'Any time. You're my favourite cousin. Good luck tomorrow. Right, I have to go now. Laters.' She hung up.

Sam smiled and shook her head. Drunk Niro was funny. Drunk Niro was also right. She would play. She would do her level best to win this tournament for herself and for Blaze. It would be her last gift to the guy whose voice got her through her teens. Once this was over, she would never watch his YouTube channel again.

Luke sat in bed, elbows resting on drawn-up knees, and scrolled through his messages from Bravura. From Sam.

Bravura: *We're in the bar now, when you're ready.*

Blaze: *I'm hoping to get this wrapped up in about half an hour. I'll come join you soon. Flick will look after you.*

Bravura: *Hi. Not to rush you, but are you coming down? We should talk strategy for tomorrow.*

Bravura: *Is everything okay?*

Bravura: *Blaze?*

Bravura: *I guess you're busy. I'll see you tomorrow. I'm meeting Flick at breakfast at 8. If you want to discuss strategy.*

He should reply, but what could he say? 'I know your real name is Samadhi.' or 'Hey, Sam, it's me, Luke'. He should tell her. The mere thought of it sent a hot wash of humiliation through him.

186

Without thinking he ran the heel of his hand up his forehead to push back the curls that were no longer there. He was a mess. He had always been a mess. He had a good job and managed to fool people into thinking he was an adult, but he had never grown out of his awkward, shy phase. That's why he needed Blaze. Blaze was everything he wasn't. Self-assured, confident, charming. It was like he stuck on a beard and green contact lenses and they injected him with fire. No wonder Sam preferred that guy to Luke the website guy!

Would she even believe him?

Besides, she fancied Blaze. Quite obviously. So even if she did believe him – and he could easily prove it by taking his hair and fake contacts off – would she fancy him? She hadn't fancied him when he was himself yesterday, so there was a good chance she would reject him all over again, only now she'd be angry because he'd lied to her by omission.

His phone buzzed. He glanced warily at the message. Flick. He relaxed a fraction. He could probably reply to Flick without screwing anything up.

Flick: *What's going on m'dude? Bravura just found out about the #Blazevura marketing plan from the Syren lady. She is NOT happy.*

Blaze: *Oh crap. Did you tell her I didn't know about it until today?*

Flick: *I tried. She was furious though. I tried to interrupt the Syren woman (Marsha? Martha?), but failed. I'm sorry.*

Blaze: *Don't be. It's not your job to mop up my mess.*

Flick: *Are you going to talk to her?*

Blaze: *I want to but there's something else that happened. I don't think I can talk to her. I'm not even sure how I'm going to play tomorrow.*

Flick: *Explain.*

Blaze: *It's complicated.*

Flick: *Well duh. Of course it is. Does this have anything to do with your lady friend from work?*

Blaze: *Yes. There's been a … development.*

Flick: *Good development? Bad development?*

Blaze: *That's what I'm trying to figure out.*

Flick: *And you ran away from meeting me and Bravura because …*

Argh. What should he say? He couldn't out Sam without her consent.

Blaze: *Like I said, it's complicated.*

Flick: *Look, you should have told Bravura about the Syren marketing thing before she found out. But you didn't. You just have to talk to her now and get it sorted. You can't just hide in your room and hope it goes away.*

It was a convenient excuse. He could go with that. He needed to talk to Bravura on many levels, it seemed.

Flick: *I take it from the silence, that's it. You're a twit, you know that?*

Blaze: *I know. I just need to work out what to say.*

Flick: *But we love you, even if you are a twit.*

Blaze: *I know that too. You have no idea how much I appreciate it.*

Chapter 16

By the time Sam woke up the next morning, the anger and sadness had fermented into icy calm. No one treated her like that. Not even Blaze. She glared at the mirror as she glued her wig back on. So what if she'd loved him for all those years? She was just a fan. A normal fan, not a possessive scary person like that woman from last night. That wasn't where she'd gone wrong. No. She carefully stuck the cheekbones into place. No. Where she'd gone wrong was thinking that Blaze in real life was the same easy-going, nice guy that he was on his channel. Obviously that was a persona. Obviously. The real Blaze was an asshat. If she hadn't won the draw for this competition and been paired with him, she would never have known. Well, she was here now. And if he thought he could ghost her all evening and get away with it, he could damn well think again.

She dragged the body paint across her face like it was battle woad. Bring. It. On.

Her anger gave her strength. She could feel it rolling off her in invisible waves as she strode down to the breakfast hall in full costume. Her blue plait swung with each step. People stopped to stare at her. Let them. For the first time ever, she was Bravura. Not the shy, stuttering fangirl that she'd been at the start, but the new Bravura who wasn't going to be intimidated by anyone.

She showed her pass to the woman at the door and was waved into the breakfast room. From across the room, Flick raised a hand in greeting. Sam wasn't a hundred per cent sure about Flick – she was Blaze's friend, and likely to take his side on things. But it was good to see someone familiar. She grabbed a tray and got herself some breakfast. In the face of the mundane things like toast and a full English breakfast, some of her anger dissipated. She joined the queue of people, some in costume, some not, to get a croissant and a glass of juice. Her appetite seemed to have disappeared.

'Morning!' Flick said. 'How are you this morning? Nervous?'

'A little, yes.' Sam sat down. She looked around. 'Where's Phil?' She didn't even bother searching for Blaze. He was probably hiding in his room.

'Oh, he doesn't do breakfast. So don't worry. You don't have to fraternise with the competition.' Flick buttered her toast.

'Hah. That won't be a problem since my own partner is ghosting me.'

Flick paused mid-spread and looked up, her knife hovering over the bread. 'Still? He didn't call you?'

'No.' Why did Flick think that he'd called her? Had he and Flick been discussing her? Oh, of course they had. Sam leaned forward. 'What's going on, Flick?'

Flick lowered her knife and picked up her coffee. 'It's … He didn't know until yesterday evening, honestly,' she said carefully.

Of course Flick would make excuses for him. Sam gave an exasperated 'tsch'.

'I suppose you need to hear it from him, really.'

'Ha. Except, like I said, he's not talking to me.'

'Silly boy.' Flick smiled apologetically. 'I'm sorry, love. Just concentrate on the game. That's what you're here for after all.'

Sam nodded. Her appetite had disappeared now, but she still

tried to eat something. The last thing she needed was a blood sugar low in the middle of the game.

'Are you looking forward to it?' asked Flick. 'The game.'

'I guess so. I'm not the best at it, so I just hope I don't embarrass myself out there. That's my main goal. To not look like a fool.'

'That's a good goal to have. Obviously, I'm biased and I want Phil to win because we could do with the money for sorting out the kitchen and upgrading a few bits around the house.' Flick smiled. 'What would you do with yours, if you won?'

She'd tried not to think about that too much because the chances of them winning were so small. But … 'I think I'd save most of it and invest the rest in my friend's business.'

'The handbag one? That's cool. If it takes off you'd be a shareholder in a small business, which sounds quite glam,' said Flick. 'More glam than teaching, anyway.'

'I think it sounds more glam than it is in real life.'

'Ha!' said Flick. 'That's exactly what Blaze would say.'

Sam frowned. 'He would?'

'I think he has a lot of small-business clients,' said Flick.

'What does he do exactly?' She knew it was something to do with computers, which was understandable since he was so into gaming and online life, but he rarely talked about it on his channel, apart from the odd comment.

Flick paused while raising her coffee cup to her lips. 'Hmm. I'm not sure exactly. Something to do with computers. Something to do with small-business clients.' She shrugged.

Sam filed that away to think about later. She imagined Blaze would be quite good at talking people into things. If he had shown up, with those amazing green eyes and that cast-iron confidence and told her to do whatever it was with her website, she'd have just rolled over and gone with what he'd said. Not like the fight she put up against Luke's suggestions. Last week, the idea of Blaze striding over and telling her what she needed to do would have sat comfortably with her, but now? Now she wasn't so sure.

Luke had made her think about what was holding her back. He had made suggestions, but the text on the website and the feelings it created were all hers. He had helped her work out what she wanted to say. But she wouldn't have known what she wanted to say if he hadn't coaxed it out of her. Blaze's way would be exciting, but Luke's way was actually better.

She looked down at the coffee cup in her hand. Poor Luke. What was he doing now? She hoped he wasn't too down about her rejecting him. If she was being honest, she was a little conflicted about it. He was so sweet and quite sexy when he was in full flow. Competence was sexy. Who knew?

Was that what she'd liked about Blaze? His competence? Probably. Also, she had thought he was a nice guy. Now she knew better.

One of the women in a Syren Corp T-shirt came up to her. 'If you've finished breakfast, Bravura. Can we borrow you for a bit?'

Sam drained what was left of her coffee. 'I'm done. Let's go.' Enough speculation. It was showtime.

Luke stared at himself in the mirror. He looked like Blaze, but he didn't feel like Blaze. This had never happened before. He normally put on the costume – or more often, the headset – and instantly stepped into character. Blaze was scared of nothing and nobody. While Luke was shy and hated conflict, Blaze ate conflict for breakfast. Speaking of which, he had missed breakfast, because he was fretting about what he was going to say to Bravura when he saw her. One thing was for sure. He couldn't tell her who he really was. Sam didn't want Luke in any meaningful way and now she was pissed off with Blaze too. Telling her they were the same person would just mess everything up even more, and probably put her off her game. He didn't know how much of Bravura was real, but he believed her when she said she was scared of letting people down. If he messed up her gameplay by dropping a bombshell on her, he would feel terrible. No. He had to wait until after the game. He would talk to her and console her about losing and then tell her. It would take her mind off the defeat.

But what if they won? Luke considered this and dismissed it. They couldn't win. Phil and Jeff were too good. Even if he and Bravura had an edge on the puzzles, Phil and Jeff were so much faster, they could take twice as long to get through the puzzles and still win.

His phone, which he'd left on the bed, rang. He picked it up. It was Marsha from Syren.

'Blaze. Where are you? We're going live in half an hour and we need to do your debrief.'

'Right, right. Yes. I'm on my way,' he said. Ugh. He even sounded wrong. Like he needed people to like him. Like Luke. He tried to pull himself back into character. 'I'll be there before you know it.'

Okay. He had to do this. He would apologise to Bravura – Sam – for being rude and avoiding her last night. He would explain how he'd known nothing about the Blazevura idea until last night. Blaze was charming. He could manage that. Then, afterwards, he would tell her he knew who she was and … maybe tell her who he was too. Right. Time to go. It was showtime.

When he got to the VIP room, it was abuzz. Phil and Jeff were standing together, deep in conversation. Bravura was in the far corner, clutching a water bottle, talking to one of the staffers. He took a step towards her.

'Blaze. There you are. We need to do your pre-game interview.' Lance appeared, as if from nowhere.

'Oh. Right. Yes.' He let himself be dragged off to a booth that had been set up in the back of the room, not far from where Bravura was standing. As they went past, she turned and looked at him. He gave her a smile. She did not smile back.

Inside the makeshift booth, he sat down. This was not going well. He had to talk to her.

'We don't have much time,' Lance said tersely.

'Yes. I'm so sorry I'm late. I ...' Wait. What was he doing? Blaze wouldn't apologise so profusely. 'You know how it is,' he said. 'Life gets in the way.' He forced a grin. That was better. More Blaze.

He got through the interview without saying anything of substance, but being convincingly Blaze. It was weird. He was Blaze. Until this morning, he had barely noticed the effort it took. Now he could see just how far apart Luke and Blaze were. No wonder women liked Blaze better.

Stepping out of the booth, he searched for Bravura. He had to go and iron things out with her before the game. He spotted her, not far from where she had been before. Her arms hung down by her sides and she was clenching and unclenching her fists. Psyching herself up. He hurried over to her.

'Bravura.'

She looked up. Her expression was defiant and annoyed. He had seen that expression on Sam before. How on earth had he not recognised her? 'Yes?' she said.

'Look. I need to apologise about last night. I'm so sorry I didn't reply to your messages. I ... had some news and it knocked me sideways. I'm sorry. I didn't mean to be rude.'

Her expression did not change. 'I see.' She wasn't exactly friendly, but at least she was still talking to him.

Okay, so far so good. He took a fortifying breath. 'There's something I need to tell you, though.'

She raised her eyebrows. 'Oh, you mean the whole "let's flirt with Bravura in order to feed the publicity machine and not bother telling her" thing? That sort of something?'

He shifted uncomfortably. 'I didn't—'

'Blaze. Bravura!'

He turned to see Harry with a bright-eyed older man in a VIP lanyard. Harry introduced him as head of Syren Corp UK.

The man clapped Luke on the shoulder and shook his hand. 'I just wanted to say what a splendid job you're doing. I was a little sceptical when they first told me about this soft launch to kids

194

and parents, but I can see they were right.' He leaned forward and shook Bravura's hand too. 'They said "word of mouth", but this campaign you two cooked up with the unrequited love story? That's a stroke of genius. Sex sells, eh? Keep up the good work. Don't close the story too early though. Unless …' He gave them what he probably thought was a conspiratorial grin. He gestured between them. 'Unless there really is something going on here?'

'No,' said Bravura, her tone icy. 'There is not.' Luke opened his mouth, but Bravura got in before him. 'It's just, like you say, a brilliant marketing plan.' Her words were clipped, thrumming with anger. 'Don't worry. We won't close the story early.'

'Excellent. I'll be watching the game. May the best team win.' The man was impervious to the atmosphere. '"It's complicated", eh? Such a brilliant strategy.' Still shaking his head in amusement, he bounced off to talk to Phil and Jeff.

Bravura turned towards him, with absolutely no warmth in her expression. 'Campaign *we* cooked up?'

'I only found out about it yesterday,' he said. 'That's what I was coming to tell you about.'

'And that's why you said it was complicated when that woman asked you if you were single.' She folded her arms.

He nodded. 'I'm sorry. I wanted to talk to you about it but—'

'But conveniently, something came up?'

He wasn't getting anywhere with this conversation. He needed to be more Blaze. 'Yes. They asked me to keep the speculation going, just before the session started. I didn't have much choice. I should have explained, but there wasn't time. I can only apologise.'

He could tell she didn't believe him.

'Okay, guys, everyone ready?' Someone opened the door to the auditorium.

'Let's just get this game over with,' Bravura said and turned her back on him. He watched as she slid her silver backpack off her shoulder and gripped it tightly in her blue gloved hand.

He reached to touch her arm. 'Sam.'

But she didn't hear him above the noise as they stepped out into the dazzling lights. Blaze looked through the door at the cheering crowd and for the first time in years, he felt nervous about playing a game.

The noise from the crowd in the auditorium hit Sam like a tidal wave. It filled her ears and surged into her head. It distorted time and space. All these people. They were here to watch her play. Next to Blaze. She turned to look at him.

He seemed worried and, somehow, unlike his normal self. Which was a weird thing to think, because she'd only met him yesterday – how on earth could she know what his normal self was like? But then again, she'd been playing online with him for days. The avatars mirrored their real-life selves. The way Blaze was moving was all wrong. Yesterday, he had been quick and sure. Today it was almost like he was cosplaying himself.

Someone tapped her arm and guided her up the steps. She stared at the crowd and fell back into the world of SyrenCon. Up the steps. Onto the stage. The long table from the day before had gone. Unlike the previous rounds, the final was being broadcast live. The stage had been set up with two cubicles, each with two game stations. There was enough space between stations so that they could wave their arms around. Above the stage was a huge screen, split into four. Four game streams, one for each player.

The staffer led them across the stage to the cubicle at the far end. Sam remembered to wave to the crowd. Blaze must have done something behind her because there was a swell of cheers.

'Okay, everybody, now you know this works,' said Lance. 'Both teams will log into the world at the same time. Whichever team grabs the flag first will win. Remember – where one goes, you both go. If one dies, game over.'

Sam nodded. Her ears were throbbing with the sound of her own pulse. Her hands felt sticky under her thin cotton gloves. She turned towards Blaze, who was returning a thumbs-up sign to Phil at the other side of the stage. Blaze's gaze moved to her. He stepped closer. 'You okay?' he asked her, with obvious concern.

'I am,' she said stiffly. 'Are you?' Now she was looking at him properly, she could see the bluish shadows under his eyes and the way his face appeared pinched.

He gave a little shrug.

'You look tired,' she observed.

'I'm bloody exhausted,' he said. 'But we are where we are. Let's have a good game.'

She nodded. 'Let's get us some prize money.'

He gave her a sudden smile. Not his usual half-smile, but a proper one. It reminded her of someone, but she couldn't work out who.

'Thanks.' He gave her a small, terse nod. 'Let's go get 'em.'

Lance said, 'Are you ready, players?'

One by one, they gave him a thumbs-up. Sam sat at her station, lowered her headset and faced her screen. A timer was counting down the last few seconds. She pulled off her gloves and put her hands on the controllers. Now she was here, her vision narrowed until there was just her and the screen. Nothing else mattered. She was going to do her best to win this game. And then she would disappear from his life and never let him worry her again. 'Let's do this.'

Luke flexed his fingers. The countdown ended and they were standing in a rocky pit. A ravine of some sort. He turned towards Bravura. The attack came almost immediately. The creatures were low and rat-like. The first one struck him behind the knees, throwing him backwards. He went for his sword, but another had his sword hand. He flailed at it with his free hand. It had a snout full of teeth and the claws were needle-like. His health bar was shrinking fast. Not a great start.

Then Bravura was there. She kicked the one holding down his arm. He used the brief respite to scramble to his feet and grab his sword. He hit out at another creature that was rearing up behind her. He paused to grab a health potion from his inventory. One of the rats came at him and nearly took him out again.

He was fighting as hard as he could, but he felt like he was moving through treacle. So slow. Normally, in the middle of a game fight he wouldn't even be thinking. His fingers did the moves without consulting his conscious brain. That was one of the things he loved about gaming. The immersion. What the hell was wrong with him today? He gasped as he turned to see a mouthful of teeth coming straight at him. He twisted out of the way, but he was too slow. He took a massive hit. Gah.

He gritted his teeth and went for it. At one point, he and Bravura ended up back to back. She was a force of nature, making up for her lack of skill with sheer drive. She fought with such fury, he could barely keep up with her. Finally the onslaught stopped.

Bravura was out of breath. 'What now?'

He glanced up towards the wayfinder diamond. 'That way, I guess.'

'Watch out.' Bravura leapt at him and pushed him to the ground. A boulder crashed into the place where he had been standing. He looked up. She was kneeling over him, hands up by his shoulders, knees either side of his hips. Her face was very close. All he could see in her expression was hardness. Angry and determined, there was nothing of the softness she'd shown him before. He had lost both Sam and Bravura.

She got up. 'Move.' There was a tremendous rumble and more rocks fell. Luke scrambled after her.

They watched from the safety of the other side of the ravine as dust billowed from where they had just been.

Luke used the opportunity to catch his breath. 'Great fighting back there.'

She glared at him. 'What is wrong with you today?'

She looked so angry, he almost stepped backwards. 'I ... don't know. Tired, I guess.'

'Well, get over it,' she snapped. 'You want to win this? Make an effort.'

She had good reason to be angry, but it wasn't his fault he was struggling. A little voice in his head asked, 'Whose fault is it, then?' There was only one answer to that. He was doing this to himself.

'You're right,' he said. He needed the prize money from this. Besides, he had been hired to be a pro, here he was being rescued by the amateur. This was not how Blaze did things. His fans would be so disappointed. Hot embarrassment flooded his veins. Everyone would be watching this. Everyone would be hearing this interaction. Everyone would be wondering why he was being such a whiny baby.

'You're right,' he said, again. He could feel Blaze flowing back into him from wherever he'd disappeared to. There was no place for Luke in this virtual world. He was Blaze now. He had to be. 'Sorry about that folks. I was having a small ... glitch. I'm back now.'

The rockslide gave them a way to climb out of the ravine. They had to work out handholds and pathways across, but at least nothing was attacking them.

'Look, Bravura, I'm sorry about before.'

'It's fine. You're back in your stride now. That's what matters.' She didn't sound so angry anymore. That was good.

'Friends again?'

She didn't reply. Oh. Right.

Sam slid down the last bit of the slope and came to a stop by a huge gateway carved into the rock. She and Blaze seemed to have reached a sort of peace as they climbed over the rubble. She hadn't forgiven him, but there was no point fuming at him the whole time.

He seemed to have recovered from his bout of incompetence now, thank goodness. He had started his patter again, talking through what was going on, chatting to his fans. She answered the odd question he threw her way, just like she had before.

Now that she wasn't so angry, she remembered that this was going to be the last time she played alongside him. It may as well be a fun time. When this game was over, she was going to walk out and there would be no more Blaze in her life. That might be a good thing. Maybe it would give her the space to consider other people. *Like Luke, maybe.* The thought snuck in before she could stop it.

She followed Blaze into the gateway. The passage grew darker and darker the farther they went. Blaze pulled a torch from his inventory and lit it. Sam did the same. The walls shifted in the dancing light. Here and there, something gleamed.

'This is very creepy,' she whispered.

'Why are you whispering?' he said very quietly.

'You're whispering too.'

'I'm not. I'm just speaking quietly. It doesn't draw attention to itself like whispering does.'

'Oh. Right,' she said, softly. 'Good point.'

'So what are we looking for?' The tunnel ended in a rough-hewn doorway. Blaze stopped just short of it.

'A device, maybe? Or a button. Or maybe even the flag itself.'

Blaze stuck his arm through the doorway and sprang back, in case something shot out at them. Nothing. They entered cautiously. The lack of anything attacking them felt ominous.

In the light of the torch, they could see they were in a cave. A raised ledge ran around its periphery. In the middle there was nothing but a rocky floor.

They looked at each other and, in silent agreement, split up. Blaze went round the cave clockwise, along the ledge, while she went the other way. She moved in a crouch, alert for any sign of movement. This felt like the end. They'd fought quite a few things to get here, so it must be.

Sam peered around the cavern. It was quiet, dry, and almost

pleasant in the glow of their torches. Somehow that made it even creepier. 'There has to be a boss here to fight.'

'I was just thinking that,' said Blaze. 'There must be a trigger somewhere.'

She reached about halfway when a shout from the opposite side of the cavern distracted her. It was difficult to make out what Blaze was pointing at from this distance.

'It's a door,' he said, his voice clear in her headset. 'Or an archway. I'm trying to work out if the middle opens out, but I can't see anything.' The light at the other end moved.

She stepped off the side ridge to go towards him. A whispering noise rose and the floor seemed to move. She looked at her feet. Hundreds of scuttling things appeared from the shadows, swarming over her feet. She yelped, 'Ants!'

'Ants?' said Blaze. 'Ugh.'

The creatures flowed, little bodies washing like waves over the floor. When they met her foot, her life bar took a hit. They were biting. 'I think they're poisonous,' she said. 'Stay back.' She leapt back onto the ledge and used her flare to fend off the ants that had clung to her boots. But the ants could follow her up here, couldn't they?

She flailed her torch at them. The moving light caught something, high up on the wall. Still stamping her feet, she reached up. 'There's a handle here.'

Sam grabbed the handle and pulled it down.

The grind of rock on rock reverberated around the cave and the door behind Blaze opened. 'Excellent work,' he said. 'Come on. If you top up your health you can probably run across before the ants kill you.'

She let go of the handle. The moment her hands came off the bar, the door slammed shut. 'What the—' She whipped out her inventory and took the health potion anyway. Those ants didn't do much damage individually, but there were so many of them that it added up.

'I think I need to hold the handle down to keep the door open,' she said.

'There must be a way to wedge it open.' The flare stopped moving. 'I'm checking my inventory. I have nothing else useful. Nothing,' he said.

'Maybe I can wedge this thing in.' She jumped down into the ants and tried to pick up a rock. 'Nope.' She tried to wedge her sword between the handle and the rock. 'Still no.'

'How on earth are we meant to have you there and going through the door at the same time?'

'I don't know. Go through and see if there's something on the other side?'

'Where one goes we both go, remember?'

Something tingled in the back of her mind. Where one goes, you both go. When one dies, you both lose. 'What if …'

'You have an idea? Something outside the cave?'

'Shh. Let me think.' She absently swiped at the ants again. 'What if … it's not an instruction? What if it's a rule?'

'What's the difference?' His voice was quiet, cautious.

'Think about it. "When one dies, you both lose" – that's a rule. It's just telling us a fact. What if "where one goes, you both go" is a rule. Where one of us has gone, the other is deemed to have been. Dammit, we could have separated and got more done, quicker.'

There was a beat of silence as he considered this.

'No, no, that can't be right,' he said. 'We do this together.'

Sam stamped her legs and flailed at the ants. She couldn't keep fighting them off. Her health bar was dropping again, slowly, but steadily, as the ants bit her. 'I can't see any other way. If there's a way to open the door from the inside, then great. If there isn't, I'll let you through and then run the hell out of here. Maybe there's something else I need to do from the outside. You get on with the quest and finish it.'

'I dunno, Bravura, that sounds—'

'Blaze. There is no time for this. Do you want to win this or not?'

'Good point. Against the clock. Stuff it. Let's try it.'

'I'm throwing you the keys.' She took them out of her inventory and hurled them in his direction.

'Got them. You have my last health potion. You'll need it to get out of this place.'

He threw it across towards her. It arched through the air and appeared in her inventory. 'Thanks. Let's hope you don't need it.'

'What's life without a bit of risk?' he said.

'Ready? Okay. Go.' She dropped the torch to free her hands and pulled the handle down. Without the flame to keep them at bay, the ants closed in.

The door opened so, so slowly. She danced, stamping to keep herself from being bitten. Come on, come on.

Blaze was pushing at the door, glowing faintly in the light of his torch. A profound sadness welled up in her chest. He was distant and beautiful. And he was not for her. She gave herself a moment to lean into that feeling. Blaze had been a comforting voice, a perfect abstract Prince Charming, for years. It had been a mistake to meet him. The real human was always going to be less than the one she'd built up in her mind. Somewhere deep inside, a teenage part of her wept. She would never see him in real life again. At least she could leave safe in the knowledge that she'd played well. That when he thought of her, if he ever did, it would at least be with respect.

Ants were swarming up her legs now and her health was dangerously low. She saw the slice of darkness by the door open wide enough for Blaze to go through. 'You're a champ.' His voice cracked. 'Thanks.'

She watched him disappear.

'I'm in,' he said.

She let go of the lever, topped up her health with the potion he'd given her, and picked up the torch again.

'I'm in a brick-lined corridor,' he said. His voice was still in her ear, as though there was no thick rock between them. 'There's nothing here that I can use to open the door again.'

'I'll head out,' she said and ran for the door. There was a huge rumble. Sam nearly fell off the ledge. A massive bang and a cloud of dust. When the dust cleared, in the dancing light of her torch, she saw that where the doorway had been, there was now a pile of rock. She swore. Then remembered she wasn't supposed to curse on Blaze's channel. Oh well, he'd have to bleep that out.

Wait. Her health wasn't declining. The ants had gone. But she could still hear them. A sixth sense tingled between her shoulder blades. This was not good. She turned around.

The ants had coalesced into one giant ant. It bore down on her. 'Oh. Shit.'

Luke was running through a maze of brickwork tunnels, trying to keep his bearings, when he heard Bravura's shout. He couldn't catch the game sounds around her, but there was a change in her breathing and her muttering. 'Bravura? What's going on?'

'They've become …' Grunt. 'One bloody massive ant.' A hiss of breath. 'You?'

'Miles and miles of corridor. I'm going as fast as I can.' He turned a corner and skidded to a halt. A doorway. Cautiously, he thrust the torch through. Nothing happened. He stepped through. 'Okay. There's a room ahead.' His YouTube voice kicked in. This is what he did and he had to finish the game.

After the darkness the light in the room felt blinding. His eyes adjusted. 'I'm in a throne room. The flag is behind it.'

'There'll be a trap,' Bravura said.

'The room is roughly square. There are square tiles on the floor. Everything else is smooth and featureless.' All he had to do was cross the tile floor. Could it be that easy? 'I'm guessing the floor is booby-trapped.'

He took another step closer and looked around. 'Let's see.' He spotted a pile of rubble. Maybe a small amount of a column had fallen. 'There's a pile of rubble. I'm going to see if I can pick up a rock or two.'

'Good idea.' Bravura sounded less frazzled now.

'Have you defeated your ant?'

'No. I found a gap in the rockfall at the entrance and climbed out. I made it out of the cave but had to come back because there's a bloody dragon circling outside. I'm regrouping.'

While she was talking, Blaze threw a rock onto a tile at random. The tile turned into a column of flame. He told Bravura what happened.

'Try a different tile,' she said.

He did. 'Same thing. They burn for a few seconds, then stop and then burn again. Which gives me a two-second window to step on it.'

'So you need to throw rocks and time it so that they match up.'

'Yup.' He started counting the seconds. 'Eight seconds of fire, two seconds off, so I need to lob the next one out at seven seconds ...'

'Oh sh— Poo,' said Bravura. 'The ants are coming through. How annoying that you ended up having to do puzzles and I had to do the running around and fighting. Not fair.'

'You're being remarkably calm about this,' Blaze said.

'That's because I've remembered something a wise person once told me. This isn't real. It's just a game.'

Once the ants found the hole Sam had clambered through, they streamed out in a long black line and met in a pool at the base. It wouldn't take them long to join up into the giant ant again. Outside, there was the whump of wings and a huge shadow drifted across the ravine.

'Oh boy,' she said. 'Here we go.' She turned and ran.

The giant ant was bigger and faster than she was. But she had a head start. A few seconds might just be enough.

Sam raced out into the rocky landscape. The ant lumbered after her. Ahead of her the dragon turned and came back for another pass. She ran over the rocky ground. The creatures closed in on her. Ant behind her, dragon ahead. The dragon opened its mouth. She threw herself to the side and curled into a ball. The dragon flame raked through the ravine, starting where she had just been, and burned everything in its way. Including the giant ant. It burst into its component critters, but the flame was too wide to escape.

The ant was gone. The flames had caught her too. Her health bar was red and flashing. She was, technically, barely alive. She had no more health potion left. She stayed where she was. Hopefully, the lack of movement would fool the dragon into thinking she was gone. With any luck, Blaze would find the flag within minutes. All she had to do was not die.

Blaze counted in his head. 'Okay. Here goes. Three. Two. One.'

Heart pounding, he ran across. He missed his stride at the last tile and had to take a flying leap, at an angle, to escape the column of flame. He landed and immediately leapt up in a crouch, ready to fight. Nothing came at him.

In his ear, Bravura said, 'Oh boy, here we go.' He ignored her, keeping his focus on his immediate surroundings.

He had a key – three pieces put together to make a triangle. All the trouble they went to get it, it must be needed. He cautiously approached the throne. The flag was planted in a hole that went into the back of the stone throne. He would have to stand on the throne to get it out. Fine.

He didn't have any rocks on hand, so he checked through his inventory and took out the spear. He reached forward and leaned it against the throne seat, putting as much weight on it as he could from that angle.

The click was barely audible. He ducked, just in time. Something whizzed past at shoulder height and embedded itself in the wall opposite. 'Phew,' he said. 'See. Always a last trap.'

He stood on the throne seat and tried to remove the flag. It didn't budge.

'Bravura?' he said. 'You okay?' He hadn't heard from her for a few seconds now.

'Hiding,' she said, very quietly.

'I can see the flag but I can't pull it out.'

'Key?'

'Can't see where. Lemme check behind this throne.' Sure enough, there was the lock. He slotted the pieces of the key together and inserted it. Then he tried to remove the flag. This time it came away easily. 'I've got it!'

Chapter 17

Game over. Sam removed her headset. Above her, on the screen, Blaze pulled at the flag. On her screen, Bravura stood, exposed in the rocky ravine, arms slack by her side. Head down, as avatars were when their players leave the controls. She looked out at the audience. Every single face was turned towards Blaze's portion of the screen, where he pulled the flag completely out of its socket and waved it. When she crept away, walking briskly off the stage and across the auditorium, no one saw her leave. The crowd unfroze and roared. Blaze had won. Sam ducked into the VIP room.

There was no one there. She grabbed a bottle of water for her parched throat and ran out into the main auditorium. A staffer, sitting by the door to keep people out, looked up. 'Everything okay?'

'Um. Yes. I'm out of the game,' she said.

'Oh, I'm sorry. Can I—'

'I just have to do something. I'll be back in two seconds.' She fled to the reception desk and asked for her bags. Luckily, they were easy to find. She thanked the concierge and bolted. All she wanted to do now was to go home, wash this paint off, and forget about this wretched tournament.

*   *   *

Luke was transported instantly from the throne room to a wide-open hilltop. The valleys they'd crossed lay spread out below them. He could make out the monolith, catching the light in the distance, the forest, the rocky gully. Their game time appeared in huge letters. 01:03:47. That was pretty good. But was it good enough? He held his breath.

The time disappeared and was replaced by WINNER. Fireworks exploded.

'We won. Bravura, we did it. We won!'

He turned to the avatar standing beside him. She was slack. No expression. Arms limp. Head bowed. The system had brought Bravura to the hilltop at the same time as him, but she must have taken her headset off.

'Sa— Bravura?' He pulled his own headset off and looked over at her booth. Her headset was on her chair, but she was nowhere to be seen. The silver backpack he'd seen her bring in was gone too. He whipped round. 'Where is she?' he asked the staffers in the Syren T-shirts. 'I need to talk to her. Where is she?'

The audience had picked up the sense of something wrong. The roar of celebration had died down and was replaced by a puzzled hum.

'She must have left,' Marsha said, looking around.

Luke ran down the steps.

Marsha followed him. 'But we have to do—'

He ran through the VIP room and burst out of the door. The bored kid at the door looked up.

'Where'd she go?' Luke demanded.

The kid pointed towards reception. He ran, straight past the reception and out into the forecourt. He was just in time to see a woman with blue hair and a blue face get into a taxi and be driven away. A Syren employee, who had presumably been trying to stop her, was talking into her headset with an air of urgency.

'Urgh.' He put his hands to his face. 'I never got to explain.'

He spent a few seconds cursing under his breath before

someone touched his arm and said, 'Um. Blaze. Could we go inside please?'

He dropped his hands and looked around. He was attracting a bit of attention having his dramatic moment, dressed in costume. 'Oh. Yes. Sure. Sorry.'

His phone was vibrating like mad. As he walked back inside, he checked his messages. There were a few congratulations but many more about Bravura. Did he need help finding her? What happened last night? One guy even offered to trace her by the IP address and find her home address for him.

He quickly posted on all his channels: *Completely over-whelmed with winning SyrenQuest. Couldn't have done it without my awesome teammate. Thank you for all your offers of help to find Bravura for me. There's no need. I know how to contact her. Blaze.*

People kept trying to talk to him. Apparently, he was contract bound to go on stage and say something about winning.

'I can't,' he said. 'Bravura's not here.'

'Regardless,' said Marsha sternly. 'We have all this time to fill.'

The head of Syren Corp UK was beside himself with glee. 'This is brilliant,' he said. 'You fulfilled your brief brilliantly! A little too brilliantly maybe because Bravura is not returning our calls, but well done.'

What was he talking about? Oh. Right. The #Blazevura thing. Oh god. Poor Sam thought he was in on this massive joke against her.

'If you could keep the speculation going …'

Luke stared at him. 'No. She's upset. I'm not going to say stuff that makes her feel even more upset. What is wrong with you?'

He looked taken aback. 'Er. Right. Yes. Of course. Well, let's get you out there talking to the fans. They're all agog.'

'Just give me one second.' He pulled out his phone and called Sam. It rang and went to answerphone. 'Hi, Sam. This is …' Who should he say he was? Blaze? Or Luke? Either way it would make no sense that he was calling her on her personal phone to ask about her Bravura persona. Oh crap. What should he do? He panicked and hung up. Damn.

'Blaze.'

'Yes, yes. Sorry. Coming.' He followed them back into the auditorium.

The cubicles had been cleared away and the stage was set with five chairs. Lance sat in one, Phil_the_Vicar and GodlessJeff were in two others. They must have decided to exit the game when notified that Blaze and Bravura had won. Luke chose the chair next to Phil. Bravura's chair was pointedly empty.

A quick sound check and they were good to go. The audience was noisy, but they settled down when Lance asked for quiet.

'To kick things off. Congratulations, Blaze! You won!'

He had to stay in his Blaze persona. 'Thank you. Couldn't have done it without Bravura. I mean, how awesome was she?!'

The audience applauded, a little hesitantly.

Luke carried on talking. 'Ha. Typical that all the way through, she was the brains of the operation and I was the sword arm. And at the end, I had to work out a puzzle and she had to fight the boss. Two bosses. Legend.'

'Speaking of Bravura,' Lance said. 'Where is she?'

He had to handle this carefully. Sam was probably going to watch this. 'She … is not here. I think she had some real-life stuff to attend to.' He gave a shrug as though to say 'whaddaya gonna do'.

The audience buzzed.

'We have to ask,' Lance leaned forward. 'What's going on?'

Luke gave the man his cheekiest smile. 'What do you mean? We won *SyrenQuest*. That's what's going on.' He looked at the camera that was trained on him and twitched an eyebrow. He knew from past experience that Lance would not let this go. He just had to keep stringing him along until their time ran out.

'Haha. Of course.' Lance shifted position. 'While you were

playing, you apologised to her for something. I think we all would like to know … what did you do?'

Luke rubbed his forehead. 'Ah. Well. This doesn't make me look good.'

'We still want to know. Am I right, folks?'

The audience roared, 'Yes.' Behind the cameras Marsha was shaking her head urgently.

Luke spread out his hands. 'Okay. Well. I was supposed to meet her last night for a drink in the bar. And I stood her up. Not very gentlemanly, I know. It was an unfortunate thing.'

'So … not a lovers' tiff?'

'Oh, come on, man. The lady and I are friends. That's all there is to it. She's a really nice person and oh my god, I've never seen anyone work harder. Did you see how she improved from game to game? Do you think that happened all by itself? It didn't. She put in the hours and practised. I can't believe you're focusing on gossip and her so-called relationship with me when you should be focusing on that. I get paid to be here. I wanted to win, obviously, because who doesn't, right? But I'm a pro. I get paid to practise and be good at this. She just entered for fun. For *fun*. And all anyone ever did was criticise her. I saw the comments that were posted.' He glared at the camera. 'You would never have said half that crap to a bloke. Every person who sent her threats and filth – you should be ashamed. No wonder women feel unwelcome in this industry!'

Lance drew breath to speak, but Luke wasn't done.

'No one expected me and Bravua to get anywhere in this tournament. But we won. I was not on top form today – I'm sure you all noticed that. So Bravura carried this game. She should get all the credit. Because she was awesome.'

He sat back, drained. The applause from the audience was deafening.

Lance waited for people to calm down. Behind the camera operator, Marsha was practically dancing.

'But where is she?' asked Lance.

'I told you. Had to go home. Personal stuff. Shall we talk about the game?'

Lance glanced across and was given the go-ahead by the man from Syren. They discussed the game at some length. Then they brought the lights up and invited audience questions.

Predictably, the first question was 'Are you and Bravura dating?'

Luke grinned. 'No.'

'Yesterday when you were asked if you were single, you said it was complicated. Is that why you stood Bravura up last night?'

Oof. Tough question. He gave it some thought. 'As I said, it is complicated. But Bravura and I are just friends. Honestly.'

Another voice. 'You said you had to find Bravura, why was that?'

Luke shifted in his seat. 'I see that you guys really want to know about Bravura. I'm sure she'll come and talk to you when her crisis is over, okay?'

'You didn't answer the question.'

'Oh. Right. Why was I looking for Bravura? Well, it was pretty rude of me to stand her up last night. And I was a bit of a hot mess at the start of the game. I wanted to apologise. I owe her a drink.'

'I hope you find her,' Lance said.

'I will. I'll get in touch with her the way I always do. Through the game DMs.' He knew where she would be. She would either be at home or, since her presentation was tomorrow, the office. Either way, he would find her. As soon as they let him leave this place.

Chapter 18

Sam looked around her office. It was early evening on Sunday. She had washed her make-up off and come into work, where she could distract herself from thinking about what had happened that morning.

Her presentation materials for Boutique Belvoir – three sample Shanthi bags that she had made and packaged herself and a set of boards with artwork on them – were now packed into her portfolio bag. She carefully copied her presentation onto a USB stick. Should she go over her presentation again? She took the USB stick out and deliberated. No. She would only fiddle with it and it was fine as it was. Luke had said that it was good and that it conveyed passion. If he thought it was good, it probably was.

She put the USB stick in her bag and sighed. Luke. She had pushed him to the back of her mind while she was at SyrenCon because she had been so blinded by Blaze. How could she have been so stupid? Blaze wasn't a real person. He was a character. He had told her so himself. But she couldn't leave behind the voice that had helped her through her grief. Blaze and his channel had always been an emotional crutch for her. A place to be safe. So she'd carried on stubbornly being in love with him, even though the real-life Blaze had turned out to be nothing like the one in her imagination. So much so that she'd said no to the lovely prospect that was Luke.

Picking up the portfolio case, she turned off the lights and locked up the office. There had definitely been something ... a moment ... with Luke when she'd shown him the presentation. She hadn't analysed it then, but now she knew she was attracted to him. He wasn't what she'd normally consider to be her type, but then, none of her past relationships had lasted very long, so what did she know? Most of her ex-boyfriends had been too obsessed with their own careers to pay that much attention to hers. Luke, on the other hand, actually cared and was proud of her. He believed in her and in this project in a way that no one else had done. Not even Niro. When she thought of the look on Luke's face at the end of the presentation, she felt like she could do anything. She hadn't realised how much she had needed that support until it made her cry.

The Nest was eerie and quiet at this time of the week. There were a few people in, even at the weekend, but the sporadic noises only made the place feel creepier. Sam signed herself out. Glancing at the door, she remembered Luke coming in wearing his suit and a new haircut. He had looked so good she'd almost not recognised him. She smiled. He was hot if you looked closely enough to notice. She thought about his fierce focus with his fingers flying over the keyboard. Dammit, she *had* noticed. Then she'd thrown it all away because of Blaze. Who was a git.

A wave of humiliation caught her. She had been so stupid to think that Blaze could feel anything for her. He had flirted with her because the company had asked him to. When she stopped to think about it, it made sense. Perhaps they'd set it up from the very beginning, pairing her up with him because she was a fan. Urgh. She felt unclean now.

As she walked out of the building, the pub down the road

caught her eye. That was where Luke had gone to drown his sorrows after she'd shot him down. Poor Luke. She walked slowly towards the pub. She could do with a drink. It had been the strangest day.

She'd won *SyrenQuest*. With Blaze. It should be the happiest day of her life. But all she wanted to do was to talk to Luke. He'd said he was away this weekend, so there was no point calling to see if he fancied a quick drink. Even if that weren't the case, what would she say? 'Hey, Luke, would you like to go for that drink I said I wouldn't go for?' She was so stupid.

The pub was open, but it was late Sunday afternoon, in the middle of office blocks, so it was quiet. Sod it. She needed a drink. She pushed the door and went in.

The girl behind the bar was clearly not busy and was watching something on her phone. When she saw Sam, she perked up. 'Hi. What can I get you?'

Sam sat at the end of the bar and tucked her portfolio case in front of her legs. 'I'll have … a gin and tonic, please.'

It was far too early for her to start drinking, but stuff it. She had just won a major game competition and she couldn't tell anyone about it to celebrate. When her drink arrived, she paid for it and took a long gulp.

'Woah,' said the barmaid. 'Bad day?'

'You could say that,' she said. 'There was this guy, who I thought was almost perfect. Turns out he's just a guy, you know. Not perfect. Not even that nice, it turns out.'

'Oh, ouch,' said the girl. 'That sucks.'

Sam read her badge. 'Yes. Thank you, Julie. That does suck. So I'm here to drown my sorrows, but not too much. I have to work tomorrow.'

A couple of other people came in and Julie went off to serve them. She came back and took her phone out again and plugged one earphone in.

'What're you watching?' Sam asked. Getting drunk by yourself was less fun than she'd thought it would be. Probably just as well. She'd go home and have a long bath or something. Even after scrubbing herself thoroughly in the shower, there were still hints of blue in her fingernails and in the creases of her fingers. She didn't dare think where else the paint might have lingered. Hopefully nowhere obvious.

'The *SyrenQuest* final. I missed the live show, so I'm catching up. It's brilliant so far.'

'Brilliant.' Sam took another sip.

'There's this bit where he took the headset off and realised she was gone,' said Julie.

'What?' said Sam.

'Sorry. It's this computer game, called *SyrenQuest*—'

'Yeah. I know about that. The guys from work are always talking about it.' Sam waved her glass, indicating that she should get on with the story. 'What about this thrilling finale?'

'So you know about the #Blazevura, thing, right?' said Julie.

Ha! Did she ever. But she said, 'Enlighten me.'

'That's the cool bit,' said the girl. 'There are these two players called Bravura and Blaze. Bravura is really into Blaze. Blaze is possibly into her ... possibly not.'

'So not,' said Sam. She finished her drink. 'Can I have another please?'

Another customer came to the bar. Julie went to serve him.

Sam was beginning to feel the gin already. That'd teach her to start drinking in the afternoon. After no lunch.

'Anyway,' Julie said, when she came back. 'They won and everybody was watching the screen. But when Blaze took his headset off, Bravura had disappeared. He was desperate to find her.'

'So you're not watching this for the game?' Sam asked.

Julie smiled, a little sheepishly. 'Not really. I started watching because this guy I like was talking about it. And then I came across Blazevura and ... got hooked.'

'Huh.'

'You know, it was obvious right from the start that she had a crush on him. There was so much chemistry between them.' Julie stared thoughtfully into the distance. 'But ... I didn't think he would be interested. Like, he's a proper YouTube star and she's nobody. She wasn't even very good at the game. But then weirdly, he started flirting back a bit. And there was this moment at the end of the semi-finals when I honestly thought they were going to snog.'

'That does sound very dramatic,' said Sam, sourly.

'I've just watched the post-game interview,' said Julie. 'He said there was nothing going on between them. I don't believe that for a minute.'

'Huh,' said Sam. 'He should be so lucky.' Had it been so obvious how she felt about him? Well, it must have been, if everyone knew and Syren asked Blaze to pretend he might like her back just to fuel the rumours. 'I feel so stupid,' she said.

'Listen to me going on about a game. What happened to you?' asked Julie. 'If you want to talk, it's fairly quiet.' She glanced behind Sam at the rest of the pub. 'I'm a good listener. I'm training to be a counsellor from next term. It's good practice.'

'Okay. Well, I ... had two guys in my life. One was hot and confident. The other one was ... also hot, but you tend not to notice because he's a bit quiet. Do you know what I mean?'

Julie nodded. 'Oh yes.'

'I had to choose and I chose the wrong one. So now I've lost them both.'

'Which one did you choose? Was it the hot, loud one?'

'Yeah.' Sam took another sip of her drink. 'I'm a shallow fool.'

'Have you got back in touch with the other guy?'

'To say what? "The guy I really liked turned out to be a bit of an arse. So I'd like to try you instead"? No. I don't think so.' She raised her glass again. 'But at least I was honest about it. I didn't string him along just because of ratings.'

'You've lost me,' said Julie.

'Doesn't matter,' said Sam. 'I've lost everyone else too.'

It was evening by the time Luke got back to his place. He had travelled across town wearing normal clothes, so no one had recognised him. He knew from experience that he didn't even have to change clothes. All he had to do was take off the contact lenses and hair and just remember that he was Luke. Being himself had its own invisibility shield.

He tried Sam's phone again. It went to answerphone. Again. He stood by his front door and tried to work out where she might be. It was nearly 6 p.m. She was likely to be at home. He didn't know where she lived. He could try and work it out, but that was getting weird and stalkery, which wouldn't make her view him any more favourably when he told her he was Blaze. He sighed and tried her phone again one last time.

To his surprise, she picked up.

'Hello?' Her voice sounded strange.

'Hi, Sam, it's Luke.'

'Luke! S'Luke,' she said, to someone she was with. 'He's my friend. No, he's the nice one.'

Now he knew why she sounded strange. She was slurring. 'Sam, where are you?'

'Pub. Near work. Very nice. I like it here.'

He hesitated. She was drunk. It was probably not the best time to tell her. But … he had to see her anyway. If nothing else, he could at least make sure she didn't go overboard so she wasn't too hungover the next morning. She had her presentation to give. 'I'll come join you,' he said.

It didn't take him long to get there. She was sitting on a bar-stool, elbows resting on the bar. The barmaid was talking to her in between serving customers.

'Sam,' he said.

'Luke!' She startled so wildly that she nearly fell off her stool. He caught her and pushed her gently back onto her perch.

He caught the barmaid's eye and asked for a glass of water and a Diet Coke for himself.

'I was just thinking about you,' said Sam blearily. 'And you appeared. Poof. Like magic.'

'I spoke to you on the phone a few minutes ago,' he said, smiling. She was very drunk. More so than he'd thought. She was going to be really annoyed with herself in the morning. 'You know what, Sam. You should probably drink some water. Have you eaten?'

'No … I haven't eaten since. You know. The thing. Breakfast. With Flick.'

'You haven't eaten since breakfast? No wonder you're wasted. Here.' He pushed the glass of water towards her. 'Try this.'

'You're lovely,' said Sam. She patted his arm. 'Really lovely.'

Luke sighed. Lovely. Yep. That was him. Blaze got to be hot. Luke … just lovely. He looked at Sam and felt the sadness yaw open inside him. She would never see him as anything other than the nice guy that everyone loves, but would never fancy. He watched her take a sip of water. It wasn't late, but he would have to make sure she got home and got to bed early. She was going to have a hell of a hangover in the morning.

In the end Luke took a taxi home with her.

'You're very lovely,' she told him, when he checked that her seatbelt was on. 'Not a git like that Blaze. He's not nice. You're nice. And lovely.'

'Right. Thank you,' he said. He sat back and did his own seatbelt up.

'You're *sure* she's not going to throw up?' asked the taxi driver.

'Oh yeah. She doesn't throw up,' he said, hoping that was true. 'We'll be fine. It's not that far anyway.'

Sam reached out and put her hand over his. 'Thank you,' she said, suddenly earnest.

He turned his hand over and wrapped it around her smaller one. 'It's okay. It's what friends do.'

She frowned, then nodded and turned away. Ten minutes later, Sam was asleep with her head resting against the window. Her hand was still in Luke's.

Luke looked down at her small brown hand nestled in his and felt the weight of his unconfessed secret pressing down on him. She didn't like Blaze now because she thought he'd been playing with her feelings. He hadn't meant to. She was going to be furious with him when she found out that he was Blaze.

He glanced at Sam, whose head had lolled backwards in sleep. Poor Sam. He must have really hurt her or she wouldn't have let herself risk not being in top form tomorrow for her big pitch. He had done this. It was up to him to fix it.

When they got to her house, he paid the taxi driver and woke Sam up. It took a good five minutes for her to find her keys. 'There's a special pocket for keys in the Shanthi bag,' she told him, while she completely failed to get her hand inside her actual bag. 'It's dead useful.'

'I can see it would be. May I?' He took her bag and dug out her keys. 'Shall I unlock the door for you?'

She nodded and leaned backwards against the wall by the door. The fresh air and short sleep seemed to be doing her some good. She wasn't slurring quite so much now.

The flat was the first door on the left. As soon as she got in, Sam took off her shoes, so Luke did the same. There was a rack by the door. He followed her into an open-plan living room with a small kitchenette at the end of it, separated by a cluttered breakfast bar.

'Niro's away for the weekend,' said Sam. She flopped down on the sofa.

221

Niro must be the cousin. The one who took the photos that were on the website.

'I'm going to make you some toast,' he told her. 'But first, here's a glass of water.' He watched her drink some. 'You need to drink a lot of water, or you'll have a terrible headache tomorrow.'

Sam took out her phone. 'Ugh. I have so many messages.'

Luke found the bread bin and the toaster and put a couple of slices in. 'Some of those are from me.' He had sent DMs as Blaze and tried to call her as Luke.

'I can't be bothered to listen to any of them. I should probably delete the whole lot. Especially the DMs from Blaze. Ugh. I can't believe I thought he liked me. It was all an act.'

'It wasn't like that—'

But she wasn't listening. 'I really liked him,' she said miserably.

'Oh, Sam. I'm sorry.' He went round and hunkered down in front of her. 'Can I ask why you liked Blaze so much? You'd never met him before.'

'It's a long story,' Sam said.

'I've got all night.'

Sam looked up at him with big, wet eyes and he almost teared up in sympathy. He put his hand on top of one of hers and gently squeezed.

Sam looked at their hands and sighed. 'He has this voice … it's comforting, you know. When Mum died, Dad was so depressed he'd just ignore us kids. So we used to hang out together. I spent a lot of time with Gihan, watching him play computer games. And he used to watch Blaze's videos. That's what Blaze reminds me of.'

That went straight through him. He knew he meant something to his fans, but he hadn't realised that he could mean so much. His heart ached for teenage Sam. It was nice to think that he had given her some comfort in her grief, even if he'd had no idea he was doing it.

'I thought he was nice,' Sam continued. 'He *sounds* like a nice person when you listen to him, right? But in *SyrenQuest*, he was

222

really snappy. Then he apologised and started being nice. I should have known something wasn't right. Do you know why he did that?' She sat up, one finger raised accusingly.

Luke interrupted her before she could mention the PR stunt. 'Sam. Listen. There's something I have to tell you.'

'I already know,' she said. 'I'm such an idiot. I turned you down because I thought Blaze was a good guy and he's not. But you are. You're nice and kind and weirdly sexy when you're in full flow at work.'

Wait, what? Did she just call him sexy? Okay, she'd said 'weirdly', which was a caveat he could have done without. But she did call him sexy. He was so distracted by this that he was taken by surprise when she leaned forward and kissed him.

It was a soft, exploratory kind of kiss and for a split second, he closed his eyes and leaned in. Then his brain kicked back in. As much as he wanted to kiss her back, it wasn't right. He gently broke contact and moved back. 'Sam,' he said, softly. 'I'd love to, but you're very drunk right now and …'

Her face was a picture of horror. She put her hands over her mouth.

'Oh, don't look like that. I'm sorry,' he said. 'It's only because you're so drunk and I don't want you to do something that you'll regret in the morning.'

She fell backwards against the sofa and covered her face with a cushion. 'I'm such a loser.'

The toaster popped. He left Sam and went to fetch it. He found the butter and spread it on the hot toast. He had to tell her. She was going to be angry, but putting it off wasn't going to make it any better for either of them. He picked up the plate of buttered toast and took a deep breath. 'Sam. I'm Blaze. He's not a bad guy. I'm not as nice as you think. We're the same person.'

She didn't respond. He walked around the sofa. She was still lying there with a cushion over her face. 'Sam?' He twitched the cushion away.

She was asleep.

Luke's shoulders dropped. Had she heard? No. She'd be shouting at him by now if she'd heard. Oh well. He'd just have to tell her again tomorrow.

He put the glass of water within arm's reach. There weren't any blankets or throws immediately obvious, so he fetched her coat and laid it over her. She was home. She was safe. That was pretty much all he could do for her tonight. He quietly let himself out.

Chapter 19

Sam woke up to a weird ringing noise. She opened her eyes and a thousand needles stabbed her head. Ow. Through half-closed eyes she assessed her surroundings. She was at home. Good. On the sofa? Why? There was a glass of water on the coffee table in front of her, she cautiously sat up and picked it up. The water washed away the disgusting feeling in her mouth. The ringing. Now, where was that coming from?

It was the landline. No one rang the landline these days, surely. Sam put a hand to her head. Ow. The phone rang out and the answerphone clicked in. 'Hey, it's Niro. Just calling to say good luck for the presentation. I guess you've already gone. I feel a bit of a berk leaving this message now. Anyway, good luck.'

Presentation! She sat upright. Shit! She looked at her phone for the time and shot to her feet. The pain in the head almost made her sit down again. Why had her alarm not gone off? She checked her phone again. She had turned it on silent mode. When? Annoyed, she switched it off silent and tried to run upstairs, which was not easy to do with a banging hangover. She had barely enough time to get changed and get to her presentation. Filling in the blanks about what happened the night before would have to wait.

Thirty frantic minutes later, she looked more presentable and her headache was receding to a manageable level. Thank god she'd laid her clothes out ready the afternoon before. Now she just needed to grab her samples and she could be off. Samples. Where were her samples?

She tried to remember exactly what had happened the night before, but she could only recall snippets. She remembered taking the samples from the office. Where had she put them? She double-checked her bag from the night before, after finding it on the bottom stair – which was where she put it when she took off her shoes. Weirdly, her coat had been laid over her like a blanket, rather than hanging up in the hall. Then there was the glass of water and the toast, so someone must have come with her. She thumped the heel of her hand on her forehead. Think. Think.

Luke. Luke had been here. She vaguely remembered. Maybe he'd know where the samples were. She called him.

'Hello?' He sounded tired.

'Luke, it's Sam. Did … you see me last night?'

'Um … yes. Are you okay? You've got your presentation soon.'

'I know. I can't find my samples. I … oh god, this is embarrassing. I can't remember much about last night. I know I had the samples when I left the office. They were in a portfolio bag.' She waved her free hand to indicate the size of the bag, even though he couldn't see it. 'I can't find them here.'

'You didn't have a portfolio bag with you when I took you home,' he said.

She tried not to cringe. She had to focus on the start of the sentence. She'd worry about the 'took you home' part later. 'I must have left it in the pub. I don't have time to go there and get to the Boutique Belvoir offices in time. The pub will be shut anyway. What am I going to do?'

Her usual composure abandoned her. How had she got herself

into this mess? It wasn't like her to go drinking the night before a big presentation, but she had. Now she was hungover. And late. And missing a vital part of her presentation. 'What am I going to do!' This came out as a wail. Tears rose.

'Sam, Sam, it's okay.' Luke's voice was reassuring. It made her feel safe.

Her subconscious tickled her. There was something she had to remember. But Luke was still talking. She grabbed a piece of kitchen towel and dabbed at her tears, trying not to add smudged mascara to her list of troubles.

'Do you have the slides?' Luke asked.

'I put them on a USB stick.' She put her bag on the kitchen counter and checked the zip pocket of her Shanthi bag. 'It's here.'

'Everything you need to say is in the slides. Deliver it with your usual passion, like you did when you showed me on Friday, and it'll be fine.'

'But—'

'You know your product, you know your vision. You can do this.'

She stared in front of her, not seeing anything. She did know her stuff. In her heart she knew that. Her product was good. It was useful. She had a small set of testimonials to prove it. 'I could show them my own bag …' she said.

'There you go! A demonstration model. You'll be fine.'

'I suppose.' Feeling better, she dabbed the last of the moisture from her eyes. 'I just have to persuade them to believe in the product like I do. I can do that.'

'Of course you can. You won *SyrenQuest* coming out of nowhere. You can do anything!'

Sam smiled. 'I did, didn't I?' Then her brain caught up with her. 'Wait, how do you know about that?'

There was a brief silence. 'I … er … don't you remember anything from last night?'

227

Damn. 'What did I say?'

'We'll talk about it later,' he said. 'Shouldn't you get going?'

'Yes. Speak to you later.' She hung up and put the phone in her bag. How did Luke know about *SyrenQuest*? Did she tell him last night? Why didn't she remember?

She looked up. That would have to wait. She had bigger things to worry about right now. Yes. Using her own bag as a demo model was a good idea. It wasn't as good as having the actual prototypes and the mock-ups she'd designed to fit with the client handbags, but she could always say she'd send them in later. She grabbed her coat and ran out.

This was her big chance to get a high-end business partner on board. She was not going to blow it.

Luke put his phone back in his pocket and took a slug of coffee. He had been sitting in his office, debating whether to call Sam when she'd called him. Now he could stop worrying about whether she was coherent enough to make her presentation. She seemed pretty much with it. Which was more than could be said for him. He had almost blurted out about his other identity. From what she'd said, she hadn't heard what he said last night before she fell asleep. He would have to tell her later. After she'd done her stressful presentation.

It was a shame she didn't have her samples with her. He glanced at the clock. It was far too early for the pub to open, but he could check if there was anyone in. It would take him only five minutes and it was a good chance to get some fresh air. He locked his empty office and went out onto the street.

As predicted, the pub was shut. Luke cupped his hands and peered in through the window. Someone was sitting at a table, doing some paperwork. Oh. Brilliant. Luke went to the door and knocked loudly.

It took a while before a man answered. 'We're closed, mate.'

'I know. I'm sorry to bother you. But did my friend leave a

portfolio case here? I'm guessing it was by the bar. She was sitting at the far end. Please. It's important.'

The man looked him up and down and gave an exasperated sigh. 'Wait here. I'll check in the office in case one of the staff put it there.' He shut the door on Luke and disappeared.

Luke stood in the doorway and fidgeted. *Please be there.* What if it was? How would he get it to Sam in time? He looked at his watch. It would be nearly impossible to do it on the bus or in a taxi, with the traffic being what it was. But on his bike … if he pedalled like fury. He might make it. Assuming the portfolio bag was still there. Knowing Sam, it would have been a good quality bag. There was a good chance that someone had just picked it up.

The door opened again. 'What does this bag look like?' the man asked, eyes narrow.

'You found it. Brilliant.' Luke realised he had no idea what the bag looked like. He could guess, but he didn't want to get it wrong. 'I don't know what it looks like. My friend didn't describe it. But I can tell you what's in it. There are three packages, with stickers on them saying 'Shanthi Bags'. Some mood boards with pictures of handbags on them. A folder with sales projections and stuff on …' What else had she shown him? 'Hang on, let me call her. She can describe the bag to you.'

He called, but he got a 'caller is not available' message. She must be on the Underground already.

The man seemed to be looking inside the bag, which was just out of sight. 'No. It's okay. You've convinced me. The contents are exactly what you said. Here.' He passed over the portfolio bag. Tan. Good job he hadn't tried to guess.

'Thank you. You're an absolute star.'

'I need your name and contact number, though. In case anything goes wrong.'

He left his business card with the landlord and legged it back to the office to pick up his cycle helmet and cycle clips. The bag had a carry strap. He slung it across his chest and tightened it. There was a chance he'd miss her, but he had to try.

The combination of painkillers and strong coffee was doing Sam the world of good. By the time she got off the Tube, her headache was a mere throb at the back of her skull. She had mentally gone over her presentation. She knew the numbers that she needed off by heart, so hopefully, the lack of her projections in paper form wouldn't matter. It was a real pain that she didn't have her samples and her lovely mock-ups of how her designs would look next to the company's bags, but it couldn't be helped. She had to hope that she could wow them by personality and visuals alone.

When she walked the short distance to the company HQ, her stride was purposeful. She could do this. She paused just outside the doors, binned her empty coffee cup, and took a moment to gather herself. This was it. If she got these people onboard, she would have a decent chance of getting Shanthi Bags to market. Last night's little wobble aside, she had done everything right. Now was her chance to shine. Sam took a deep breath and climbed the first step up to the doors.

The screech of bicycle brakes. 'Sam! Samadhi!'

She turned to see who was calling her name. A cyclist jumped off his bike, hoiked it onto the pavement, and rushed towards her, apologising to annoyed pedestrians as he went. He grappled with the bag slung on his back and removed it. Her portfolio bag. She finally recognised the red face under the cycle helmet.

'Luke?'

'I went to the pub.' Luke panted. 'They had it. Here.'

Her samples! She had samples now. And mock-ups. She reached forward and took the bag. 'Oh, Luke. You're a proper lifesaver. I could kiss you.' A memory kicked in. She *had* kissed him. Her smile dropped. She had kissed him last night and he'd pushed her away.

Luke's expression was serious. 'Go do your presentation. You have everything now. Knock 'em dead.'

She shook herself. Focus. She had a job to do. Everything else could be dealt with later. 'Thanks. I owe you.' She gave him a quick wave and ran up the steps.

Luke got back to the office and wished he'd changed into his cycling gear before he'd rushed off. He was all hot and sweaty now. He flapped his T-shirt as he went to sign in. Maybe he could have another shower. Thank goodness he didn't have any meetings. He went over to the reception desk.

'Where did you rush off to in such a tearing hurry?' said Kim, eyeing him up and down.

'I had to deliver something to a friend.'

Kim raised her eyebrows. 'A friend? Would this "friend" happen to be a pretty young thing called Sam?'

Luke sighed. Normally he would roll his eyes at her, but there wasn't enough fight left in him now. 'Yes,' he said. 'It was.'

Kim's expression softened. 'You really like her, don't you?'

He made a rueful face and shrugged.

'You should ask her out.'

'I did.' He signed in and pushed the book away. 'She said no.'

'Oh, Luke. I'm so sorry.'

'Yep. Story of my life.' He put his hand up to push his hair back and was surprised afresh to find it short. 'I'm hot and bothered from cycling across town. I'm going to go and splash my face with cold water until I cool down. I'll see you later, Kim.'

In the office, Pete was on the phone. Luke, his face still slightly damp, opened the window and sat down to work. He had just got into the flow of it when the office phone rang. With Pete already on the other line, Luke had to pick it up.

'Hi, Luke. It's Kim. You have a visitor.'

A visitor? Who could that be? 'I wasn't expecting anyone.' Had he made an appointment and forgotten about it with all the excitement? He pulled up his diary online. Nope. Nothing for this morning.

'It's Bradley.' Kim sounded happy. She liked Bradley. Everyone did, it seemed. 'Meeting room three is free so I've booked it for you.'

'Thanks. I'll be there in a minute.'

He hung up and sat back. What did Bradley want? Luke still had a few days left before the deadline they had agreed on. He allowed himself a small smile. He'd won *SyrenQuest*, which meant that he would have the money within the next week or so. He could tell Bradley that today. He stood up, tucked his T-shirt in, and went out to see his partner.

As soon as he saw Bradley, Luke could tell that he was nervous. To a stranger, it wouldn't have been obvious – he was leaning against the reception desk, chatting to Kim – but all those years of friendship meant that Luke could still read his body language with no effort. The way he held his shoulders and the set of his jaw suggested he was tense. What could he have to be nervous about?

'Everything okay, Brad?' he said. Kim handed him the key to the meeting room. He acknowledged her with a grateful smile.

'Hmm. Yes. Good to see you again, mate.'

They made stilted small talk until they were inside the meeting room. Bradley sat down, fidgeting a little. Luke sank into a chair at the opposite side of the table. 'What can I do for you?'

'It's about buying out my share of the company,' said Bradley.

'I won *SyrenQuest*,' said Luke. 'I have enough money to buy you out now. It'll just take a week or so for the money to come through from Syren and then we're all good. I'll speak to the lawyers to draw up the agreement of sale—'

'I've had another offer,' said Bradley.

Luke stared at him. 'So …?'

'If you can't get the money to me immediately, I'll have to go with their offer.' Bradley picked at the sleeve of his suit.

'What? You can't do that.'

'I said three weeks, right? Which is … in three days' time, so …'

Thoughts chased each other through Luke's mind. They coalesced into one word. 'No.'

'What? No, as in you won't have the money? Well, then.' Bradley made as though to stand. 'I guess this meeting is over.'

Anger overrode Luke's natural instinct to de-escalate. 'No, as in you can't do this.' He stood too. 'You OWE me, Brad. I've been carrying this company by myself for the last year. The least you can do is give me an extra week to get the money that you know I'm good for.' He leaned forward, eyes narrowing. He was so angry, he could feel it rising up his face and making his eyes burn. 'If you go ahead and try to sell your shares from under me, I will use the money from *SyrenQuest* to pay for a lawyer and I will sue you for breach of contract. Do you understand me?'

Bradley drew a sharp breath. The look of fear in his eyes lasted only a split second, but Luke registered it. They stared at each other.

Normally, Luke would have been the one to back down. Not today. This time, it was Bradley who looked away first. 'A week,' he said.

'Thank you.' Luke nodded.

Bradley turned to leave. The anger subsided a little. Luke forced himself to relax his shoulders. 'Listen, Brad. If you need money in a hurry … we can draw up an agreement and I can put down some sort of deposit.'

Bradley gave him a strange look. 'I'll think about it. I might take you up on it.'

Luke didn't follow his friend out. He stood still, breathing hard. It would take Bradley a few minutes to leave. He counted to a hundred under his breath. Whatever was going on with Bradley, it was making him behave oddly. He almost didn't recognise his former friend.

Carefully, Luke locked up and returned the key to reception. Kim was dealing with an elderly South Asian man who was visiting, so he escaped without having to explain anything. The adrenaline draining out of him was making him feel weak and shaky.

When he got back to the office, Pete asked him how it went.

'So ... I'm still employed?' he asked, after Luke explained.

'Of course. Even if things had gone wrong, I would have made sure you had your notice period.' Luke sank back into his chair. He raised his hands in front of his face. 'I am really not good with confrontation.'

'I dunno,' said Pete. 'You seem to have managed okay. Maybe you're channelling Blaze.'

Luke laughed. 'Maybe I am. That's probably a good philosophy for me. Take a leaf from Blaze's book when it comes to handling confrontation.'

'Hashtag Be More Blaze.'

'I wouldn't go that far,' said Luke.

Pete looked over his shoulder and nudged the office door shut. 'So, what happened with Bravura? Why did she run off?'

'What are people saying?'

Pete shrugged. 'Speculation varies. The general consensus is that something happened between you two on Saturday night. Like, more than you said in the interview.'

Luke sighed. He couldn't out Sam, so he said, 'No. That was pretty much it. She thinks that I was flirting with her because Syren asked me to. I hadn't even realised that I was flirting with her.'

'How can you not realise?' Pete shook his head. 'Impossible.'

'Honestly, I didn't. I was a shit to her to start with, then I got over myself and now I'm quite fond of her. There's nothing more to it than that.' Honesty compelled him to add, 'At least, there wasn't anything more on Saturday.'

Pete perked up. 'And there is now?'

'I don't know,' said Luke. 'I mean, I like her. She's nice. But I haven't had a chance to speak to her about things and I honestly don't know what's going to happen.' He checked his watch. Sam should be coming back from her presentation about now. He had to tell her. Since he was in her good books now, today was probably the best time to do it.

Chapter 20

Sam had an extra bounce in her step as she walked the last bit from the Underground station to The Nest. She wouldn't know whether her pitch had been successful for a few days. The fact that they were deliberating wasn't the best sign, but it had gone as well as she could have hoped. She had thrown herself into the presentation and demonstrated using her own bag, talked about the company's own handbag designs, and shown them how her product would complement theirs. It had been the most exhilarating experience. She couldn't wait to tell Luke about it.

Even if he hadn't arrived in the nick of time with her samples, his total belief in her had given her the exact boost she needed. Somewhere along the line, she'd absorbed her father's fears about the risks of striking out on your own and the hustle being somehow demeaning. It was Luke's guidance that had helped her stop being apologetic about her product. Without his mentorship, no matter how annoying it was at the time, she wouldn't have found the faith in herself that she needed to face those business people. She could tell they were taken with her presentation. Whether they took on her suggested partnership was down to the numbers, but her presentation had been great.

Once inside The Nest, she joined the queue at the cafeteria.

Celebratory biscuits were in order. She wondered what Luke would like. It was funny how she knew his choice of breakfast food, but not much else about him.

Again, her memory nudged her. She had kissed him last night, hadn't she? She was almost sure of it. The memory was a little clearer now. He had stopped her. She couldn't remember why. Perhaps he was still annoyed with her for turning him down when he asked her out. But he had come through for her in a big way that morning, so he couldn't be that annoyed with her. It was all so confusing. What was even more confusing was that she really, really wanted to kiss him again.

She peered at the various cookies and muffins that were on sale and tried to untangle her feelings. It was as though her obsession with Blaze had overshadowed all her relationships, including the one with Luke. Now that it was gone, she could see what was in front of her all along. It was her turn to be served. She chose two white chocolate cookies, because who didn't like chocolate?

She was so wired, she took the stairs instead of the lift. When she walked through the doors, she stopped dead. Sitting in reception, arms folded, was her father.

It took her a few seconds to stop gawping. Kim was on the phone, but her eyes darted from Sam to her father and back again. Thatha stood up, stiff and angry.

'Hi,' Sam said, with forced cheer. 'What are you doing here? I thought you were working today.' She hadn't been expecting to see him until that evening. She hadn't had a chance to plan what to say.

'I had a cancellation, and your stepmother is with friends, so I thought I would come and see you,' her father said. His gaze did a quick scan of the foyer. 'Here. In your place of work.'

The words fell into place, accusing her. She hurriedly signed them both in. 'Come. I'll show you my office,' she said.

As they walked down the corridor, she tried to break the silence. 'I didn't know you were coming,' she said, pointlessly.

'I tried to call you, but you weren't answering your phone.'

All those messages that she'd ignored. Damn. 'I'm sorry. I had a big pitch today, so I turned my messages off.'

'I went round to your house. Nirosha claimed she didn't know where you were, but I found this.' He held up one of the brochures she'd had made. She had left a stack of them in the living room. She could kick herself.

She let him into her office, which was relatively tidy, thank goodness, and braced herself for the row that was bound to follow.

'So.' Her father managed to fit a whole load of *I'm very angry with you* and *explain yourself, young lady* into that one word.

Sam backed against the desk and looked at her feet. 'I'm sorry. I should have told you,' she said. 'It all happened quite quickly. I got made redundant and—'

'You got made redundant and you didn't tell me?' Her father wasn't shouting. He didn't shout. But the low growl was somehow worse.

'I got a year's salary as part of the package—'

'And you used it on *this*?' He waved a hand encompassing the tiny office, the boxes of sample fabrics, the sewing machine in the corner, the piles of paperwork.

Coming fresh on the heels of her confidence high, she found the contempt in his voice too much. 'Do you even know what *this* is, Thatha?'

'A craft business? Making and selling … what – not even handbags?' He pulled himself to his full height, making her feel like a child. 'And worst of all. You're using your mother's handbags as *advertising*?' He made the word 'advertising' sound like something you scraped off your shoe.

Sam drew a sharp breath. How dare he? He had no idea how difficult that decision had been. No idea what Amma's handbag collection actually meant to her. He just assumed that her pain was less than his pain. Just like he always had.

'Honestly, Samadhi, I'm disappointed in you. Have you so little respect for your mother's memory?'

It was the mention of Amma that did it. She shot straight through angry to furious. Right until that moment, she'd had no idea how she was going to handle this. But handle it she must and she was going to have to do it by shouting.

'It's my memory of her,' she snapped. 'You're not the only one who lost her, you know. Even though you like to act like it. I lost my mother and how dare you suggest that I don't care about her memory. I was a child and she was *my mother*.' Tears stung her eyes, hot and angry. She ignored them. 'You think you're the only one who misses her? You're wrong. We miss her too. Every day. We wanted to talk about her and remember her and celebrate all the things that we loved about her, but you wouldn't let us, because it interfered with your grief. And your grief was all that mattered. When she died we didn't just lose one parent. We lost both of them.'

He recoiled as though she'd slapped him. Sam felt the shock ripple through her too. She had never, ever spoken to her father like that. Never. But now that she'd said it, she couldn't unsay it. Tears ran down her face. She brushed them off with the back of her hand. She should apologise, but she didn't want to. What she'd said was true.

Thatha was staring at her as though he had never seen her before. His eyes reddened and swam.

'I'm not sorry,' she said hoarsely. 'I mean it. You stopped being there for us when she died. We were children. We needed you. Aunty-amma knows that. She cared. Why do you think we go to her when we have a problem and not you? It's not because she's a woman. It's because she listens. She actually cares about us as people. Not just as an idea.'

'I care,' he said, in a voice she almost didn't recognise. 'I care about you three, so much.'

She shook her head. 'Not as we are now. You love the memories of us from when Amma was alive. We're not kids anymore. You like to give us advice and provide "guidance".' She did air quotes with her fingers. 'We don't need a careers adviser. We needed a parent. Thank god for Aunty-amma.' She swiped at the tears on her face again.

Thatha slowly sat down in her office chair. He seemed to shrink into himself as she watched, getting older by the second. Her father had got old. Why hadn't she noticed? Perhaps she was as guilty of not noticing change as he was.

'This isn't me exploiting Amma's memory. This is my tribute. I ... can't always remember her face, but every time I use one of her bags, I feel a connection to her. You once told us that she would never be gone, so long as we kept remembering her. This is me, remembering her.'

Thatha frowned. 'I said that?' He sniffed.

Sam nodded, her throat suddenly felt tight. 'You did.'

Thatha looked around, his gaze resting on various things in the room. The paperwork she'd scribbled on, the pictures of bags, and finally, the small photograph in the corner of the noticeboard. He nodded. 'I see.' The words were flat, almost without intonation.

Fresh tears welled up in Sam's eyes. Her nose was all snotty now. She picked up her bag and looked in it. The pocket that normally held tissues was empty. 'I need a tissue,' she said and fled the room.

Leaving the little office was a relief, but it made the tears come freely. She headed for the bathroom. Thankfully, there was no one else in there. She washed the tears away, hastily dabbed it dry, and headed back to face her father.

She loved him. Obviously, she did. But her mother's death had driven a wedge between them that even the arrival of her stepmother hadn't been able to repair. They had each retreated from the other, hiding behind the walls of respect and familial duty so that they did what was expected of them, but she hadn't seen the Thatha who teased and tickled and sat on the floor building Lego houses again.

When she got back into the office, he was examining one of her older sample bags with an air of bewilderment.

'That's an old prototype,' she told him.

He looked up. 'Did you make this?'

She nodded. 'I have Amma's old sewing machine.' That, too, had been banished to the loft. When she mentioned wanting to buy a machine, her stepmother had quietly pointed out that there was a perfectly good one she could have. The fact that it was Amma's didn't need to be said.

He nodded.

Sam cleared her throat. 'Listen. This morning, I gave a presentation to a handbag company to see if they would partner with me to produce a range of inserts that worked specifically with their bags. Would … would you like me to go through it for you? It might answer a few questions.'

The nod from her father was reluctant, but she took it. She fired up her laptop and ran through the presentation. It wasn't the same as delivering it that morning, but she still felt that tingle of pride. Her plan was good. She had created it from nothing. Even if this business went nowhere, she could still be proud of having got this far.

When she finished her presentation, Thatha was quiet. Sam fidgeted, resisting the urge to say, 'Well, what do you think?' like she was showing him a crayon drawing.

'Is this something you really want to do?' he asked.

'Yes. I would like to bring these bags to market. And I think I'd be good at being my own boss.'

His small smile caught her by surprise. 'Yes. I can see that.'

There was a moment of quiet and Sam couldn't sense the mood of the room. She wasn't even sure how she was feeling. Perhaps they both needed a bit of time to digest all this.

'Can I get you … a tea?' She remembered the cookies she'd bought for Luke. 'I have some biscuits.'

She gratefully made her escape to the small communal kitchen

241

at the far end of the corridor. Being rude to her father didn't come naturally. There had always been a healthy level of respect towards him. But she had snapped and now she was starting to feel bad about it. At least it had gone well and he wasn't angry any more.

She had intended to tell him about it all, at some point. She really had. But that right time had never come. She shook her head while she made the tea. What would he say when he found out about *SyrenQuest*? Games were a hobby. Not something to waste time on. But she had won several thousand pounds off it … so maybe he'd change his mind.

There were emails from Syren unread on her phone. She should catch up with all of those. They would want to know what she was doing. She was supposed to do publicity if she won. It was in the contract. At the time, the prospect of winning was so ridiculous that she hadn't even bothered thinking about it. But now, the idea of seeing Blaze again and being interviewed with him was … awful. Things had been okay while they were playing, but the betrayal still stung. He had behaved so oddly, too. For the first half of the game, it was almost like he was a completely different person.

Well, she would deal with that when she got to it. Right now, she had to make sure Thatha wasn't too angry at her. She found a tray and put the mugs and an empty plate for the cookies on it. In her pocket, her phone buzzed. She checked it. Another email from Syren. Just below it, two notifications of missed calls from Niro.

She put the phone back in her pocket, leaned her head against the doorframe, and took a moment to appreciate just how much of a mess her life was. Her father, her business, her feelings, everything was a complete mess. She could do with a day to sit down and work out what was going on with each one. She needed a mind map. The thought reminded her of Luke, which made her smile.

She pulled herself together. First things first. She had to deal with the problem that was in front of her right now. The fact that Thatha had gone quiet was a good sign. Hopefully, he was coming round to seeing things her way. Or at least tolerating them.

When she got back, he was looking at the board with all her planned designs for the Boutique Belvoir pitch.

'You did all this? All by yourself?' He didn't sound angry now. Merely interested.

'Well, I had a bit of help. Niro did all the photographs and a friend of mine, Luke, helped with the website and the presentation, but yes … it was mostly me.'

He shook his head. 'What I don't understand … is why you gave up your career for this. It's so risky.'

This one, she knew the answer to. 'I didn't give up my career,' she said. 'My qualifications are still there. I still have my skills and I've gained a few more doing this. If this business fails, I can always go back to working as a project manager.'

'How long have you given yourself?'

'Two years.' She explained how she'd split the money from the redundancy settlement for two purposes: to keep her bills paid and to use as start-up capital. She also explained the concept of crowdfunding.

He asked her more questions as they drank the tea. The atmosphere loosened. By the time the last of the tea was drained, things were almost relaxed.

'Send me the link to your crowdfunding thing,' said Thatha, as he stood up to leave. 'I know some people who might be interested.'

Really? Wow. 'Um … sure. Of course.'

'We're around for a few days,' Thatha continued, as though he hadn't just said something unthinkable. 'We're taking you and Nirosha out for dinner tonight, but it might be nice to meet just the three of us, on a different night. We could go for Thai food, maybe?'

'That would be nice.'

Thatha made for the door. Sam followed him. 'So … you're okay about all this?'

Thatha turned. 'I would have preferred it if you'd told me and not lied.'

'I'm sorry. I wanted to. I just knew you'd be angry and I wanted to wait until it was a success before I showed you.'

'And what if it wasn't a success?'

'Then I was going to pretend it just took a long time to find a new job.' She braced herself.

To her relief, he laughed. 'As you keep reminding me, you children are adults now.' He patted her shoulder. 'For what it's worth, I think you'd be happier working for yourself, too. You never did take kindly to being told what to do.' He stepped out of the office. 'You take after your mother that way.'

'I do?'

He nodded. 'Hmm.' He took a deep breath. 'Your mother's memory is still precious to me … to us all. Be careful what you do with it. Okay?'

The tightness returned to her throat. Sam nodded. 'I will.'

By the time Sam had washed up the cups from her father's visit and sat down, it was well past lunchtime. She went downstairs and got herself a sandwich. On the way back, she went up the extra floor to see Luke. She didn't have her biscuits, but she still needed to thank him. And maybe work out exactly what happened the night before.

As she turned the corner, she ran into Pete, coming the other way.

'Oh, hi, Sam.'

'Hi, Pete. Is Luke around?'

'He's in the office, in a good mood, too.'

Sam raised her eyebrows. 'Oh yes?'

'He's been a badass in a meeting and it's gone to his head a bit,' Pete grinned. He tilted his chin in the direction of the office. 'Go see for yourself.'

Sam grinned back. 'Luke' and 'badass' didn't really go together. She carried on down the corridor. Or did they? What did she actually know about Luke? She knew he was kind and loyal and extremely good at his job. He had saved her bacon that morning and quite possibly the night before, too. Her memory from the night before was still a bit patchy, but she was pretty sure something had happened between them.

The door to the office was open. Luke had his back to her. He was standing at his desk, typing and humming to himself. The tune was familiar. She had been hearing it all weekend. It was the theme tune from *SyrenQuest*. He must have watched the final—

Luke hit the return key and turned with a flourish. Something about the movement was electrifyingly familiar. The flourish, the set of the shoulders, the music. Suddenly, it all clicked into place. Porridge for breakfast. The half-finished tattoo. The way he knew she'd won *SyrenQuest*.

'Blaze.'

If there had been any doubt, the way his head snapped towards her would have sealed it. Luke looked straight at her. 'Bravura,' he said, and dipped his head in a bow.

Emotions buffeted Sam in the chest. Surprise, anger, embarrassment, disbelief. 'You're Blaze?'

He nodded. 'I told you we needed to talk. Come in.'

She stepped inside and kicked the door shut with her foot. 'But … how is that possible?'

'The usual way,' he said. 'Beard, contact lenses. It's not hard. You should know, Bravura.'

He knew about her. Did she really tell him that last night? Or had he known for longer?

'How long have you known? About me?'

'Since Saturday night, in the bar. I was coming to join you

245

and then I saw you pull out your bag and show it to Flick and … I recognised you.'

In her mind she saw Blaze's face as he stared at her across the bar, the look of horror, the way he turned heel and walked out. 'And that's why you blanked me?'

'I panicked. I didn't know what to do.'

She stared at him, anger catching fire. Now she could see both men in the one face. Blaze had hurt her. But Luke had known that it was her and he'd let Blaze hurt her anyway. 'Why didn't you just tell me?'

He pushed a hand over his forehead to flick away the hair that wasn't there anymore. No wonder that gesture had looked so familiar. God, was she stupid to have not seen it sooner?

'I was coming in to tell you that Syren were trying to construct a "will-they-won't-they" romance narrative about Blaze and Bravura. Us. And that they were pressuring me to go along with it. You liked him … me as him. Whatever. And I had to tell you that he didn't feel the same way. And then I realised that Bravura was you.' He stretched a hand out towards her. 'You. Whom I like very much. And that is a serious headfuck.'

It was. 'But surely, that made things easier?'

'How, Sam? *How?*' He threw his hands up. 'I asked you out and you turned me down. You didn't like me as me. You liked me as him. How do you think that makes me feel? He's not real. I am. And I'm not the one you wanted.'

'Well, I don't want him now. He's a narcissistic wanker,' she said. 'I don't know how you can even be the same person.'

'We are and we aren't. I told you. He's a persona. He gets to say and do stuff that I can't.'

'You didn't tell me that. He did.'

'Same thing!' His voice was tight, like he was fighting to keep it under control.

The weirdest thing was, the angrier he got, the more she could hear Blaze. Blaze made her angry. But the man standing in front

246

of her, gesticulating wildly as he talked, was Luke. Who made her feel safe … and other things.

She tried to map it all in her mind and ran into her memory from last night. 'I kissed you last night,' she said. 'You pushed me away.'

'Yes. Because you were very drunk and on the rebound. From him.'

This was getting ridiculous. 'But *he* is *you*!'

'Can you see why I freaked out?!'

Now she didn't know whether she wanted to smack him or kiss him. Blaze had hurt her. Luke had known who she was. He must have known he was hurting her. How could he not? Blaze could have spoken to Bravura or Luke could have spoken to Sam. He had chosen to do neither. Which was cruel, regardless of which persona it was.

All her feelings coalesced into a ball of hurt and anger. 'All I know is that you hurt me. You had more information than I did and you chose not to share it with me and let me carry on feeling like shit.' She pointed a finger at him when he opened his mouth to retort. 'And don't give me crap about how he isn't you. He is you. And you were being a coward because you hate confrontation. So you ran away rather than face it and didn't spare a thought for how it might affect me.'

His expression was of pure horror. Exactly as it had been as he stared at her across the bar. Anger flared. She wasn't putting up with that again. Yes, Luke had helped her. But he had also been complicit in hurting her and that was not okay. 'You disgust me. Both of you.' She wrenched the office door open and walked out.

When she got to her office, she was so angry, the room seemed to pulse with it. She looked behind her, at the door. She couldn't stay here where he could come and find her. It's not like she was going to get any work done here anyway. She grabbed her bag and stormed off home.

Chapter 21

Luke glared at the door that Sam had just walked out of and fumed. How unfair! It was all very well people saying 'you should talk to her'. This was what talking to her led to. She'd called him a narcissistic wanker! He'd looked out for her and tried to do his best for her and this was what he got? He had cycled across bloody London for her. It was so infuriating. He kicked a table leg. Ow.

He sat down and wriggled his toes inside his shoe to check he hadn't broken anything and spent a few minutes swearing at the world in general. He was mid-expletive when Pete came back.

'What did you do to Sam?' said Pete. 'I just saw her march out of the building with a face like thunder.'

'She ...' How could he explain this without outing Sam as Bravura? 'Um ... You know how I like Sam?'

'Yes ...' Pete frowned. 'And?'

'Then there's Blaze and Bravura.'

Pete's eyes widened. 'Wait, when you said "it's complicated", did you actually mean that you were starting to have feelings for Bravura?'

'Not exactly, but sort of. It is complicated. Syren wanted me to help them feed a "will-they-won't-they" narrative. I didn't want to, so I sort of half-arsed it with "it's complicated". But then she found out about it and thought I was in on it all along and got angry.'

'But what does this have to do with Sam?'

Good question. He couldn't give her away, not even to Pete. It wasn't his secret to tell. 'She's annoyed with me as well,' he said, weakly.

'So, you've managed to annoy both the women in both your lives. That's quite special.'

'No one screws up like I screw up.'

'Okay, okay.' Pete leaned forward. 'But which one are you interested in? Who is more important?'

'Sam, obviously.' What a stupid question. 'Blaze isn't real. Bravura probably isn't either.' Except, she wasn't very different from Sam. She didn't change her behaviour at all. The only difference between Bravura and Sam, apart from the appearance, was that Bravura had fancied him at some point.

'So, what's your problem? Fix things with Sam, forget about Bravura.'

Luke shook his head. 'It's not that easy, is it? I don't know what to say to her.'

'What did you do?'

'Doesn't matter. All that matters is that I've alienated her.' His anger had lost its edge now and it was turning into self-pity. 'I'm not good with talking to people at the best of times. I'm useless at talking to women.'

'Again,' said Pete. 'How is it even possible that you're Blaze?'

'I keep telling you. He's not me. He's a persona. A character.'

'But you can play him effortlessly, right? So what would Blaze do?'

What would Blaze do? 'He would stride over to her and kiss her.' Probably. Not that Blaze had ever done that. But it seemed like the sort of thing he would do, if the situation arose.

'Well then, there's your answer,' said Pete. 'Be more Blaze.'

Could he channel a bit of Blaze into his real life? He normally tried to keep them separate, but with Sam, that boat had well and truly sailed. Blaze wouldn't let the woman he loved go without a fight.

Luke nodded. Blaze would not. Neither would he. 'Be more Blaze.' He stood up. 'I'm taking the rest of the day off, Pete. Make sure you lock up properly when you leave, okay?' He grabbed his coat.

Pete gave a little cheer. 'Good luck, mate.'

'Thanks.' He was going to need it.

Sam was still angry when she got home. She stamped into the living room and startled Niro, who was sitting on the sofa with her laptop balanced on her knees.

Niro pulled out her earbuds. 'Sam! I'm so sorry. I wasn't expecting to see him and I didn't have a chance to hide everything before he saw.'

Sam stopped, halfway to the kitchen. 'What are you talking about?'

'Your dad.' Niro frowned. 'Didn't he go to your office? Isn't that what you're so angry about?'

Her dad. That had been only that morning. Sam shook her head. 'So much has happened today. That feels like long ago now.' She pressed a hand to her forehead. 'What a day.'

'What happened?' Niro shut her laptop and sat up.

Sam changed course and flopped down on the other chair. 'With my dad? It was okay in the end. I think he might actually be onside.'

'That's brilliant!' said Niro. 'See. I told you you should tell him.'

'Hmm.' Ordinarily, she would have been so relieved. She *had* been relieved and everything was going so well until this bombshell with Luke. No, Blaze. Both. 'Arrgh.'

'What's going on, Sam? Did the presentation not go well?'

'Oh, that went fine. I won't know for a few days, but I don't think I could have presented it any better.' Sam waved a dismissive hand.

'Then what on earth are you so upset about?'

Sam groaned and tipped her head back against the chair. 'I don't even know where to start.' She lifted her head and looked at Niro. 'You know Blaze …?'

Niro clapped her hands together. 'Oh! What happened there? You have to tell me.'

Sam just groaned again.

'I'm serious, Sam. My friends had a watch party to see the *SyrenQuest* final. A watch party! I had to be on guard the whole time in case I blurted out something by mistake. And … what the hell happened between you? I tried to call you, but you weren't answering. I was really worried until you texted to say you were home. You owe me. So spill.'

Sam sighed. She quickly explained about Blaze going along with Syren's plan to string Bravura along and make her look like a complete idiot.

'Wait, but—' Niro shook her head.

'That's not all,' said Sam, getting into her stride now. 'Turns out, Luke – my so-called friend Luke – and Blaze are the same person.'

'Woah. No way!'

'I'm so angry with him – both of him – I can barely think straight.'

Niro stared at her for a second. 'I think this calls for biscuits. There are a few things I'd like to point out to you, but first, I think you need something to drink and a biscuit. Sit there. Don't move.'

Sam covered her face with her hands and stared into the red and black darkness. The anger had morphed into something softer now. She no longer wanted to hit someone. Now she wanted to curl up and cry. How had she not seen that Luke and Blaze were the same person? How had she managed to have feelings for both of them? She felt stupid and humiliated and most of all, miserable.

Niro made her a cup of tea and waited while she took a few

sips. Then she sat on the coffee table and leaned forward, so that Sam had no choice but to look at her.

'Tell me, slowly, what happened,' Niro said.

Sam told her again, in detail. Humiliation and hurt igniting all over again in the retelling.

Niro shook her head. 'I am finding it hard to believe that Blaze was in on this whole "spin" thing.'

'I know, right! How could I have been so wrong about him?'

'And then there's what he said in the post-win interview.'

She was supposed to have been in that interview. It was part of the publicity she'd agreed to do if she won. 'What did he say?'

'I think you should watch it.' Niro opened her laptop and started typing. 'Here we go. It's on YouTube.' She turned the laptop round so that Sam could see the screen. 'I reckon he was just being himself. After all, he's well known to be a kind of flirty personality. And you said he apologised for being part of it. He clearly has a level of respect for you.'

Sam sat forward as the interview clip began. She watched Blaze angrily defend her and denounce the focus on their relationship or lack of it, rather than the game itself. 'Legend?' She felt the anger drain away. 'He said I was a legend.'

'See. Not such a demon after all,' said Niro.

'I guess. But what about Luke?'

'I dunno,' said Niro. 'It must have been a hell of a shock to find out you liked him as Blaze, but not as himself. If you think about it.'

Sam looked down at her hands. 'I did like him as himself. I just thought I liked Blaze … more.' She thought about Luke. Even with her hazy memory, she knew that he had come to find her, brought her home, gently dissuaded her before she did something she knew she'd have regretted. Those weren't the actions of someone who was laughing at her. Those were the actions of someone who cared.

'He cycled across London to get my portfolio case to me. I left

252

it in the pub last night. He picked it up and got it to me. Just in time, too.' She scrunched up her face. 'I was going to thank him, but then I realised he was Blaze and … Oh god, I've messed up so badly.'

'Possibly,' said Niro, with an apologetic smile. 'You said he was shy. Is it possible that he chose Blaze to be the opposite of him?'

That made sense. 'Blaze is larger than life and confident and Luke is so shy he can barely talk to people. But once he relaxes, he's friendly and approachable and really, really helpful. I guess Blaze is too, once you get past the bluster. A good guy at heart.' Sam gestured towards the biscuits and, when Niro held out the packet, took three.

'Is that what attracts you to both of them?'

She nodded. 'That and the fact that they are so good at what they do. I watched Luke rearrange my website. It was like he was playing the piano. I've never seen anything like it.'

Niro said, 'If you had to choose, which one would you go for?'

'They're the same person, remember?'

'For the sake of argument, if you had to choose.'

Sam didn't have to think about it for long. Blaze was delightful, but it would be exhausting keeping up with him. Luke, on the other hand … 'Luke. Definitely, Luke.'

Luke got as far as standing outside Sam's front door before Blaze failed him. He stared at the door, heart pounding, hands clammy. What was he doing? He couldn't do that 'striding in and kissing a person' thing. Who did that? How did he even know she wanted him to kiss her? This was stupid. He turned around, took one step, and stopped.

No. He couldn't go back to his life like today hadn't happened. He couldn't face another morning waking up and thinking of Sam. Of feeling his heart rise when she walked in and sink when she left. He had to do something. Otherwise he'd regret it forever. He turned back to face the door. Right. Be more Blaze.

He gulped down the ball of terror in his throat and rang the doorbell.

A South Asian woman with purple and black hair answered the door. This must be the cousin Sam lived with.

'Hi.' His voice came out all squeaky. He cleared his throat. 'Is Sam in?'

She raised her eyebrows. 'You are?'

'Luke. I'm Luke. I'm—'

'Come in!' She practically yanked him inside. 'Brilliant.'

In the flat, he toed off his shoes and pushed them against the wall.

Before he could explain further, the woman shouted, 'Sam! You have a visitor. I'm just going to my room to listen to music *really loudly*.' She gestured to the door to the living room and mouthed 'good luck' before disappearing up the stairs.

Luke took a deep breath and went in.

Sam was coming out of the kitchenette. 'Luke.' She wasn't shouting. That was good.

He had to get this out before his head exploded. 'Sam,' he said, speaking quickly, 'I'm sorry. I'm sorry I hurt you as Blaze, I'm sorry I didn't tell you sooner. I'm sorry about everything and I understand that you're angry with me. But I have to tell you how I feel.'

She tipped her head to one side.

He ploughed on. 'I am completely mad about you. I wake up in the morning thinking about you. Everything in the office reminds me of you. Even *SyrenQuest* made me think of you.' He raised his hands to his head and made an exploding sign. 'You're everywhere in my life. Those few days when we had breakfast meetings were the best, most exciting days of my life. I … I get that you like Blaze more than me. But. But I just needed you to know how I feel. Because I think I'm in love with you.' He stopped, out of breath.

Sam took a step closer to him. She wasn't running away or

254

frowning. That was good. But she wasn't smiling either. What did that mean? His heart was hammering like it was trying to run away. It probably had more sense than he did.

Sam stopped, a couple of feet away from him. 'My feelings for Blaze,' she said, slowly, as though she were weighing up the words. 'They're tied up with all kinds of other stuff to do with grief and healing and … being a teenager.' She met his gaze. 'So you were right, when you said it was complicated. To you, the online world and the real world are two separate things. To me, the distinction is … blurred. I don't think you can disown everything Blaze did on the basis that you feel he's not you.'

'I'm not excusing what he said or did. I didn't know about Syren's PR twist until Saturday. Honestly. And I genuinely was coming to tell you. I just panicked when I realised who you were.' This was what he'd been trying to tell her before. 'I didn't mean to hurt you. I would never do that. Not as me nor as Blaze. And once I figured out it was you, I wanted to tell you I was me.' He had to make her understand. 'You probably won't believe me, but I even told you about it last night.'

Sam winced. 'You did? How did I take it?'

'You fell asleep.' He braced himself. He had no idea how she would take that.

To his relief there was a small smile. 'I meant to say thank you,' she said. 'It was very kind of you to look after me last night. And thank you for bringing my portfolio case across London. I owe you one.'

Okay. This was going well. He seized his chance. 'You could repay me by going out for that drink.' He waited, heart trying to climb out of his throat.

Sam smiled. 'I'd love to.'

Luke nearly collapsed with relief.

Sam took another step forward. She was quite close to him now. He could smell her perfume. All he could focus on was her mouth.

'Just so you know,' she said. 'If I had to choose between you and Blaze …'

His heart thundered in his head. He forgot how to breathe.

'I would choose you.' Sam went up on tiptoes and kissed him.

It was a soft kiss, but it was dizzying. When she drew away, he put an arm around her waist and pulled her to him so that he could kiss her back. He put everything into that kiss. All the weeks of wanting to talk to her, the longing, the need. Her arms went up around his neck. Her fingertips trailed in his hair. Every fibre in his body fizzed.

When they finally drew apart, she rested her forehead against his and murmured, 'Wow.'

Luke grinned. 'I have wanted to do that for ages.'

She smiled and moved back a little. 'I'm sorry I got so angry with you. It was …'

'Confusing?' he said. 'I found it really confusing.'

'Yes. Confusing.' She gave one of his ears a gentle tug, making his breath hitch. 'I mean, we were both two people.'

'But we're not. I'm just me.' He moved closer, until his lips were millimetres away from hers. 'And you're just … you.'

She made a little noise and kissed him. Luke pulled her closer and happily kissed her back.

Sam snuggled up against Luke, her head resting on his chest. They were sitting on the sofa watching Blaze's stream of the *SyrenQuest* final. 'This is surreal,' she said. 'I spent so many hours watching you and listening to your voice on the screen and now you're here, next to me. It's weird.'

Luke laughed and she heard it rumble through his chest.

'Sorry.' He kissed the top of her head. 'It's just that neither of us remembers what we said or did in the final game very clearly and we should get our story straight if we're going to be interviewed.'

'Yeah. I know.'

They had talked about a great many things that afternoon,

but mostly, they'd discussed how to deal with Syren and their media requests. Thankfully, Bravura didn't have any social media accounts, but some of the stuff on her in-app messages was pretty toxic. If Luke hadn't been with her when she finally read them, she would have been genuinely frightened. He had helped her block and report each one. This, more than anything, had helped her decide that she would do the *SyrenQuest* publicity interviews. The idea was to drown out the negative comments with positive stuff about the possible romance between two strangers who had met because of a computer game.

Sam had drafted something and Luke had sent it in. Now they were watching the gameplay to make sure they didn't say anything that would contradict their suggested narrative.

There was a loud knock on the living room door. 'Is it safe to come in?' said Niro.

'Of course it is.' Sam turned her head, but didn't bother getting up.

Niro came in. 'Hi,' she said to Luke. 'I'm Niro. I'm the cousin who lives here. We didn't exactly meet properly earlier.' She reached over the back of the sofa to offer her hand.

Luke leaned up and shook it. 'Nice to meet you properly, Niro. I've seen your work on Sam's brochures. You're a talented photographer.'

Niro grinned. 'Aw. I like you. You can stay,' she told Luke. 'What are you two watching?'

'The gameplay from yesterday,' said Sam. 'God, was it only yesterday? It feels like weeks have gone past.'

'So, you've just got together and you're spending your time watching a replay of a computer game?' said Niro. She shook her head. 'What a pair of dorks. You deserve each other.'

'It's important,' said Sam.

'Yeah. Yeah. Whatever.' Niro wandered off. Sam could hear her putting bread in the toaster.

On the screen, Blaze and Bravura got to the bit where she

worked out that they could split up within the rules of the game.

'I still don't understand how you figured that out,' said Luke. 'It's really not obvious.'

'There were clues in the song all the way along. I only properly understood when we didn't kill the baby dragon. The line about sparing the young resonated all day the next day and when I saw Flick's game, the penny dropped.'

'I don't think any of the others figured that out. And no one worked out that they could split up. That's what stymied Phil and Jeff,' said Luke. 'You're amazing.'

Sam grinned and tightened her arms around him.

'Don't inflate her ego,' said Niro, walking past with a plate of toast. 'She's going to be impossible to live with.'

Luke looked down at Sam, his expression so soft that it made everything in her melt. 'I don't think that'll be a problem.'

Sam laughed. She didn't think she'd ever been happier.

Chapter 22

Sam looked at the mirror and Bravura stared back. The make-up artist was fluttering around her, making sure the wig was on and there were no brown bits peeping out from under the blue skin paint. Having a pro do her make-up showed Sam just how amateur her own attempt had been.

They were at the studio that Syren used for their interviews and broadcasts. Lance, who was still hosting all the promo shows for Syren, had been delighted with their suggestion that they come on together. He had suggested they end with the big reveal that they were a couple.

She heard Luke's voice off to the side and turned. This was the first time she'd seen him dressed as Blaze after finding out who he was. How had she not noticed the similarities? The facial hair and the green eyes were a massive distraction, but really …

He turned and smiled at her. Luke's smile, which was so much more attractive than the half-smile he'd perfected as Blaze. Not many people got to see that smile on Blaze.

Sam glanced at the make-up artist, who indicated she was done. She hopped off and padded over to where Blaze was talking to Marsha from Syren. She looked up at him and felt a thrill through her body. This man had seemed so unattainable just a few weeks ago and now he was hers. Even better, the man he was when he wasn't dressed as a green-eyed pirate was hers too. If she ever had to choose, she knew she'd always choose Luke. But it was really, really nice that she didn't have to.

'Well, my YouTube views have rocketed,' Luke told Marsha. 'And all the social media numbers are up.'

'Everyone loves a love story,' said Marsha. 'We have a lot of new followers coming in to find out what happened between you two. We'll lose them soon enough, because they're not here for the games and such, but we're hoping that it'll be good for name recognition, which we can use come Christmas.'

Sam listened. 'Can I mention my friend's business on the show?' she asked. 'I'm helping her crowdfund for her handbag insert business. I'd love to give her a plug.'

'So long as it's only a mention and not a long spiel, I should think so,' Marsha said. 'Keep it short through, yeah?'

'Oh, of course.'

They had agreed that keeping their real identities private was a good idea. Especially for Bravura. But the chance to tell such a huge audience about Shanthi Bags was too good an opportunity to pass up, so she had decided to frame it as a friend she was helping out.

'Okay, people. Are we ready?'

Before she knew it, she was sitting in front of a small studio audience. Blaze was at the other end of the long interview sofa. Lance was in a matching armchair opposite them.

They stuck to the running order that they'd agreed to beforehand. They discussed the game, the twists, and the hidden clues that Bravura had worked out. Syren unveiled the extended version of the game that now came with the headset. There would be an online leaderboard for the fastest players.

Sam glanced at the clock behind the camera. Things would be wrapping up soon. This was the bit she'd been dreading.

'And what's next for you two?' Lance asked.

'I'm going to be helping Syren with their new expanded game,' said Blaze. 'And getting on with real-life stuff.'

'What about you, Bravura? Will you be joining a group that plays on Twitch and YouTube?'

'Funnily enough, Flick has already invited me to be on her team,' said Sam. 'But no. I'm going to leave that to the professionals. At the moment, I'm helping a friend with her crowdfunding campaign. She makes handbag inserts, so that you can change handbags without leaving vital things behind. They're called Shanthi Bags. S-H-A-N-T-H-I Bags.'

'They're very useful,' said Blaze. 'Especially if you have a secret double life.'

There was a ripple of movement in the crowd. Hopefully, that was the sound of a hundred people typing 'Shanthi Bags' into Google.

'So basically, going back to your old lives?' said Lance, getting them back on track.

'Pretty much. Except that I'll be using the Syren3 headset now, obviously,' said Blaze, smoothly. 'The older games don't use it to its full capacity, but I've got used to it now and I like it a lot.'

Lance nodded solemnly, then made a big show of looking at the audience. 'And finally ...' He paused and glanced at the audience with a smile. 'The bit we've all been waiting for. You have agreed to talk to us about your partnership ... with some behind-the-scenes details.'

Sam sat up straighter and glanced at Blaze, who flashed a grin at the camera.

'So, you met as strangers, got to know each other through playing the game. Things were rocky at first, then you mellowed to each other. Let's have a look at some clips.'

Watching the clips was painful. In the heat of the moment, she hadn't realised quite how obvious her crush on him had been. Sam tried not to shrink away and hide behind her hands. When she looked at Blaze, she found him gazing at her, with tenderness in his eyes. They had been told to keep things ambiguous until the very end, so she shot him a warning frown. He bit his lip and looked away with mock shyness. She had to stifle a laugh. That reaction clip would probably end up in the show, but it did make her feel better.

They came to the end with a close-up of Blaze's face as he turned this way and that, searching for her on the stage of the *SyrenQuest* final. He appeared frantic. Sam leaned forward, intent on the screen. 'I haven't seen this bit before,' she said. She watched him throw the headset on the chair and run off after her. No wonder the girl in the pub had been so struck by it. It was pretty dramatic stuff. Her own heart had quickened seeing it and she already knew how it turned out.

The clip ended and Lance turned to them. Sam stared at her hands and tried not to grin. She could feel the increased interest from the audience. It sucked at them, pulling them in.

'Something happened the night before the final. Can you tell us what it was?'

'Well,' said Blaze, leaning forward. 'Bravura and I have opposing views about how real online life is. You see, I think that who we are online is not the real us. It's a made-up version of who we are.'

'Whereas, I think it is real. Sure, not identical to the real-life you, but close enough,' said Sam. 'The faces are made up, but the feelings are real.'

'And which one of you is right?'

Blaze laughed. 'She's the clever one in this partnership. So she was.' His expression turned serious. 'Bravura reminded me that I've made some incredible friends through gaming and YouTube. Some of them, like Flick and Phil_the_Vicar, I've met in real life and there's lots of you whom I haven't met but could genuinely call in an online emergency. So in that sense, it's all real.'

'On the other hand, we do get to escape and be a different version of ourselves,' said Sam.

'I get to have tattoos without passing out,' said Blaze, raising his arms. This got a laugh and a small round of applause.

'And this caused a rift because …?'

'Clearly, this was a big difference of opinion,' said Blaze. 'And as an indirect result of that disagreement, I managed to stand her up at the bar on the night before the final. Which was not cool of me, because she didn't know anybody. I'd just left her alone at a party with all my friends.' He put a hand over his heart and mouthed 'I'm sorry' to her.

Sam smiled and shook her head. 'I was already very stressed out because of the final. I didn't expect to be there and it was totally overwhelming. So I overreacted. I'm sorry too.' She couldn't see the audience behind the spotlights, but she could feel them listening. The atmosphere did not feel hostile, like it had at the convention. 'Once I got away from the stress, I calmed down and we got back in touch. It's all sorted out now.' She looked across the sofa. 'Right, Blaze?'

'Oh yeah, definitely. No hard feelings,' he replied.

'And what about soft feelings? You obviously get on very well. I think the real question is … *how* well? Are you romantically involved?'

She and Blaze exchanged glances.

'Would you believe it if I said it's complicated?' Blaze said. This got a laugh.

Lance was not to be fobbed off this time. 'But seriously, though.'

Blaze nodded. He stood up and straightened out his jacket, flicking it so that it flipped dramatically behind him. Sam fought the urge to laugh. He was loving this. This was who Luke wished he was. He would never pose when he was being himself, but as Blaze … as Blaze he could do anything. The first claps from the audience started the minute he moved, but when he took a few steps across the stage to come and sit next to her, they became a full-blown round of applause. When he took her hand, they went wild.

He looked at her, brought their clasped hands up to his face, and placed a kiss on her hand. From behind their hands, he mouthed, 'Okay?' and Sam felt her whole body warm up in response. She managed a quick nod.

Lance waited for the noise to die down. 'I take it that's a yes.'

They both nodded.

Sam said, 'We had a slight misunderstanding at the con, but we're good now.'

'Slight misunderstanding.' Blaze rolled his eyes.

She nudged him in the ribs. The audience laughed. Lance beamed at them.

It looked like it had been the best result for everyone.

Epilogue

Sam ran up the steps to The Nest and looked at the queue at the cafeteria counter. Hmm. May as well go check her email and come back when things were quieter. She went upstairs to her office. Luke had left at the crack of dawn because he needed to catch up with some work. They had been together over a month now, but they'd agreed to keep their relationship secret for a bit. Not least because they were worried about some bright spark working out how Bravura was connected to Shanthi Bags and then making a connection to Luke.

She put her shoulder-bag on the reception counter and signed in.

Kim peered at it. 'Mandarina Duck. Nice,' she said. 'Is it actually vintage 1990s? I didn't know you had one of these in your mum's collection.'

'I didn't. I got it off Etsy,' she said. 'It's a little treat to celebrate busting through the crowdfunding goal.' She grinned. Mentioning Shanthi Bags on Syren's show had brought the website up on the radar of a lot of people, including a few lifestyle bloggers who had got in touch. A few promotions later, she'd passed her crowdfunding goal and was still raising money. At Luke's suggestion, Sam had opened a Facebook group for Shanthi bag enthusiasts, where people mostly got together to talk about handbags. Checking in with them was now her favourite task of the day.

'Oh, you were interested in the whole *SyrenQuest* thing, weren't you?' asked Kim. 'Have you seen this?' She pulled out a magazine from under her desk. 'Look. They got together. Isn't that lovely.'

It was a picture of Bravura and Blaze, sitting at opposite ends of the couch, facing each other. He had his bottom lip caught between his teeth and she was looking amused.

'That is lovely, yes.' She couldn't help but smile at the picture. The headline said, 'An antidote to Gamergate: The online romance that captured the nation's heart'. Cute. A quick scan of the article showed that they had not mentioned Shanthi Bags anywhere. Less cute.

'Says here that it's been a boon for gaming companies that have been trying to get more women to play,' said Kim. 'I guess not so many women play computer games.'

Sam thought of Flick. Some women did play professionally. It took a certain amount of courage to put your head above the parapet and be counted though.

Kim turned the paper around and peered at the photo. 'Mind you, I'd play if I thought it would net me a bloke like that. Just look at the way he's looking at her. If only I were single. Phew. The things I would do to a bloke who stared at me like that.' She pretended to fan herself. 'Lucky cow.'

Sam grabbed her bag. 'I'd better get going,' she said, and fled to the safety of her office.

Her phone was ringing in her bag by the time she opened her office. She answered it while awkwardly shrugging off her coat at the same time.

'Samadhi? Hi. It's Raven Millehouse. We met a few weeks ago when you proposed a partnership with our bags.'

'Oh. Hi. Yes. I did get your note to say that you weren't interested.' Why were they contacting her again? Had something changed?

'We were wondering if you would be interested in coming for a meeting with us next week. We've … noticed the attention you've been getting since working with Bravura from the online game *SyrenQuest* and we think there might be some synergy between your product and an idea that's still in development here.'

'Okay …' This was sounding interesting, especially given how circumspect Raven was being. 'When did you have in mind for this meeting?'

'Next Wednesday afternoon?'

'Sure. I can do that.'

'Would your friends Bravura and Blaze be interested in doing some advertising work with us?'

Sam suppressed a laugh. 'I … can ask.'

She finalised the details and hung up. She and Blaze had done a few interviews as a couple, mostly by phone, so that they didn't need to costume up. Modelling might be a whole different kettle of fish. She would have to talk to Luke about it. In the meantime, she had prototypes to organise. She sat down and went through her work. The need for caffeine was just getting to crisis point when Luke knocked on the door and let himself in.

She spun her chair round to face him. 'Hi.'

He had his coat over his usual work uniform of jeans and company fleece. His hair was a bit longer now and was sticking up on end where he'd run his fingers through it. She gazed at him affectionately and smiled. How on earth had she thought he was unremarkable? Right now, his eyes shining, he looked like a bundle of energy barely contained in a human body.

'What's up?'

He beamed. 'You are looking at the sole owner of L&B Online Event Services! Ta-daah!'

'The sale went through. Congratulations!' She stood up and hugged him.

He kissed her.

'Luke! I thought we agreed to keep it quiet.'

'Right now, I'm too happy to care. I'm going out to get a celebratory piece of cake. Want to come with?' Luke gave her Blaze's trademark half-smile and passed her her coat.

Sam hesitated.

'I was thinking of somewhere other than the cafeteria downstairs,' he said.

'Okay.' She pulled on her coat. 'Actually,' she said. 'I had a very interesting phone call earlier.'

She told him about the bag company on the way downstairs. They were still discussing it when they went to the reception desk to sign out.

'Off out at the same time again, you two?' said Kim.

Sam rolled her eyes. Kim always did this to wind Luke up. Normally, Luke would look embarrassed and scurry off. Except now, he had that gleam in his eye that said he was still channelling Blaze. He did that more and more these days. Sam took up the pen to sign out and smiled. Things were always more fun when Luke was a little bit Blaze.

'It's almost as if you're leaving together,' said Kim, still teasing.

Luke looked her in the eye. 'It is, isn't it?' He turned to Sam. 'Should we tell her?'

'Sure.' Sam grinned.

Kim glanced from one to the other, her eyes narrowed. She seemed to reach a conclusion. 'Oh, you're trying to wind me up. Nice try, buddy.'

Luke threw his hands up. 'Seriously? You don't believe me? Kim!'

'You're just trying to get me back for teasing you. I see you.'

Sam laughed and linked her arm through his. 'Come on. I'm dying for that coffee.'

'But Kim doesn't believe we're together.'

She dragged him towards the door. 'Does it matter?'

'Yes. I mean, not really. But yes. It does a bit. Why is it so preposterous that you might go out with me?'

She stopped at the door and turned to face him. A quick glance showed her that Kim was still watching. Luke seemed genuinely annoyed.

'Does it really mean that much to you?' she asked.

He reddened. 'It's stupid, I know. But I've been here for nearly seven years and Kim has teased me about all kinds of women who have worked here. I don't mind being made fun of when it's true, but now that it's n—'

She put her hands either side of his face, pulled him towards her, and kissed him. When she finally let him go, he was wide-eyed. She glanced over at Kim, whose mouth had dropped open.

'Can I have my coffee now?' she said to Luke.

He cleared his throat. 'Yes. Coffee. Sure.' He opened the door for her, still looking adorably flustered.

As they took the lift down, she laid her head against his shoulder. 'All things considered,' she said, 'if I had to choose between you and Blaze, I'd definitely still choose you.'

Luke took her hand and kissed it. 'I'm very relieved to hear that.'

Sam smiled. The lift came to a stop and hand in hand, they walked out into the brightness.

Acknowledgements

Playing For Love was about a lot of stuff that is beyond my sphere of experience. I haven't played many computer games (not since the 90s, anyway). But, luckily, I have a daughter who could help. I also have friends with helpful offspring. I would like to say a special thank you to Diarmuid Fanning and Emily Fanning for all the tremendously useful tips and links about games, YouTubers and other sundry information about the modern online world. Thank you also to Tom Johnson for helping out with details about cosplayer etiquette.

Thank you to Phil_The_Vicar for letting me use his gamer tag for a fictional gaming vicar. Hat tip to Dangerous, Jimothy and Rahuligan – I hope you don't mind your silly nicknames being immortalised in a rom com.

Thank you to my agent, Jo Bell and to my editors Dushi Horti and Abi Fenton for all the advice and encouragement along the way. As always, thank you to the Romantic Novelists Association for being generally awesome and to Jenni Fletcher and Jane Lovering for tea and cake chats. A special thank you to the ladies of the Naughty Kitchen for chivvying me along and letting me wail when the writing was going particularly slowly, (even when Zoom made me sound like a Clanger).

As always, thank you to my family for putting up with me wittering on about imaginary people all the time. Most of all, thank *you* for reading!

Hi. Thank you for reading *Playing For Love*. If you enjoyed it (or even if you didn't, I guess), please could you leave a review? Reviews help other readers decide if this book would be the sort of thing they'd enjoy (or not). It also helps me work out what I should write more of (or not).

So, the next time you're in your favourite book retailer, please leave a review. It doesn't have to be long, just a line or two will do. Or tell your friends about the book – that works too!

It would mean a lot to me. Thank youuuu!

If you would like to read a deleted scene from the book (it didn't fit the story, but I had such a lot of fun writing it, that I kept hold of it), sign up to my newsletter and I'll send it to you. https://jeevanicharika.com/pfl/

Jeevani

Dear Reader,

We hope you enjoyed reading this book. If you did, we'd be so appreciative if you left a review. It really helps us and the author to bring more books like this to you.

Here at HQ Digital we are dedicated to publishing fiction that will keep you turning the pages into the early hours. Don't want to miss a thing? To find out more about our books, promotions, discover exclusive content and enter competitions you can keep in touch in the following ways:

JOIN OUR COMMUNITY:

Sign up to our new email newsletter:
http://smarturl.it/SignUpHQ

Read our new blog www.hqstories.co.uk

🐦 https://twitter.com/HQStories

📘 www.facebook.com/HQStories

BUDDING WRITER?

We're also looking for authors to join the HQ Digital family!
Find out more here:

https://www.hqstories.co.uk/want-to-write-for-us/

Thanks for reading, from the HQ Digital team

If you enjoyed *Playing for Love*, then why not try another delightfully uplifting romance from HQ Digital?